JESSE STUART

Over the past fifteen years, Jesse Stuart has written twelve books. He has won innumerable awards, prizes, fellowships, a Book-of-the-Month Club selection, and the highest critical praise. William Saroyan said: "Jesse Stuart is a genius. What's more, he's natural." Mark Van Doren: "His stories are strange and powerful. A great deal happens in W-Hollow ... and now the world may know." William Du Bois, *New York Herald Tribune:* "Jesse Stuart is a natural-born writer, whether he is performing as a poet, a story teller or a creator of moods." Lewis Gannett: "His pen picks up magic ... his story has the mountain ballad quality." Whit Burnett, *Book of the Month Club News:* "He writes as easily as he breathes." Jesse Stuart is one of the truly great regional novelists of contemporary American fiction.

HIE TO THE·HUNTERS

HIE to the HUNTERS

BY JESSE STUART

WHITTLESEY HOUSE

MCGRAW-HILL BOOK COMPANY, INC.

NEW YORK   LONDON   TORONTO

HIE TO THE HUNTERS

PUBLISHED BY WHITTLESEY HOUSE

A division of the McGraw-Hill Book Company, Inc.

Printed in the United States of America

To
Deane and Jane

PART ONE

I

SIXTEEN-YEAR-OLD Jud Sparks walked slowly down the street with his hands in his overall pockets, looking first to his right, then to his left at the pretty houses and the neat yards fenced with rows of well-trimmed hedge. Many of the hedge fences were high but Jud could look over them. He was so tall he slouched when he walked and his broad shoulders sagged. Instead of letting his arms swing like the pendulums of clocks alongside his legs, he rested them in his hip overall pockets until he had ripped one of the pockets loose and had sagged the other. Beneath his sun-tanned, fuzz-covered jaw he carried a quid of light burley leaf which he didn't bother to chew or change over to the other side of his mouth. The quid of burley looked like a ripe peach.

As he walked along the street he stopped, aimed, and squirted something into a pooch's eye. The well-dressed lady sitting on her porch wondered what this long, lanky, odd-looking boy carried behind his jaw when she saw her dog take off with his tail between his legs, yelping as if he had been sprinkled with shot.

More than one woman wondered why her cat ran away squalling, or her dog took off yelping, when this young man, dressed in overalls, jumper, cap, and brogan shoes, passed her house. Where there were no cats or hounds, Jud was content to walk lazily along, listening to the hobnails in his brogans click alternately on the gray smooth-concrete street.

2

DOWN THE STREET, Jud saw something going on. He stopped suddenly. For a few seconds he watched two boys fighting one. They were twins. Each twin would weigh approximately a hundred and sixty pounds. The boy they were fighting would not weigh more than a hundred and thirty pounds. Jud heard the small boy scream as one of the twins held his arms pinned to his sides and the other stood off and punched him in the face as if he were practicing on a punching bag. When Jud saw this he started off with long increasing steps. This was trouble and he had always taken to trouble. When the small boy's screams grew louder, Jud broke from his lazy gait into a run. A crowd of smaller boys had gathered to watch the fight.

"What's a-goin' on here?" Jud asked.

"Maybe you'd better make somethin' of it?" said the twin who was holding the small boy's arms.

"It ain't no fair way to fight," Jud said.

"Help me, big boy," the small boy begged, spitting some blood from his battered mouth.

"You big hillbilly, get into it if you want some of the same thing," said the twin who was doing the beating. "You'll be sorry if you do. You won't like the sort of medicine we dish out to the boys around this town!"

"It won't be good for you if you help this rich little sissy," said the twin who was doing the holding.

"Medicine, huh," Jud said, putting his hands back in his hip pockets for balance. "Speakin' of medicine, I got some of my own."

Jud aimed at the boy who was doing the pounding, puckered up his lips while the small boy looked on.

Squirt!

"Oh! oh!" screamed the twin. "Fire in my eye!"

While he covered his burning eye with both hands and danced up and down on the street, Jud puckered his lips and aimed again.

Squirt!

Then this twin jumped two feet high and clicked his heels together twice before he came down to the street with a hand over each eye.

"I'm blind as a bat, Dee," he screamed. "Fire in both eyes!"

"That wasn't a good shot," Jud said, turning to the small boys who were watching, wide-eyed. "He wouldn't stand still."

Since the twin who was doing the holding had turned his face away, Jud slowly took his hands from his hip pockets.

"Turn him loose," Jud demanded, as the small boys looked on in amazement. "If ye don't I'll give ye some of my medicine."

"Make me, you big hillbilly!"

Jud reached out with his long arm, took the boy's cap from his head, and threw it on the street. This was a challenge for the twin to strike him. But he didn't. Jud got a handful of hair on his head, shook him with one hand while he boxed first one cheek and then the other with his big hand.

"Ye think yer tough, huh," Jud said; "two big men fightin' a boy!"

3

"What's that you put in my eyes," screamed the one Jud had just put out of the fight. He stood there rubbing his eye-sockets with the back of his hands.

"Only burley terbacker ambeer," Jud said. "It ought not to smart yer eyes like that. Ye can't stand as much as this little fellow yer tryin' to beat up! Take it like a man!"

"But my eyes won't quit smartin'," he screamed as he opened one eye enough to see the light.

Squirt!

The twin started to run and the gob of ambeer spattered just below his eye. He ran out the alley toward the railroad tracks, with one eye open and a hand clasped over the other eye. At every step his heel would come up and hit him behind, he was running so fast.

"You're not runnin' out on me are you, Dee?" screamed the twin brother, who was still holding the little boy.

"He's had enough," laughed one of the boys who was watching.

"Twist him round till I can see the whites of his eyes!" Jud said to the little boy who had taken the beating. "I'll give'im some of the medicine I give his brother. I don't want to use my fist on him."

The small boy twisted and squirmed, while Jud stood back, rested his hands in his hip pockets, and waited for his chance.

"Bite his arm, little boy," Jud said.

When the small boy bent over to bite the big arm that was pinned around his small arms and body, he twisted the big boy around until Jud could get a shot at the corner of his eye.

Squirt!

"He's got old Dennis too," one of the small boys laughed.

"Gee, how he can spit."

"Lord, have mercy on me," Dennis screamed, letting go of his small prey and slapping both hands over his eye.

While he still had one good eye, Dennis took off as hard as he could go. Jud took after him, giving him three boots

4

with his brogans before he reached the railroad tracks, while the small boys clapped their hands and shouted.

The boy Dee and Dennis had beaten leaned against a twisted elm shade tree and pulled a handkerchief from his pocket. He wiped blood from his battered nose and swollen lips as he watched Jud go over the railroad tracks, kicking Dennis every time he got close enough and squirting at him every time he looked back. He and the other small boys watched the two go out of sight across the tracks and up an alley beyond the station.

"Did they hurt you this time, Did?" one of the small boys asked.

"They've nearly beaten me to death," Did told them as they gathered closer to look at his swollen face.

"Who was that hillbilly, Did?"

"I don't know."

"Gee, he's some fighter!"

"Wonder where he's from?"

"I don't know!"

"Wonder if he'll be back?"

3

THEY SAW JUD turn the corner from the alley into the street, with his hands in his hip pockets. He walked slowly along whistling, stopping every few steps, looking back to see if there was anybody behind him. The small boys ran to meet Jud as he crossed the railroad tracks.

"I want to thank you," Did said. "You've saved me from a worse beating than I got. What's your name?"

"Jud Sparks is my name. Sparkie, that's what everybody calls me. What might yer name be?"

"My name is Didway Hargis," Did said, trying to smile with his thick swollen lips. "Just call me Did. Did Hargis."

"Sparkie, you whipped the best fighter in this town," said a small boy.

"What do I owe you, Sparkie, for helpin' me?" Did asked. "I've been whipped many times by them before."

"Oh, ye don't owe me nothin'."

"Gee, how you can fight, Sparkie," said a small boy admiringly. "Wish I could fight like you can!"

"Oh, I can't fight much," Sparkie said, looking at the street, scraping a leaf with brogan-shoe toe. "But I've got a way to take my part!"

"You've just whipped the twin bullies of Greenwood," Did told him. "They've beaten every boy in town!"

"Bullies, huh?"

"That's right! I can't walk down this street that they don't wait for me."

"Why do they jump on ye?"

"Just because I'm easy to whip!"

"I'll tell you why they jump on Did," said one of the small boys. "It's because Did's pappy owns the biggest store in town."

"No, it's because Did's a sissy," another one said.

"It's because they're older and bigger," said another. "They're sixteen years old, Did's just fourteen. They're a lot bigger'n Did too."

"Don't ye have anybody to hep ye fight 'em?" Sparkie asked.

"No. I'm the only one. Don't have a brother or a sister."

"I don't neither."

"It'd be wonderful if I had you to help me."

6

"I'd shore like to be around to hep ye."

"But where do you live?"

"Outten the hills. Ever hear of the Plum Grove hills?"

"Sure. That's where that war's going on between the fox hunters and the tobacco growers."

"Yep. It shore is."

"That's where they're burning tobacco barns and poisoning hound-dogs."

"Yep. The farmers shoot and pizen the hunters' hounds fer runnin' the fox through their terbacker patches and a-breakin' the leaves. Then the hunters burn the farmers' terbacker barns. Yep, it's shore some war out there."

"I saw in the paper last night where a thousand-dollar reward was offered by the Sheriff for any man caught settin' fire to a barn."

"We don't take a paper," Sparkie said, "but I ain't surprised."

"Which side of the war are you on?" Did asked.

"Dogs' side."

"Thousand dollars is a pile of money," one of the small boys said.

"Sounds big to me," Sparkie said, squirting ambeer at a knothole on a tree.

"Just like a bullet," one boy laughed. "I don't want you to squirt that stuff in my eyes."

"Why don't ye go home with me, Did?" Sparkie said, taking the big quid of tobacco from behind his guinea-egg-colored jaw and throwing it down on the street. "Ye don't have anybody to hep ye fight yer battles. I'll see no one harms ye. I'll do yer fightin' fer ye."

"Oh, I couldn't do that," Did said.

"I'll go home with you," said one of the little boys.

"No, ye won't," Sparkie said. "Now all ye little fellers go along home." They looked at Sparkie and then at each other before they walked silently down the street.

7

"We don't want 'em to know what we do," Sparkie told Did. "If ye decide to go home with me, they might go tell yer pappy."

Sparkie stood looking down thoughtfully at Did while he pulled a long brown burley leaf from his front overall pocket and crammed it into his mouth, neatly placing it with his tongue behind his jaw.

"See, this is my second year in Greenwood High School and Mother and Father wouldn't let me quit," Did apologized. "I'd have to run away from home if I went with you."

"Ye're high up in larnin'," Sparkie said. "To look at ye, one wouldn't think it."

"Don't you go to school, Sparkie?"

"I ust to. I got to the Second Reader; then I quit."

"What do you do now?"

"I hep Peg a little with the terbacker patchin'. I hunt, trap, go to a few dances."

"Have you got hound-dogs?"

"I got four left. I had four pizened by the terbacker men."

"Why?"

"Because they run the foxes through their green terbacker, uprootin' it and a-breakin' the ground leaves. Ye see why I'm on the dogs' side. Drive, Lead, Topper, and Scout got pizened on fried taters; but I got four left—Shootin' Star, Lightnin', Fleet, and Thunderbolt."

"Have you got a gun?"

"Couple of shotguns and two pistols!"

Did stood for a minute in silence. He looked thoughtfully at Sparkie.

"Will you teach me to hunt and shoot if I go home with you?"

"I'll shore larn ye."

"Do you suppose Father and Mother would find me?"

"What if they do find ye," Sparkie said. "Where we live there's lots of good places to hide."

"I'll have to wear what I've got on. I can't go home and get my clothes. I'd be afraid to."

"Yer clothes are all right," Sparkie said, looking Did over. "They look like Sunday clothes to me. But ye can share my clothes."

"Let's don't go down past the Hargis General Merchandise Store," Did warned, as he walked beside Sparkie down the street. "Father is there. He'll see me!"

"Oh, I know yer pappy," Sparkie said. "Bought many a trap and shell from him. I didn't think about ye a-bein' his boy when I saw ye in that fight. But yer pappy don't know me."

4

BEFORE SPARKIE AND Did reached the Hargis General Merchandise Store, they turned left, went up an alley, crossed the railroad tracks, and took up the back road that ran on the west side of Greenwood and connected with the Plum Grove Turnpike. Soon they reached the turnpike where automobiles passed like bullets, leaving them hidden in clouds of swirling dust.

"If we only had our car!" Did said, after he had stood a minute holding his breath and then spit out a mouthful of dust.

"Ye'd better fergit about a car if ye're a-goin' home with me," Sparkie said. "Where I live, ye won't need a car. I don't know what we'd do with one."

The two boys fought their way through the clouds of dust

under the October sun for seven country miles along Plum Grove Turnpike. Did didn't understand what Sparkie had told him about their not needing the car until they left the turnpike and walked three miles over a jolt-wagon road. When they left the jolt-wagon road, they walked up a narrow path under the scrawny pines until they came to a deep hollow where Sparkie grabbed a grapevine and swung across, for it saved going down one steep bank and up the other. When Sparkie had swung to the other side, he shoved the grapevine back to Did. Did gripped the vine, took a run-and-go, and swung across the hollow beside Sparkie.

"This is fun," Did said, "a lot more fun than driving a car. Father will never find me here. Good-by, Dee and Dennis. No need hiding along the streets to beat me up anymore. Good-by Greenwood streetcars and automobiles and high school and the stuffy old Hargis General Merchandise Store."

As they started up the hill, following a little fox path beneath the tough-butted white oaks, a rabbit jumped up from his bed beneath a greenbrier stool.

Squirt!

"Missed 'im," Sparkie said. "It's awful hard to hit a rabbit's eye unless I ketch one a-settin'. When I do ketch one a-settin', I pop the juice into one of his eyes. See, he sleeps with 'em open."

"I didn't know a rabbit slept with his eyes open."

"He sleeps with his eyes open, and I hit 'im in the eye and when he starts turnin' over and over, I run over and pick 'im up. Ketch lots of rabbits that way."

They climbed slowly toward the ridge road, up the little fox path where greenbriers lapped over to stick their legs. Saw briers wrapped around their ankles. The carpet of bright October leaves rustled beneath their shoes.

"We certainly wouldn't have any use for a car here," Did said as they reached the ridgetop. "How do you get your tobacco hauled from here?"

"On a mule's back."

"What a country!" Did's face beamed. He looked to the wild region beyond this ridge and at the deep valley below. Here and there were log shacks with thin streams of smoke ascending from their brown field-stone chimneys, spiraling above the many-colored autumn leaves and thinning on the blue air. "I'll love this country!"

"See that little shack down yander with the big barn around the slope from it," Sparkie said, pointing. "That's where we'll live."

"Looks like a wonderful place," Did said. "I've read in books about a country like this, but I didn't know it was this close home."

"It's the home of the hound-dogs and the foxes and the tough-butted white oaks. It's where ye find greenbriers and the terbacker. And now we got our hound-dog pizeners and our barn burners and our Eversoles. Them last's a crazy fambly," Sparkie went on. "There's Brier-patch Tom, Turkey Tom, and Jest Tom."

"Those are funny names," Did laughed. "How'd they get them?"

"All three Toms live in Eversole Hollow," Sparkie explained. "Had to tell 'em apart some way. Brier-patch Tom got his name when he let the wild blackberry briers grow up in his corn. Turkey Tom's got a long red neck like a turkey gobbler. Then there's Jest Tom. Brier-patch Tom's the craziest one of the Toms. He's got the wildest laugh ye ever did hear. And he goes around a-carryin' a little piece of dirty rag in his hand that he plays with all the time. Sure are a crazy fambly."

Did felt his knees buckle as he followed Sparkie down the slick-worn path toward the shack. Sparkie walked easily with his hands out of his hip pockets. His long arms were swinging like pendulums alongside his legs, almost reaching his knees. When his brogan shoes slipped on the dry leaves, Did watched Sparkie's arms, quicker than a striking copperhead, reach out and grab a sassafras sprout beside the path. Did knew his knees were weak in comparison with Sparkie's, as he slipped, caught himself, and slipped again, trying to keep up with Sparkie.

They followed a path that wound among the sassafras sprouts and persimmons, entwined with blackberry briers, saw briers, and wild grapevines until they reached a single-room log shack with a lean-to for a kitchen. Did knew it was a kitchen, for it had a rusty stovepipe supported by three rusty baling wires wrapped around it and tied to the turned-up clapboards below. A thin, sweet-smelling wood smoke was easing from the pipe and an October wind was driving it groundward, so that Did's nostrils could catch a draft of smoke that smelled strong and pleasant.

"That wood smoke smells good," Did said.

"It ain't all wood smoke ye smell," Sparkie told him. "Ye're a-smellin' vittles cookin'. Arn's gettin' supper."

"Who's Arn?"

"That's Ma," Sparkie said, staring strangely at Did.

I couldn't call my mother by her first name, Did thought. She wouldn't stand that a minute. Did had always called his mother "Mother" and his father "Father." They wouldn't even let him call them Mom and Pop, and certainly not by their first names.

"Before we go inside the shack and meet Arn and Peg," Sparkie said, "I want to take you out here and interduce you to the best hound-dogs in these hills."

PART TWO

I

SPARKIE WALKED TOWARD the barn with Did following him.

"Thunderbolt," Sparkie said softly as they approached a lean-to kennel made of clapboards alongside the barn, "come out to git interduced."

Did heard the chain rattle as the lanky, blue-speckled hound squeezed out the small door. Sparkie thrust his hand down, and Thunderbolt put his nose in Sparkie's palm, wagged his brier-scarred tail, and whined.

"Fastest foxhound among these hills," Sparkie bragged. "He's got the right name. He's a bolt of thunder the way he roars and runs. He's the one the terbacker men would most like to pizen."

"He's a little skinny, isn't he?" Did asked.

"Any good hound-dog stays skinny," Sparkie said. "I feed him plenty of good grub that sticks to the ribs. But twelve hours of hard runnin' takes off every ounce of it. Look at the scars on 'im where he's been cut a-goin' through fences and brier thickets and thorn bushes."

"He's a good-looking dog," Did said, thinking that Thunderbolt was the skinniest animal he ever did see.

"Now I want to show you Fleet."

Fleet was out of her clapboard kennel ready to greet them. She whined as the boys approached her. Sparkie held out his hand and stroked her black-and-tan head. Did held out his hand, which looked soft and white next to Sparkie's. Fleet's long ears almost reached the ground.

"She's a good cutter," Sparkie said, patting her head while she looked up out of huge brown eyes and whined.

"What do you mean by a 'good cutter'?"

"She won't follow the track with the other hounds. She knows these fox woods and foxes so well she makes for the places where the foxes cross the ridges and the low gaps. You know foxes have certain places they cross on the circuits they run. Fleet not only gits ahead of the other dogs, but she gits ahead of the fox and she sits and waits on 'im. And when he gits close, she gives him a sight chase. Then we hear her open up with all that purty music. Wait until you hear her bark! Purtiest hound-dog music anybody ever heard. The other hunters don't like Fleet because she cuts on their hounds. I only use her when Thunderbolt can't outrun another dog."

"I didn't know dogs were that smart," Did said.

"When ye start huntin' you'll larn a lot about dogs and foxes. Ain't many hound-dogs that are as smart as foxes. But Fleet can jest about outwit any fox. I call her Fleet because she's fast as the wind."

"When do we go fox hunting?"

"Not right now. I'm afraid my hounds will get pizen taters scattered all over the Plum Grove hills. See, that's why I have 'em all tied. But we can go a-possum huntin'. Would you like to possum hunt?"

"I guess so. I never went possum hunting in my life."

"Then we'll go after supper. Come down here and I'll show you our possum dog."

When the boys left Fleet's kennel, she tucked her tail between her legs and went back to her bed of leaves.

14

"Shootin' Star," Sparkie called at the next kennel. "Come, boy! Shootin' Star!"

"Why do you have to coax him to come out?"

"He's a retired foxhound. That's why he's treein' possums. He ust to be a powerful foxhound. He was a better dog than Thunderbolt. But when he got to be seven years old, he lagged in the chase. He couldn't stand that. So he started treein'. Now he tries to put more possums up the trees than any other tree dog in the woods. And I believe he can."

"Bring him out. I'd like to see him."

Sparkie slapped the kennel with his big hand, rattling the boards. "Shootin' Star, come out," he said in a loud tone of voice.

A skinny hound-dog, whose heavy wrinkled lips doubled over his toothless gums, slowly slunk out the small kennel door. His ears had been split in many places until they looked like curtain fringes. His mouth and head were almost as white as frost and his body was salt-and-pepper colored. His black eyes looked weak and he closed them often to keep out the sunlight.

"He doesn't look like he could tree a possum."

"He's nine years old," Sparkie said. He reached down and opened the dog's mouth. "See, his teeth are whetted off even with the gums, and he's nearly gray as a possum. Yet old Shootin' Star can crush a polecat's head at one bite. Ye know that's somethin'. I'll show ye what he can do tonight!"

While the boys talked, Shooting Star turned around and eased back through the door of his kennel to his warm, soft bed of dry leaves.

"Look down here, Did," Sparkie said, pointing. "Ain't old Lightnin' a pretty hound!"

Did looked at a tall brown-reddish hound with black spots above his eyes and small black patches on his ribs. He had long ears, a slender nose, and long legs. He was wagging his long, reddish, black-tipped tail and whining.

15

"He's got the speret," Sparkie said, as the hound reared up, put its forefeet on his chest, and looked him in the eye. "That's why I call 'im Lightnin'. Ye'd think he'd outrun Thunderbolt. But he can't. He runs like a lightning flash while he runs. I use him as a burn-out dog."

"What do you mean by 'burn-out'?"

"I hold him out until Brier-patch Tom Eversole's War Horse cold-trails the fox and gets a hot track," Sparkie said. "When the fox hunters untie their hounds and the chase is on, I turn old Lightnin' loose. He takes the fox a couple of circles like a streak of lightning and then he's through. He comes in and lays by the fire. But he's done his work. He's nearly busted all the other hounds a-tryin' to keep up with him, and then I send Thunderbolt in and he finishes 'im. If he can't do it, I turn Fleet loose and she does the cuttin', and that will fix 'em.

"Ask anybody about me in these hills," Sparkie continued. "I'm a fox hunter and I know how to run my hounds. Anything is fair in this game. And the hunter with the best dogs don't often see his dogs win the chase. A fox hunter's got to figure. He must know how to put his dogs into the chase. A lot of fox hunters don't like old Lightnin'. They know he's a burn-out dog. He makes it possible fer Thunderbolt to lead the pack. Dogs must have teamwork. And I have it with mine. That's why fox hunters from far and near come to these parts to beat me. And when they speak of a good hound, they'll always measure 'im with one of mine."

"Gee, there's a lot to this fox hunting," Did said.

"Ye'll larn more here than you did in high school," Sparkie said, pushing Lightning away from him. "Go back to yer sleep, Lightnin'."

Lightning went back into his kennel.

"Your hound-dogs mind you. I've heard hound-dogs weren't very smart."

"Sharpest dogs in the world," Sparkie said. "Ye can really larn a hound-dog anythin'."

Sparkie took the big quid of burley leaf from behind his jaw, threw it down on the leaves, hiked his throat, and spat.

"Now that ye've made the acquaintance of my dogs, there's one more thing I want to show ye," Sparkie said.

2

DID FOLLOWED SPARKIE around one end of the barn, where there weren't any boxings up the sides. It was filled with tiers of tobacco. The tobacco tips were hanging downward with only a little space between the tiers and between the stocks for the wind to play among these curing, brown, shriveling plants.

"Looks like you'd be on the side of the tobacco men in this fight," said Did.

"It was awful hard fer me to decide which side of this war to take. I do like to chaw my terbacker. It's a wonderful weed to chaw and smoke. And I've found it's a wonderful weapon to fight with. But I love my hounds."

Did followed Sparkie past the half of the barn filled with tobacco until they came to the half that was made of logs.

"Ye may not like it up here, Did," Sparkie said as he opened the barn door. "But it'll be nice after ye once get ust to it. Did ye ever sleep in a barn before?"

"No, I never," Did said, following Sparkie inside the door. "Reckon ye can git ust to it?"

"I think I can. The mules look friendly enough."

The gray-nosed mule in the front stall put his nose across Did's shoulder and nuzzled his cheek, while the mule in the second stall stuck his head across the partition and brayed.

"Dick and Dinah know me," Sparkie said. "They'll soon be a-knowin' ye."

Sparkie climbed up on the manger, put his hands up through the scuttle-hole, and pulled himself up into the barn loft. Did looked beyond the mules' stalls at the cattle on the other side of the barn. He took a good breath that smelled of cattle's breath, mules, hay, and dry manure. It was good to smell. I don't mind this, Did thought, thinking of his room at home, his soft bed, his full-length mirror, his dresser where he kept his shirts. The bathroom was just across the hall from his room, and now what would he do?

When Did climbed up through the scuttle-hole, he saw a barn loft filled with cane hay, fodder blades, and soybeans, with the exception of one corner where a couple of pitch-forks leaned against the wall. Here and there were pockets made in the hay where somebody had slept.

"How do ye think ye'll like yer new bed?"

"Well, I—fine!"

"Ever sleep in the hay?"

"No."

Did peeped through a big crack between two barn logs. He could see the two-room shack just across the barnyard and the smoke rising slowly from the rusty stovepipe. He could see clouds of it spiraling toward the blue evening sky from the big field-stone chimney. Now that the sun had gone down and night was coming on, he could hear the cattle and mules stomp impatiently in the stalls beneath him.

"I think this is going to be wonderful," Did said.

"Glad to hear ye say it. I was afraid ye wouldn't like the way we live after yer comin' from a fine home and after havin' plenty of money to spend and a car to ride in. Ye have lived like city people. We don't live that way here. I was a-thinkin' as we climbed the mountain ye wouldn't like to sleep in the shack since we just got one room and a kitchen. We've just got one bed too. Arn and Peg sleep in it. Ye'd haf to take your clothes off in front of Arn and Peg if we slept in that room. We'd haf to sleep on a pallet made down on the floor. So I thought the barn loft would be better. I slept in this barn loft fer years, ever since I got too big to sleep with Arn and Peg."

"How does it feel—uh—sleeping with the dogs and cattle and mules?" Did asked slowly.

Sparkie laughed. "Ye'll see. Let's go meet Arn and Peg." He swung down from the scuttle-hole to the manger. "We'll sleep in the barn loft and we'll eat in the shack."

3

SPARKIE LED THE way across the barnyard to a paling gate that opened when he pulled hard. It was fastened with a trace chain that was attached on the other end to a stake and was weighted with worn-out bull-tongue plowpoints that kept it closed. He held the gate open for Did until he was through, then let it swing back into place with a bang. They walked up to the log-shack door that was made of unhewn rough-oak lumber. Sparkie pulled the drawstring and shoved the door open.

"Walk in," he invited Did.

Did removed his hat and walked in. A short woman, slightly stooped, wearing a blue dress with a white flower in it and a checked apron with a pocket in the upper right-hand corner came through the door that went into the lean-to. She had a long-stemmed clay pipe in her mouth. A small stream of smoke went up from her pipe. Every step she took, she puffed a little cloud of smoke as natural as if she were breathing. One of her upper front teeth was a little long and pressed against her lower lip.

"Arn, this is Did," Sparkie said. "Did . . . Did . . . let me think. . . ."

"Did Hargis," Did said, as he shook Arn's rough wrinkled hand.

Arn looked strangely at Did's gray suit of clothes, his white shirt spattered with blood around the collar, and his striped necktie. She looked at his face, the swollen lips, and the dark little half-moon under each eye.

"Did's come to stay with us, Arn," Sparkie said. "He's jest met my hound-dogs."

"Where did ye come from, Did?" Arn asked, letting go of Did's soft hand.

"From Greenwood."

"City folks?"

"I—I guess so."

"Do ye aim to stay with us?"

"Shore he aims to stay," Sparkie broke in.

"I'm afeard yer fare won't be what ye're ust to," Arn said.

"I think it's going to be all right," Did said.

"This ain't a pleasant place to be just now," Arn warned Did. "There's a war a-goin' on here. Did Sparkie tell ye about it?"

"Yes, ma'am, he did."

"And ye come anyhow?"

"Yes, ma'am."

"Arn, there's a war goin' on against Did in Greenwood," Sparkie said. "That's how I met him, hepped 'im fight."

"But the people around here are a-burnin' barns and a-takin'

20

shots at one another from the brush," Arn said. "Don't ye think it's dangerous to bring him here, Sparkie?"

"No, Arn, I don't. He may look soft, but he can take a powerful beatin' fer a fourteen-year-old."

"Sure, I can stand it if I'm with Sparkie. I saw him fight today."

"What did he do, squirt terbacker juice in somebody's eye?"

"That's it," Did said with a smile.

"But ye can't fight barn burners and dog pizeners with terbacker juice," Arn said. "And Sparkie is in this war up to his eyes. He's lost half his dogs. He's on the fox hunters' side."

"Then I'm on the fox hunters' side with Sparkie."

"I hope it works," Arn said, as she turned to go back into the lean-to kitchen. "Ye've brought home stray hound-dogs, cats, guns, roosters, ducks, and hides, but this is the first time ye've ever brought home a boy."

Did stood with his hat in his hand and looked over the room. There was one big bed in the room, a homemade stand table and an unpainted dresser with a broken mirror. There was a big fireplace with sticks of wood stacked in the corner. There was a churn on the hearth before the burning wood fire. The house was papered with newspapers, and a few pictures of old men with long beards and old women with wrinkled faces decorated the walls. The people in these pictures looked as if they had come from another world. One picture showed an old man with long black beard covering his chin and a big broad-brimmed black hat sideways on his head, and he was holding up an ugly pistol in his hand.

"Peg'll be here in a little while," Sparkie said. "He's across the mountain a-shuckin' corn."

"It's time fer Peg to be here now," Arn spoke from the kitchen. "The sun has gone from the mountain."

"He tells time by the sun," Sparkie said to Did. "He never misses. Come winter, spring, summer, fall, long as there's a sun, he can tell the time of day almost to the minute."

21

From the only window in the shack, a window near the door, Did looked out over the foothills into the blue chill air of an October evening. He could see the brown hills, with great splashes of green where the pine groves were. He could see flaming red and light brown and dark brown mixed with a golden yellow where the tall poplars grew in the hollows. He had never seen a prettier country. While he looked at the hills dressed in their autumn colors, he thought about the home he had left and wondered if his mother and father were hunting for him. While he thought about his parents and his home, he saw a man walk slowly across the barn lot on a wooden leg.

"I see Peg a-comin' now," Arn said. "Ye boys git ready fer a little bite to eat."

4

DID FOLLOWED SPARKIE into the lean-to where they watched Arn setting an oilcloth-covered table with steaming dishes of strong-smelling food. Did felt pangs of hunger and a weakness in his stomach. He walked toward the lean-to door that lead out onto a little porch. He noticed a flat-topped cookstove in one corner of the kitchen and around it, hanging to nails driven in the walls, were strings of bright red pepper pods, shuck beans, leather britches, dried apples, drying peaches, and drying ears of white and yellow corn.

Sparkie poured cold water from a wooden bucket into a big white washbowl. Then he dipped his hands into home-made soap and spread it over his hands and face.

"Come on, Did," he said. "Take the soap and then we'll dive into this water together. Wash together and dry together and we'll be friends forever."

Did dipped into the soap as Sparkie had done before him. As soon as he had spread the soap over his hands and face, the two boys splashed themselves with cold water. The homemade soap didn't have a sweet smell like city soap, but it sure was powerful. Did felt a stinging around the corners of his eyes and on his swollen lips. He rubbed his face with his hands and dipped blindly into the water to wash away the soap.

"Any blood left?" he asked Sparkie.

"Not a speck."

Sparkie pulled a meal-sack towel down from the nail, and he dried on one end while Did dried on the other.

"Well, Sparkie, ye're back," said a rough voice at the corner of the shack.

"Yep, I'm back, Peg!"

"Who's yer friend?"

Did looked at the man with the wooden leg, a tall man wearing overalls, a corduroy coat, and a big black umbrella hat. His face was covered with long black beard. He had wide brown eyes that looked straight at Did. His calloused hands fell limp at his side.

"Come to live with us, Peg," Sparkie said.

"Just so ye don't bring any more hound-dogs around here," Peg said. "I'm glad ye brought home a boy. Somebody took a pot shot at me from the brush today. One of yer fox hunters I know. One of the Eversoles, I think. . . ."

"Is that the gospel truth, Peg?"

"The bullet plowed the dirt so close I could've spit on the hole it tore in the ground. I tell ye it's dangerous around here since this war started. Every night a terbacker barn goes up in smoke! It'll be ours next!"

Peg walked up toward the porch where the boys had finished drying their faces.

23

"What's your name, son?" Peg asked, reaching his big hand down to Did.

"Didway Hargis. Sparkie calls me Did."

"Mighty glad to meet ye, son," Peg said, pumping Did's small hand a few times with his big hand until Did flinched from the pressure. "Ye boys git in there and git yer feet under the table. I'll be in as soon as I do some dabblin'."

When Did pulled up his bark-bottomed chair at the end of the table, he was surprised at the food before him. There was a dish of steaming hot soup beans, a dish of fried potatoes, pork ribs, kraut, pumpkin, a dish of apples, two small dishes of jelly, and coffee and milk. There was a flat plate of brown corn-pone with steam oozing from the places where the brown crust was broken. This steam smelled sweet to Did's nostrils, giving him an appetite he had never had before.

"Don't wait on me," Peg said. "I'll git my feet under the table."

Did helped himself to the soup beans. When he saw Sparkie eat beans with a big spoon, he did the same. He watched Sparkie put away one glass of milk after another and struggled to keep up with him. They kept Arn busy pouring milk and passing corn bread. When they emptied their plates, she saw that they were filled again.

Did's stomach began to stretch. The little city boy began to feel blood in his veins for the first time. He'd never tasted better food in his life. He'd never enjoyed eating so much before.

5

AS SOON AS Did had finished supper, he pushed his chair back from the table and let his belt out two notches. Sparkie pulled a leaf of burley from his hip pocket, crammed it into his mouth, and worked his jaws slowly, as he leaned on the table with his elbows, his face resting in his hands. Peg pulled a home-rolled cigar from the inside pocket of his corduroy coat. He moistened the outside of the long cigar with his tongue, put it in his mouth, removed the smoked globe from the oil lamp, and leaned over the table putting the end of the cigar into the flickering blaze. Then he pulled fire into the cigar and blew clouds of smoke up to the low, rain-circled, newspapered ceiling.

"What do ye boys aim to do tonight?" Peg asked.

"Did's never gone a-possum huntin'. Thought I'd take 'im."

"Ye boys be mighty keerful," Arn warned. "Might git hurt."

"I ain't a-worryin' so much about gittin' hurt as I am a-takin' old Shootin' Star where the hills are strowed with pizened fried taters," Sparkie said. "I wouldn't lose that dog fer love ner money."

"Keep off the ridges," Peg warned. "Keep away from the fox woods. That's where the fried taters are scattered. Possums don't stay on the ridges. They go down in the hollows where the wind don't rustle the leaves. They stir down in the valleys where the wind is still and where there's wild grapes and cimmons and pawpaws."

"Did can't hunt in his good clothes," Arn said, as she filled her pipe.

"I'm goin' to dress Did up in my old clothes."

"Reckon yer clothes 'll fit 'im," laughed Peg, blowing out a cloud of smoke.

"I can wear about anything," Did said, watching Arn send a cloud of smoke from her wrinkled lips to the ceiling.

"Do you use the fragrant weed?" Peg asked Did.

Did looked at Peg but didn't answer.

"Don't ye smoke or chaw?" Peg asked him.

"Oh, no . . . no. . . ." Did stammered as if he were sorry that he didn't.

"That's fine," Peg said. "I don't do a lot of worryin' when ye sleep in the hayloft."

"That's the only rule Peg has around here," Sparkie said, turning to Did.

"Feed's awful hard to raise here," Peg said. "A body has to take keer of all the feed he raises. My terbacker, cattle, mules, and corn are in that barn. About everything I've got but my fambly and the house plunder's out there. That's why I haf to be keerful."

"About what time is it, Peg?" Sparkie asked.

"About seven," Peg answered, after he thought a few seconds.

"Did, we'd best be gittin' dressed," Sparkie said. "We want to be in the woods by eight. Big possums stir early. I don't like to ketch little blue midnight possums."

"Ye git dressed," Arn said. "I'll fix the grub fer yer hounds."

Sparkie pushed his chair back slowly with the support of his hands on the table. Did followed him to the door. Soon as they had gone into the other room Arn got up from the table to prepare plates of bread scraps for the hound-dogs.

"I suppose that boy's all right?" Peg spoke to Arn in a low voice.

"He appears to be a boy of good raisin'," Arn said, as she divided the remainder of the dish of soup beans into four plates.

"Don't reckon he's out here a-spyin' about this hound-dog and terbacker war?"

"He's too young fer that, Peg," Arn said. "Don't be suspicy."

"Wonder how he got that pair of black eyes and the busted lips?"

"Two boys in Greenwood nearly beat him to death and Sparkie took his part. That's why he come home with Sparkie!"

"He's not our people. He talks so funny!"

"He talks proper. City folks talk proper! They don't talk like us. That proper talk is quaire to us."

"Don't reckon we'll git into trouble with the Law fer harborin' 'im if he's a runaway?"

Just then there was a roar of laughter. Did walked into the kitchen wearing Sparkie's overalls with the suspenders taken up and the legs rolled. They looked like a baggy pair of bloomers. Sparkie's hunting coat fit Did like an overcoat, but his hunting cap was almost too small for Did's head. Did had his hands in his overall pockets and he pushed the pockets out, showing that the overalls were twice too large for him. Arn, Sparkie, and Peg bent over laughing at this pale-faced city boy in hunting clothes that hung onto his slender body like clothes fitting a scarecrow.

"Do you think I'll get through the brush in these?" Did asked, laughing as he worked his hands in and out of his pockets like working a bee smoker.

"Ye got the speret, son," Peg said, blowing a small cloud of smoke from his cigar stub.

"Don't let him git hurt, Sparkie," Arn warned. "He ain't

27

ust to these hills. He ain't ust to a war like's a-goin' on here."

"We ain't afraid of anything in these hills, Arn," Sparkie said.

"Here's grub fer the hounds."

"Ye'll have to fetch the other two dishes, Did," Sparkie said, picking up a dish in each hand.

The dishes were filled with corn pone, beans, and fried potatoes. Each dish was heaped as long as a crumb, bean, or slice of fried potato would lay on, with the exception of one dish Did picked up.

"Why so little in this dish?" Did asked.

"It's fer Shootin' Star," Sparkie said. "I never feed a dog too much before he hunts."

"I'll open the door fer ye," Peg said, getting up from his chair. His wooden leg made a loud sound on the floor as he walked over to open the lean-to door to let Sparkie and Did out.

"Can ye make it through the gate?" Peg asked.

"Shore can, Peg," Sparkie answered him as they stepped out onto the little porch where the late October moonlight was shining as bright as day. "I've opened it many a night with a dish in both hands when it was so dark I couldn't see the path!"

"Have good luck, boys," Peg said. "Ketch a sack of possums."

"Do be keerful, Sparkie," Arn warned him, as she stood in the doorway chewing on the stem of her long pipe.

PART THREE

I

SPARKIE BACKED AGAINST the gate and pushed it open for Did and himself. When the hound-dogs heard the plowpoints jingling on the gate chain, they came from their kennel beds, charging against their chains and barking. Sparkie and Did had to yell to one another when they talked.

"Ain't that purty music?" Sparkie yelled.

"It sounds good to me!" Did screamed.

"They think they're all a-goin' a-huntin' tonight."

Sparkie put one dish down to Thunderbolt and the other to Fleet. Did gave Shooting Star the small dish and Lightning the full dish. While the greedy hounds gobbled up their food, Sparkie took Did to the corncrib where he opened the door, lifted a lantern from where it was hanging on a nail inside. Then he picked up a coffee sack.

"Hold these," he said, handing them to Did.

"We won't need a lantern, will we?"

"Ye never know. Deep hollows are dark. Pine woods are dark. A cloud might come over the moon. And we may be out past midnight when the moon goes down."

Sparkie got down on his knees, looked back under the corncrib floor, and pulled out a mattock.

"We might need this mattock too," he said. "It's always

best to go prepared. If Shootin' Star puts one in a hole, we'll have to dig it out. If he holes one in a hollow log, we can use the ax part of the mattock to chop him out. A mattock is a handy tool!"

By the time they had their possum sack, mattock, and lantern, the hounds had finished their grub and had started charging at the chains again.

"I'll give ye all ye want, Shootin' Star," Sparkie said, unsnapping his chain.

While Lightning, Thunderbolt, and Fleet barked like a roar of thunder, Shooting Star jumped up and tried to kiss Sparkie's face. Sparkie had to throw up his arms to guard his face. The dog ran a circle, whining and barking. Then he leaped over Did's head.

"He doesn't act old to me," Did said. "What's the matter with him?"

"He's tickled to get to the woods. He knows where we're a-goin' when we take a coffee sack, mattock, and lantern. He knows what we want him to do and he's a-rarin' to go!"

Now the barks of the other hound-dogs turned plaintively into howls.

"They know they ain't a-goin' to git to go," Sparkie lamented. "That's why they're howlin'. I feel sorry fer 'em. But this is old Shootin' Star's night out. He's my possum hound."

Shooting Star still ran circles and barked with joy. He ran toward Sparkie, barked, and then he ran away.

"What does he want now?" Did asked.

"He wants to know the way we're goin'," Sparkie said. "There may be a lot of difference between dog talk and man's talk, but I can almost understand what my hounds are a-sayin'. And they can almost understand my talk."

"What does a dog say?" asked Did. "Are you sure you understand them?"

"Shore do," Sparkie assured Did. "And I'll larn ye someday." They walked down a path toward a grove of giant beech trees around a rock-walled spring. "This way, Shootin' Star."

Shooting Star observed the direction Sparkie had pointed, and he was off like a flash toward the beech grove where the moonlight made the many-colored leaves look like decayed percoon petals.

"See, he knows where we're a-goin'."

The moonlight played upon the autumn-colored hills like foamy white breakers of water splashing upon a river bank of golden sand. The wind was still as a cornfield mouse. Did looked around him at the world he never knew, that was only a few miles from his door. It is a beautiful world, he thought, as he walked beside Sparkie, his feet hardly making a rustle of sound as he stepped on the dew-wet carpet of dead leaves. Did thought about the hayloft, the hounds, Peg, Arn, and Sparkie, and their way of living which was so different from his own.

He wondered where his parents were hunting for him now. He knew that they had missed him, for he couldn't get out of their sight unless they knew where he was going. Now he was in a world of rough hills and valleys and he was free as the wind, going into the moonlit night with Sparkie and Shooting Star, a coffee sack across his back and a mattock in his hand.

"It's a good night fer possums," Sparkie said, breaking the silence before they reached the beech grove. "Not a stir of wind and there's enough dampness so that Shootin' Star can carry a track."

"Where's Shooting Star?"

"He hunts far away," Sparkie said. "Sometimes he hunts a mile away. I don't like a close hunter."

When they reached the beech grove, Did looked up through the beech branches at the stars. They looked farther apart and much cleaner and brighter in the sky above these folded hills

31

than they ever looked to him before. Seeing a beech tree limb across the big wagon wheel of moon, he breathed deep of clean wind that had the damp fragrance of autumn leaves, and it was pleasant to breathe.

"Ah ooh!" A dog barked some distance.

"What's that?" Did asked.

"Shootin' Star," Sparkie replied, catching his breath as he stopped suddenly and put his cupped hand up to catch the sound. "That's the cold-trail bark."

Shooting Star barked again and again.

"He's cold-trailed that possum to the top of the Kotcamp Hill," Sparkie said. "He's been down in the deep Dysard Holler."

"Dysard Hollow and Kotcamp Hill," Did repeated. "I've heard of them."

"Eversoles live in this hollow," Sparkie said. "Brier-patch Tom, Turkey Tom, Jest Tom, and Cief Eversole all live in this hollow. They're always in trouble and they git their names in the papers. That's where ye seen 'em."

Now Shooting Star was barking every breath.

"We'd better be a-movin' toward him," Sparkie said as he started walking fast. "He's about ready to put that possum up a tree or in a hole!"

"Bioo, biooo. . . ."

"His bark has changed," Did said.

"He's treed. Let's git to 'im."

Sparkie broke into a slow trot down the ravine. He went between the rusty wires of a fence and crossed a field where there were rows of tobacco stubble, with Did following at his heels. Then he climbed a pasture slope and over a little ridge into Dysard Hollow.

"Ain't that purty music?" Sparkie said to Did with a half breath as they were running toward Shooting Star.

"It sounds good to me. First time I ever heard a hound-dog treed."

"Listen to 'im bark up that tree."

Sparkie spoke between puffs of short breaths. Did was getting his breath hard and fast but he didn't mind. He wiped the sweat from his face and forehead with the sleeve of his hunting coat.

"Here we are," Sparkie said as he rushed up the slope on the other side of Dysard Creek. "It's in a little pawpaw tree."

"I see it!" Did yelled.

"It's a buster," Sparkie said. "He's fat on cimmons."

"Do you mean persimmons?"

"Cimmons to me," Sparkie said.

Shooting Star jumped as high as he could, for the possum was in sight. There wasn't a leaf on the low bushy-topped pawpaw. The possum was resting where three branches forked in the top and he looked like a big hornet's nest with the moon shining upon his fluffy gray fur.

"Shake 'im out," Sparkie told Did. "Let me take keer of Shootin' Star. He's hard to take off a possum."

"Okay!" Did took hold of the tree and shook it with all his power, but the possum held on.

"Shake jest a little harder," Sparkie told him. "How much will he weigh?"

"I don't know."

"Can't you tell by feelin' his weight in the tree?"

"No."

"Let me feel."

Sparkie shook the tree easily.

"He'll weigh about twelve pounds," Sparkie said, walking away from the tree. "I can always tell one's weight where I can shake the tree. Now, shake 'im out."

Did took hold of the tree with both hands, braced his feet against its trunk, and shook with all the strength there was in his body, yet the possum held on.

"Give the tree a little jerk," Sparkie said. "Sorta flip the top!"

33

When Did gave the pawpaw a little jerk with less strength and more ease, the big possum rolled from the top down through the twigs to the ground where Shooting Star was waiting.

"Lay off, Shootin' Star," Sparkie said calmly. "That's enough. Ye've sulled him."

"Did he bite it?" Did asked.

"He didn't hurt it."

Did watched Sparkie take the dog from the possum. He had to slap the dog to make him let go. Then Sparkie held the big possum up by its long hairless tail.

"He'll weigh twelve pounds all right," Sparkie said, his face beaming in the moonlight. "Look what a big fat possum and what purty fur!"

Did looked at the possum.

"Is he dead?"

"Dead!" Sparkie repeated. "Ain't ye ever heard of playin' possum? That's what he's doin'. He's just sulled and when he comes to life, he'll reach up and grab my hand! Hold the sack open!"

Did opened the sack and Sparkie put the possum in.

"Ye want to carry the game?"

"I'd like to."

"Then I'll carry the mattock! And we'll go toward Shackle Run. That's good possum country. There's a good many old apple orchards down that way!"

Just as they left the pawpaw tree, Shooting Star ran over the hill, barking.

"He may be after a stray dog that's followed us here," Sparkie said.

But before he reached midway of the slope on the side of Dysard Creek, the way Sparkie and Did had just come, he barked treed.

"Another possum," Sparkie said, breaking into a run.

Sparkie ran faster than the wind could blow across an empty

34

mountain cornfield. He leaped over rocks, logs, stumps, and saw-brier stools. Did could hardly keep up with him, for his legs were shorter and the possum in the sack bounced up and down on his back.

"He's barkin' up this little sourwood," Sparkie said. "Can't see anything fer the leaves."

Did stood back and peered up among the red sourwood leaves that looked like flames in the moonlight.

Sparkie put his hand on the tree and shook it a little.

"Gosh-old-hemlock, but he's up there," Sparkie said. "I feel him. He's another big possum."

A shower of leaves slithered down like big drops of red autumn rain. Did looked up and the leaves hit his pale face.

"Let me shake him out," Did said.

"All right, ye shake him out. I'll keep Shootin' Star from gummin' him to death."

Did laid his sack on the ground, walked up to the small sourwood, and gave it a little shake, enough to flip the top, and then something started tumbling down through the leaves. Shooting Star pranced beneath the tree, squarely under the swishing sound as the big possum tumbled end over end through the air. He fell into Shooting Star's mouth.

"Gosh-old-hemlock, what a possum," Sparkie said. "Lay off, Shootin' Star. Lay off before I slap you!"

"That's some dog," Did said. "I didn't think I'd like him at first. He looked old and no good to me. But what a dog!"

"And what a possum," Sparkie said, holding the possum up by the tail. "Untie yer sack."

Did untied the sack and Sparkie put the big sulled possum down into the sack beside the other possum.

"What do you do with the possums?" Did asked as he was tying the sack.

"If they're a little skinny, I put 'em in a pen and feed 'em buttermilk, pawpaws, cimmons, and apples," Sparkie said. "I fatten one like I would a hog. Then I sell 'em to people along the railroad tracks in Greenwood. They kill and skin the possums and give the hides back to me. I spread the hides over boards, cure 'em, and sell the pelts."

"What will these possums sell for?" Did asked.

"I can git a dollar apiece fer the possums," Sparkie said. "I'll git about a dollar apiece fer the hides. I could git more fer the hides if it was later in the season."

"Do you sell many?"

"About thirty-five or forty pelts in a season. But they ain't all possum pelts. Before this hunt is over we may go home with a couple of polecats. We may git a weasel, mink, coon, wildcat, muskrat, or a fox."

"Is Shooting Star good for all these?"

"He's an all-around dog if I ever seen one!"

Did put the sack across his shoulder. Sparkie picked up his mattock and lantern and they were off. As soon as they put the possum in the sack, Shooting Star had disappeared into the shadowy woods, where only splinters of moonlight got through the leaves still hanging on the trees. Sparkie and Did walked back toward the open field where Shooting Star treed the first possum.

They had climbed to the top of the hill and were walking out Eversole Ridge that divided Dysard Hollow from Eversole Hollow, and then they heard Shooting Star barking every breath on a warm track.

"He's crowdin' somethin'," Sparkie shouted. "Be ready any time to hear him tree."

Did stood beside Sparkie while the possums wiggled and growled at each other in the sack on his back. Did didn't mind as he listened to the beautiful barks that came one after the other from Shooting Star's toothless mouth and reechoed against the distant hill. Did could feel his own heart pound and he didn't know why. This was a night that he would always remember. He had heard boys in Greenwood talk about going possum hunting and they had gone out and stayed all night, but they didn't bring home any game. Now he waited impatiently as Shooting Star's barks came almost together.

"There," Sparkie shouted, "that's the bark! Treed!"

They ran down into Eversole Hollow, and there they found Shooting Star barking up a big tree with a wild grapevine running up into it.

"Can't see a thing," Sparkie said, looking up among the mass of grapevines and treetops. "It's a smart possum that goes up a grapevine."

"Can't we get him?"

"Can ye climb?"

"I used to beat most of the boys climbing telephone poles."

"But I don't think ye can climb this sycamore. Ye can't reach around it, and it's not got a limb on it fer twenty feet."

"Maybe I can climb the grapevine up into the tree."

Did laid his possum sack down, pulled off his hunting coat, and took hold of the big grapevine that swung loosely from the ground into the sycamore like a giant cable. He started climbing the grapevine like a squirrel. He climbed almost midway where the vine got steeper, and then his feet and hands began to slip.

"Don't think I can make it on up," he yelled down to Sparkie.

"Slide back down. I've got a idear."

Did slid back down the vine, and as soon as he reached the ground he rubbed his burning hands on his overall legs.

"Pull off yer shoes," Sparkie said. "Put these gloves on. Go over there to the creek and wet your socks and gloves. The way ye can climb, ye'll go up that grapevine like a squirrel."

While Did took off his shoes, gloved his hands, and went to the creek, Sparkie lit his lantern and stood under the tree's shadowy darkness. He held the lantern above his head and looked up into the tree.

"What are you doing, Sparkie?"

"A-tryin' to shine the possum's eyes."

37

"I'll try to climb it again," Did said, getting hold of the grapevine and starting up it like a cat. Sparkie watched. Did slowed on the steep part of the vine where it ran from an elbow straight up into the sycamore top, but he finally reached the first sycamore limb where he held on and rested.

"I didn't know wet socks and gloves would make such a difference," Did said.

"I've climbed many a grapevine and many a slick-barked tree without a limb that way," Sparkie yelled to Did.

"Have you seen any possum's eyes up here?" Did yelled down.

"I got a glimpse of a small beady eye on the limb above ye."

Now rested, Did went from limb to limb up into the tree-top, where he looked like a very small boy to Sparkie standing below.

"You're right, Sparkie," Did said excitedly, "I see him."

"Do be keerful now," Sparkie yelled up to Did. "Walk out on the limb the possum's on, hold onto the one above, and shake the possum limb with yer feet. That's the only way ye'll be able to shake him out."

Did took Sparkie's advice, walked carefully out on the possum limb, feeling with his feet in the strips of moonlight as he held tightly to the limb above him. After he had walked out where the limb began to have a little spring, he pulled up with his arms to the limb above him and then came down on the possum limb with his feet, giving it quick shakes. On his third jump the possum let go, tumbled through space, catching at the limbs and vines below as he rolled over and down like a soft gray ball.

"He's comin'," Did shouted.

"Jest as I'd expected, a little blue midnight possum. They're the ones that do the climbin'."

Did climbed down the limbs until he reached his grape-vine and then he slid down the vine to the ground.

"A lot of climbin' fer this little midnighter," Sparkie said,

38

holding the little possum up by the tail for Did to see. "He's a smart little feller. We'll have to put 'im up and feed 'im buttermilk."

"But it's worth it to me," Did said. "I've done something I didn't think I could do."

"Ye've done somethin' I couldn't do."

"You don't mean that," Did said.

"I mean it," Sparkie said seriously. "I couldn't climb that grapevine."

Did untied the sack and Sparkie put the possum in.

"Now let's head toward Shackle Run and the old orchards," Sparkie suggested. "Midnight possums stir in the woods. The big possums stir in the old fields and the cimmon groves and apple orchards!"

The possum safely in the sack, Shooting Star was off into the night. Sometimes they could see him run across an open pasture field with his head high in the wind, sniffling as he ran. A few times they saw him walking slowly with his nose close to the ground sniffling a cold scent beneath the pawpaws and the persimmons.

"I'm carryin' a lighted lantern now," Sparkie said. "Ye may think it's funny when the moon's as bright as day, but Shootin' Star will know the way we're goin' when we carry a lighted lantern."

2

WHEN THEY REACHED the Young Ridge, overlooking Shackle Run Hollow, they stopped suddenly. There was a light in a barn.

"Is it a lantern light?" Did asked.

"Too much light to come from a lantern," Sparkie said.

Then a blaze shot up and they heard screams from the nearby farmhouse.

"Barn's a-burnin'," Sparkie said. "Hunters are at work."

"The barn burners," Did shouted. "If we could only capture them, Sparkie, we could collect a thousand dollars."

"It would take a lot of animal pelts to fetch that much," Sparkie said. "But I've a hot spot in my heart fer the hunters. Look what the terbacker men did to my hounds!"

The dogs barked at the farmhouse below. The people screamed. Did and Sparkie saw long streaks of fire shoot from the double-barreled shotguns and steady blazes belch from roaring automatics. They heard pistols barking that sounded from a distance like many loud-clucking hens.

"It's Tid Barney's terbacker barn," Sparkie sighed. "Tid and his fambly's worked hard this summer fer all that's a-goin' up in flames!"

"What are we goin' to do, Sparkie?"

"Call Shootin' Star and leave here!"

"Will this end our hunt?"

"It shore will," Sparkie said, raising the lantern globe, blowing out the lantern.

"Why leave us in the dark?"

"A lantern is a good target to shoot at," Sparkie warned. "These woods are filled with men totin' guns. They're riled and ready to shoot."

While Sparkie pulled a horn from his pocket and blew a lonesome sound, Did looked down into Shackle Run Hollow, where he could see fodder shocks on the bottoms and on the slopes that looked like Indian wigwams. He could see a log shack here and one there and barns near these shacks. It's a peaceful-looking valley, he thought, why is everybody fighting? What a strange way to fight!

The guns barked again and there were some more screams as the flames from the barn shot high toward the sky, lapping up the tobacco barn, the cattle in it, and a loft filled with hay. Cattle and mules started running across the field. The mules were braying. The cattle were lowing plaintively. There were screams from the men who were trying to drive more cattle from the barn.

Though the hollow was flooded with moonlight, it was not quite as bright as day; yet one could see to shoot a rabbit on one of the slopes since the flames from this barn lighted the fields bright enough for one to read a newspaper a quarter of a mile away. Beyond this radius the reflection of light was brighter than the moonlight, fading to semidarkness in the far distance against the timbered foothills on either side of Shackle Run. Did had never seen anything like this.

While Sparkie blew his horn, the guns started blazing again, and Did watched lights coming on in the shacks all the way down Shackle Run and upon the slopes where he didn't dream there was a house.

"Everybody is gittin' riled," Sparkie said when he rested from blowing his horn. "We want to git our dog and git away from here."

"Do you think they'll shoot at us?"

"Not if we skint away in a hurry!"

"Wonder how many men are burning these barns?"

"Can't tell," Sparkie said, taking a long breath for another toot on his horn. "Maybe a dozen men are messed up in this barn burnin'. Maybe only one."

Now there was a roar of voices near the burning barn. They could hear men shouting: "Clear out. It's ready to fall in!" They heard someone shout: "Did you get all the cattle out?" and the answer: "Not all of 'em!" They could see the people, about twenty-five gathered around the barn, running this way and that but always back from the heat of the burning barn. They could see more people coming up the Shackle Run jolt-wagon road toward the fire.

"They're the terbacker men," Sparkie said. "They're a-gittin' riled. Ye'll hear a lot about this!"

"Here comes Shooting Star," Did said. "Look! He's walking on three legs!"

"Come, boy," Sparkie spoke softly, running down the slope to meet the dog, who was holding up his hind leg.

Shooting Star limped up the slope and when he reached Sparkie, he whined, dropped to the ground, and started licking a wound through the muscle of his left hind leg.

"He's been shot," Sparkie said, examining the wound by moonlight. "The bullet's gone in on one side and come out on t'other. He's been shot with a soft-nose bullet. Look at this hole through his leg."

Sparkie took Shooting Star's chain from his pocket and snapped it to the ring on his collar.

"If anybody shoots ye now," Sparkie muttered, "he'll have to shoot me too."

Sparkie turned back over the Young Ridge leading Shooting Star with one hand, carrying the mattock with the other. Did followed with the possum sack across his shoulder.

"Let's git away from this as soon as we can," Sparkie said,

stopping long enough to put a burley leaf behind his jaw. Then he picked up his lantern and led Shooting Star toward Eversole Hollow, where the moon had gone down beyond the timber-tops and had left it in twilight darkness.

"Listen," Sparkie whispered, stopping suddenly. "I thought I heard steps!"

Pow! pow! pow!

A pistol barked just across the slope on the other side of the creek, and Did and Sparkie heard three bullets hit branches in the treetops above their heads.

"Fall flat," Sparkie whispered, sprawling on the leaves.

Both boys lay flat on their stomachs while Sparkie patted Shooting Star's head and whispered to him. In this silence they heard a man running around the slope among the trees. They could hear each step he made by the rustling leaves and they could hear the greenbriers catching his pants legs and his hands breaking the twigs on the brush as he ran. They lay there breathing as lightly as they could while the runner's steps got fainter and fainter.

"Do you suppose that was the barn burner?"

"It's suspicy," Sparkie whispered. "I don't know what to think of it."

They lay there several minutes listening to a hoot owl's "who-who's" in the Gatson woods beyond Eversole Hollow. It had been some time, they didn't know how long from the time they had heard the last footstep until the big owl flew over them, its great wings spread, just above their heads.

"That man skeered this hoot owl," Sparkie whispered. "He went in that direction. But that's where the Eversoles live. They raise terbacker, fox hunt, and make moonshine. They wouldn't be out barn burnin'."

Sparkie got up and brushed the leaves from his clothes. He raised the lantern globe, took a match from behind his cap bill, raked it across the seat of his pants, and lit the lantern.

"Is it safe to light the lantern?" Did asked with a trembling

43

voice, as he got up brushing the damp clinging leaves from his clothes.

"We're not safe anymore around here jest now," Sparkie said. "We've got to have light to git outten these woods. Shootin' Star's leg's a-gittin' stiff."

Sparkie led the way back up the hill toward Eversole Ridge. Shooting Star followed him, whining painfully after each step. Did walked behind with his possums that had started growling and fighting in the sack.

"Ye've probably got two stud possums in the sack," Sparkie said. "Pay no attention to their fussin'."

"Ow! It bit me!" Did screamed. "I felt its teeth through the sack." He pulled the sack from his shoulder and shook it.

"Ye're a hunter and a vine climber now," Sparkie said. "Ye mustn't pay any attention to a bite from a possum."

Did carried the possum sack in his hand, shaking the possums until they stopped fighting. Then he put the sack back across his shoulder and continued to push his way through the brush behind Sparkie.

Sparkie lifted Shooting Star into his arms and carried him over the brier stools, the log heaps, treetops, and fences until they reached the Eversole Ridge, where a narrow jolt-wagon road wound between slopes of heavy timber and there he set Shooting Star down carefully.

"Glad to git back to this road," Sparkie said. "Shootin' Star's a good load and I'm glad to let 'im walk on his own three legs!"

Their breath came short and they stopped talking for the walking ahead. Did tried not to think of the walking he had done on this day and night. He tried to think he was in his own soft bed at his good home in Greenwood dreaming that all this had happened. He tried to pretend that he would wake up in the morning and Betty, the maid, would have his breakfast ready for him, his clean shirt and socks laid out for him to wear to school. As soon as he had eaten his breakfast, he would get in the car with his father and mother and he would drive with his father down to the office from their big home just at the edge of the city limits.

"Look here!" Sparkie shouted, ending Did's dream. "Look at these tracks, won't you?"

"What tracks?"

"Man tracks."

"What's so odd about 'em?" Did asked, sleepily.

"Look, Did," Sparkie pointed toward the wooded slope on their right. "On that slope yander's where we heard the man shootin' and runnin'. On our left is Tid Barney's terbacker barn that went up in flames! These tracks are right between!"

"I never thought of that! Guess I'm too sleepy even to have seen them!"

"See where he come from the woods on that side," Sparkie said, "and went back into the woods on this side! Why didn't he follow the ridge? Ye can tell he's been a-runnin'. Look how he's skint-up the ground! Look how his shoe heels've sunk into this clay! Why was he runnin'?"

While Did laid his possum sack down and leaned wearily against a tree, Sparkie walked over to the brush and broke a straight limb from a sourwood.

"Looks suspicy to me," Sparkie said. "I aim to measure these tracks!"

Did held the lantern for Sparkie while the latter bent over the tracks measuring them with the stick.

"Whoever made these tracks has a mended shoe heel," said Sparkie excitedly. "We may ketch this barn burner yet. Quaire though, I've always thought there was more than one burnin' all these terbacker barns."

Sparkie carefully marked the length of the track on his stick by cutting a little nick into the sourwood bark. He measured the breadth of the track at the arch of the shoe and at the widest part. Then he put his nose right down in the mud and looked at the deeper spot on the left heel where it

45

had been patched. He measured the length and breadth of the little hole the patch had made. He found a track in the clay at the edge of the road where he could get a good measurement.

"Ye can't tell," Sparkie said, "this little sourwood stick with these notches may come in handy!"

Sparkie put the stick in his coat pocket, picked up his lantern, and started around the Eversole Ridge on the last lap of the journey. Did, tired from so much walking, followed slowly toward the hayloft.

3

"SPARKIE, GIT OUTTEN there," Did heard Peg yell. "Git up before yer breakfast is cold!"

Did raised up from his bed on the hay.

"Roll outten there now, boys," Peg yelled again. "It's almost four o'clock!"

Did arose from the hay and brushed the loose grain straws from his face and hair. He saw the yellow glow of lantern light moving toward the barn door. Did heard the big step and the little one as Peg's wooden leg and his leather shoe hit the frozen ground alternately.

This is awfully early to get up, Did thought as he tried to rub sleep from his eyes. I feel like I've never gone to bed.

"Sparkie, roll outten there," Peg yelled as Did listened to the barn door screak on its rusty hinges.

"Sparkie," Did said sleepily, reaching over the hay and shaking Sparkie who was snoring away. "Peg is trying to get us up!"

"Why's he tryin' to get us up before the roosters crow?" Sparkie asked, rubbing his puffy eyes with the backs of his hands. "Peg knows I always git up with the chickens! Peg's no right to wake me sooner!"

Sparkie yawned, turned over for more sleep.

Did sat up listening to Peg put ears of corn into the mules' feed boxes. He heard him talking to the mules, asking each one how he felt this morning. He listened to Peg talking to the cattle when he poured baskets of corn nubbins into their feed troughs. He heard him call each calf, steer, and cow by name as he fed them.

Then Peg put the lantern up through the scuttle-hole and climbed up into the loft.

"Good mornin', Did," Peg said. "See you're up!"

"Yes, sir!"

"What about Sparkie?"

"He's asleep over there!"

"Did ye boys git any possums last night?"

"Three, sir."

"Biggens or littlens?"

"Two big ones and a little blue midnight possum!"

"That's not very many!"

"We would've caught more but we were right up on the hill above when we saw a blaze shoot from Tid Barney's barn!"

"We saw the light plum here. That must've been some fire!"

"It was, sir! And while we watched the barn burn, Sparkie blew the horn for Shooting Star, and Shooting Star came on three legs. Somebody put a bullet through his left hind leg!"

"Ye're lucky one of ye boys didn't get a bullet through yer leg," Peg said, shaking his head sadly. "We heard the guns a-barkin' down that way like thunder!"

47

Peg walked over to the corner of the barn loft and picked up a pitchfork.

"Be careful, Mr. Sparks," Did called, "Sparkie's asleep there in the hay. Don't run that pitchfork in him."

"I've been a-havin' to watch out fer Sparkie a long time now," Peg laughed. "Once when it was in the dead of winter, I stuck the pitchfork down in the hay and Sparkie come out a-yellin'. I thought he'd slept in the shack that night. But Sparkie's always liked to sleep in the barn loft. He's made it his bedroom. How 'bout yerself? Think ye're going to like it?"

"I think I will, sir!"

"Stop that a-sirrin' me! Call me Peg."

"All right, Peg."

Just then one of the gray game roosters arose from the leafless white-oak limb where he had been warmly perched between two hens, flapped his long wings, and let out a lusty crow that broke the silence of the frosty morning. Before the echoes of this crow had died away, a black game rooster in a leafless black oak on the other side of the barn stood up, flapped his wings, and crowed. Then it seemed to Did that a rooster crowed from every tree around the barn. He could understand what Sparkie had told him when he said that he got up with the chickens. Did had never heard such chicken music in his life. It was like the barking of many foxhounds.

"I hate gittin' up in the mornin'," Sparkie said, raising up to a sitting position and rubbing sleep from his eyes.

It's mighty early for me to get up, Did thought as he sat up yawning, stretching his arms, and rubbing his face to get himself awake. Then he thought about how he'd lie in bed at home until the morning sun slanted its ray through his window half across the room. Not the crowing of a rooster nor the yelling of a beardy-faced, one-legged man awakened him then, but the gentle tapping of the maid on his door and her saying softly, "It's time to get up, Mister Did! Breakfast's on the table."

Sparkie arose, shot his arms up and down a few times above his head, and stretched like a hound-dog when first untied from his kennel. Did got up and brushed the straw from his baggy clothes.

"Now ye boys git to yer breakfast as soon as ye can."

"O.K., Peg," Sparkie said.

Sparkie jumped down through the scuttle-hole onto the pile of hay and Did followed him. Sparkie almost jumped on Dick's head where he was nibbling hay. But when Dick sniffed the familiar smell of Sparkie, he unconcernedly went back to nibbling his hay.

"What a mornin'," Sparkie said as he stepped out at the barn door.

The air smelled cool and good, for it tasted of frost. Did took a deep breath and felt new life surge into his body. Even the hound-dogs came from their kennels, sniffed the morning air, and charged against their chains and barked.

"That's the way they say good mornin' to us, Did," Sparkie said.

"That part of dog language is not hard to understand," Did replied.

Did heard the cattle lowing as Peg threw hay into their mangers. And he heard the mules braying soft-spoken words to Peg as he gave them fodder. He was rubbing their noses with his big hands. Did heard the hogs grunting to each other as they ate the corn Peg had thrown into their pens. The roosters crowed fiercely. Each one, with his flock of hens around him in his tree, tried to crow louder than the rooster in the next tree.

I'll never believe all that stuff I've heard about the country's being lonesome, Did thought, as he walked through the gate Sparkie was holding open for him. Every hog, chicken, cow, mule, and dog greets a person early in the morning.

"We'd better dabble, Did," Sparkie said, stepping upon the porch. "It'll wake all the sleep left in us!"

Sparkie broke the thin layer of ice with the gourd dipper. He dipped the water, mixed with thin slivers of ice, from the big wooden bucket and poured it into the pan.

"Do ye wash in hot or cold water at yer home?" Sparkie asked. "If ye use hot water, I'll fetch some from the kettle."

"Never mind, Sparkie," Did said. "I use the same kind of water you use."

"I was worried about ye last night when I heard all that shootin'," Arn said as Sparkie and Did entered the kitchen. "The sky was lighted from the burnin' barn!"

"Never worry about us, Arn," Sparkie said.

"I worried about Did," Arn smiled, as she took her pipe from her apron pocket.

"Don't worry about Did. He's goin' to make a great hunter. Arn, he can climb a grapevine like a squirrel. Ye ought to've seen him a-goin' up a grapevine to git a little midnighter last night!"

"Glad to hear that!"

"Jest never worry about Did as long as I'm with him."

"Ye boys git your feet under the table," Arn said, dipping into her apron pocket to get light burley crumbs for her pipe. "I've got ye a breakfast that'll stick to yer ribs. Get to the table while the coffee's hot!"

"I don't drink coffee, Mrs. Sparks," Did said.

"Ye mean you don't drink coffee fer breakfast?"

"No, ma'am."

"Would ye like a glass of milk?"

"Milk or water, ma'am."

"No, Arn, Did don't drink anything stronger than milk," Sparkie laughed as he sat down at the table. "He don't even smoke or chaw."

"I'm glad ye have Did fer a friend, Sparkie," Arn said. "He'll be a lot of help to ye."

"But Sparkie's a lot of help to me," Did said.

50

"Ye can larn a lot from him all right," Arn said. "But some of the things Sparkie does ye don't want to larn."

"Arn, ye wouldn't be a-tellin' anything on me," Sparkie said, lifting six fried eggs from the platter onto his plate. "I'll never be givin' Did bad advice. I'll be a-lettin' Did larn me some of the good things he knows!"

Arn walked to the flat-topped cookstove, lifted the cap from the firebox with the cap-lifter, and dipped wood embers into her pipe bowl. She drew a cloud of smoke from her pipe, put the cap back over the fire, and walked toward the table.

"It's light enough fer me to see how to milk," she said. "I'll go milk while ye eat yer breakfasts."

Arn gathered milk buckets from the nails on the kitchen wall and went through the kitchen door while Did and Sparkie put away the fried eggs, country ham, gravy, hot biscuits and butter, fried potatoes, sorghum molasses and wild grape jelly. Sparkie drank hot black coffee without cream or sugar, while Did drank milk.

4

"THE SKIN ACROSS my stummick feels tight as a banjer head," Sparkie said, getting up from the table, stretching his arms above his head. "I feel like I could go out and turn a hill upside down to see what is under it. How do you feel?"

"Well—sort of full and heavy, Sparkie," Did said. "I've

never eaten this way before. Not this early in the morning."

While Did pushed his chair back from the table, Sparkie pulled a burley leaf from his hip pocket and put it behind his jaw.

"Good ye've eaten a big breakfast," Sparkie said. "I don't know what we'll haf to do today. May haf to do some hard work. Will ye mind?"

"The harder the better. It'll take me all day to work this meal off."

"We'll go to the barn now and see what Peg wants us to do today."

Sparkie picked up his cap.

"What about feedin' the dogs, Sparkie?"

"Arn feeds the dogs and the possums in the mornin's," Sparkie said. "She gathers up the scraps from the table and mixes 'em with buttermilk fer the possums. She bakes corn bread fer my hounds."

Sparkie and Did walked out to the barn where the white mists of the cattle's breath floated between the barn logs into the cool air like mists drawn skyward by the sun. All the stars had gone from the clear-as-ice sky. Trees around the barn and on the hills beyond were as white with frost as if they had been painted.

The fattening hogs gave contented grunts from their log pens. The cows gave playful moos and the cattle lowed contentedly to each other. The roosters walked about the barn lot with flocks of hens following. One rooster flogged another rooster for getting too near his hens. Did watched the sights and listened to the sounds of this new world. The hound-dogs, standing outside their kennels at their chains' length, whined loudly as Did and Sparkie passed on their way to the possum pen.

"Look at the possums," Did said, smiling as he watched the possums running around in the big pen Sparkie had made of rough planks. He had covered the pen with fine-mesh-woven wire. He had buried a hollow log in the bottom of the pen and filled it with dry leaves.

"Got about twenty-five or thirty," Sparkie said. "I'll tell ye, there's money in possums when ye get 'em good and fat."

Did stood close to the front of the pen with his face against the small meshed wire looking at some of the larger possums sleeping outside the log on beds of leaves. Others ran around, their long noses down against the leaves, sniffling like cats while their long hairless tails dragged on the leaves behind them.

"See, when the weather's a little damp, a possum likes to stir and he goes through the brush a-draggin' his tail," Sparkie explained to Did. "He leaves a lot of possum scent on the ground and Shootin' Star can trail 'im easier."

"There's a lot about hunting I don't know," Did said, "but I think I'm learning from you, Sparkie. You don't have book knowledge, but you sure know hunting and fighting."

"Ye're the first person ever to say that," Sparkie said, his face beaming. "I guess maybe I do know more than a lot of people think I do. But I'd gladly trade what I know fer the book eddication ye have!"

Two of the possums standing at the empty buttermilk trough got into a fight. They growled, gnashed their teeth, and locked their jaws, holding each other with death grips while a stream of blood trickled from each one's jaw.

"Possums are powerful things with their jaws," Sparkie said. "I've had 'em bite me. I've had to choke 'em loose. That's the reason I never stick my hand back in a hole. Look at this scar one put on me!"

Sparkie showed Did a two-inch scar across the back of his hand where one had bitten him.

"Are you telling me? When one bit me through my coat and a coffee sack last night?"

"Stop yer fightin'," Sparkie said, rattling the wire in front of the box.

The possums let go of each other and ran into the hollow log.

"See, that's why it ain't good to hunt on windy nights. A possum is afraid of sound. He's afraid of the wind in the brush and the pines. If ye hunt on a windy night, it's better to hunt in the hollows and the old fields and places where the wind can't hit. There ye'll find the possums!"

When a milk bucket banged against the door, Did turned around to see Arn coming through the barn door with a big bucket, filled to the brim with milk, in each hand. Then Peg opened the barn door and let the cows out for water.

"What do ye want us to do today, Peg?" Sparkie asked.

"I've jest been a-thinkin', Sparkie, we need some wood cut," Peg said, rubbing his big gnarled hand over his beardy mouth. "But I don't think Did'll be able to hep ye pull a crosscut or use a double-bitted ax. Ever use an ax or crosscut, Did?"

"I never have, but I'm willing to try."

"Did wants to do somethin' to put muscles on his arms, Peg."

"That'll do it."

"But don't let Did work too hard, Sparkie," Arn said, standing before the barn door holding the milk pails in her hands. "He might be a little keerless with an ax. Ye watch over 'im."

"Ye boys will find the tools in the woodshed," Peg said. "I'm goin' back to the field to shuck corn today!"

"Don't shuck any in the big Buzzard Roost patch," Sparkie said. "We want to save that fer the corn shuckin'."

"I'm a-shuckin' in the Poplar flat," Peg said. "Don't worry, Sparkie," he laughed louder than the wind among the leaves. "I'm a-savin' all the corn in the big Buzzard Roost cornfield fer the corn shuckin'."

5

IT WAS THE first time in Did's life that he had ever gone out to do a day's work. He had never cut a stick of wood in his life. In his home in the big fireplace they had imitation sticks of wood, a forestick, backstick, and the fillers between that were heated with gas. Little blue and orange flames leaped from the imitation knotholes giving the sticks of wood the appearance of living embers.

I wish Mother could see me now, Did thought, as he followed his new friend along a dim path under the frost-white trees. I wonder what she would think of me if she could see me going into the woods to cut real sticks of wood for a real fireplace.

Sparkie's big overalls flapped around Did's pipestem legs like wind-whipped clothes on the stick-legs of a scarecrow. Did had to roll his shirt sleeves because Sparkie had such long arms. Sparkie's overall jumper fit him like an overcoat. Did wore his own shoes, for a pair of Sparkie's number elevens would have looked like sled runners on his feet. Did looked like a little pale-faced city boy dressed in a full-grown farmer's clothes.

The big crosscut saw swayed as Did carried it in one gloveless hand while he warmed the other hand in his pocket after blowing his breath on his blue knuckles. He looked at Sparkie striding ahead with long steps along the frosty path, whistling, carrying two double-bitted axes in one bare hand, a mallet and two wedges in the other. Sparkie's knuckles were not blue but red as a radish. Not once did Sparkie put his tools down and blow his breath on his knuckles or put one of his hands in his pocket.

Sparkie turned from the path into the white-oak timber. At each step his big shoe smashed down into the half-frozen leaves, making a screaking noise.

"Here's where we begin, Did," Sparkie said, leaning his axes against a white oak that was decaying at the butt. "Peg wants us to cut the bad trees and leave the goodens!"

Sparkie looked the white oak over from the brace roots to the topmost twig.

"I'm jest a-lookin' to see the best way to fall that'un," Sparkie said. "I want to pertect Peg's young trees all I can."

Did looked about him at the wood that had been cut and stacked. Scattered here and there beneath the tall timber were cords of firewood and stovewood.

Did watched Sparkie stick his ax into the butt of the white oak, then take a step backward and sight the way his ax pointed.

"That's about the right way to fall it."

"What do you call that, Sparkie?"

"Notchin' a tree, Did!"

Sparkie chopped a notch into the tree close to the ground. The big chips flew as Sparkie swung the ax high above his shoulder with his long arms and struck just where he wanted it, sinking it to the eye each time, until he cut a notch that was so smooth it looked as if it had been sawed.

When Sparkie finished notching the tree, he dropped his ax, spit on his hands with ambeer-colored spittle, whetted his hands together, and picked up the crosscut.

"I'm startin' ye on tough work," Sparkie warned. "But I'll go along easy until ye get the hang of it!"

Sparkie showed Did how to get down on his knees so they could saw the tree close to the ground.

"Frozen ground makes fer hard kneelin'," Sparkie said. "Rake some dead leaves under yer knees."

Did graveled in the frost until he'd found enough leaves to make cushions for his knees. He dropped to his knees on his side of the tree. Sparkie knelt on his side, and they held the crosscut between them.

"Now don't worry about yer hands gittin' cold," Sparkie told him. "This will warm 'em. First thing you know, ye'll be takin' off yer jumper. Ye'll have yer shirt off before the day is over! Let's go."

The big cutting teeth gritted against the bark at first, and the drag teeth spit out little slivers of brown and gray bark. Did watched the mark the saw made across the tree and then watched the saw teeth bury halfway, and then the drag teeth started spitting out little white slivers of white-oak wood that were good to smell.

"Never bear down on yer saw," Sparkie warned him. "Let it run just as smooth as ye can."

Sparkie wasn't getting his breath any faster than he did when they started the saw against the tree, but he stopped a minute, straightened up from his bent-over position.

"Straighten yer back a minute, Did, and ketch yer second wind."

"Whooie." Did straightened up and looked at Sparkie.

"First time I've ever seen any blood come to yer cheeks, Did."

Did just stood there, gasping for breath.

"Yessir," Sparkie said, shifting his quid of burley to the other side of his mouth. "Now let me tell you somethin', Did. Somethin' that'll make it a lot easier on both of us. Don't push the crosscut fornenst the tree. Don't try to crowd it. It'll eat into the wood fast enough. Don't try to cut slivers too big fer the drag teeth to draw out; if ye do, we'll gum up the whole works. Let the saw do the work and don't push it."

Did breathed deeply and warmed his blue knuckles.

"All right, let's go again."

The saw ate into the white oak until the crosscut got too hard to pull.

"What's the matter with it now, Sparkie?"

"The wind is a-blowin' against us. Tree is bindin' the saw. But we'll take keer of that!"

Sparkie put the thin edge of the wedge into the sawed groove and drove it in with the mallet. Did looked up and watched the treetop lean forward against the wind each time Sparkie hit the wedge.

"Now the tree 'll be easier to saw," Sparkie said, dropping his mallet.

Did and Sparkie dropped to their knees again and ripped the crosscut quickly through the leaning tree until it started snapping and popping.

"There she goes!"

Did and Sparkie jerked the crosscut from the tree and stepped back to watch it go lumbering to the earth, breaking a few limbs on other trees and crushing a few small trees beneath it. When it hit the ground, a shower of frost rose up like a snowy mist.

"We'll saw as long as ye can stand it, Did, and then we'll start usin' our axes."

"How long will it take us to cut this tree into wood?"

"Today if we're lucky."

Sparkie took his double-bitted ax and chopped away a few of the bottom limbs on the fallen tree. With his hands he measured a two-and-a-half-foot measuring stick, laid it on the log, and marked several lengths for sticks of firewood.

"The butt of this tree won't make good stovewood," Sparkie said. "It'll be too hard to split. Never saw off a white-oak block fer stovewood if it's knotty."

Did listened and as soon as he had measured the sticks, he picked up the crosscut from the white-oak stump and brought it over to the log. He found that the crosscut was easier to start since they could stand up on each side of the log and look directly down on their saw. All they had to do was stand and pull the crosscut back and forth until the log started pinching the saw and then they drove a wedge into the saw groove and spread it far enough apart that the saw ran easily through the wood. Did felt a warmth in his hands and face he had never felt before. It was fun to work in the woods with a crosscut saw, to saw down a big white oak, to see it tumble to the earth, and then to trim the limbs with an ax and measure the firewood sticks to saw from the trunk. He had seen men cut timber in the movies and they were called lumberjacks. Now Did was thinking of himself as a lumberjack and a hunter and a man of the out-of-doors, something he had dreamed of all his life.

"You know, Sparkie, I like this work."

"I'm glad ye do."

"I like to work with real wood out in the woods. I don't like to sit around a fireplace filled with artificial wood."

"What kind of wood is that?" Sparkie asked, looking across the log at Did, slowing down with the crosscut. "I've heard about every kind of wood too!"

"We burn gas at home," Did explained to him. "And it comes through something that looks like sticks of wood."

"Must be a funny fireplace," Sparkie shook his head, then speeded up the crosscut to their normal rate.

"Not after you get used to it," Did said. "But I'd much rather have your fireplace and sit before a real wood fire."

"Do ye really think ye'll like it here, Did? Think ye'll like our ways?"

"Like it?" Did repeated. "I love it already."

"Think if yer pappy finds out ye're here, he'll let ye stay?"

"No, he won't let me stay if he finds out I'm here."

"What'll ye do if he finds ye and takes ye home?"

"I'll come back again! For the first time I'm doing something on my own, and I like it."

59

"Don't ye think ye'll miss yer home and yer car and the high school?'"

"Yes, I miss them all right. But I like it better here."

"But sometime ye'll want to go home?"

"Maybe," Did said.

"Never thought I'd like town life," Sparkie said. "Couldn't git enough huntin' to do. Wouldn't have enough space fer me. This may just be a notion I've got in my head. I may like it better than I think."

Just then the saw went out at the bottom part of the log, letting the stick fall that held the tree upon the stump.

"See, we won't need the wedge when we saw the next stick," Sparkie said.

The trunk of the white oak was off the ground, about at Did's waist. The limbs beneath the white oak, farther up toward the top, and the many heavy branches in the top overbalanced the trunk.

"This'll be nice sawin'," Sparkie said. "We can rip these blocks off purty fast."

Just as the red ball of sun had peeped over the range of frost-colored hills, Sparkie and Did had sawed the firewood lengths up to the heavy white-oak top.

"This is about the time ye'd be gittin' to school if ye were back at Greenwood, ain't it?"

"I was just thinking the same thing myself. And, here, I've done a good half-day's work."

"Now we've got to try another kind of work," Sparkie said. "I hope ye can use the ax as well as the crosscut saw."

Did dropped his saw handle, spit on his hands as he had seen Sparkie do, picked up his double-bitted ax.

"I'm ready to try," he said.

"Let me see ye chop that first limb," Sparkie said, pointing to a big tough white-oak limb.

Did took a wild swing at the limb, his ax striking a glancing lick.

"Don't chop like that, Did," Sparkie warned, rolling the quid to the other side of his mouth. "If ye were to let go of that ax, it would cut me in two. If ye chop like that, neither one of us will be here much longer to do any choppin'. Ye'll kill both of us. First, ye must control yer ax."

"Like this?" Did asked, striking more slowly, hitting the limb squarely.

"No. Not like that."

"What's wrong with that lick?"

"Ye chop like a stiff-armed woman," Sparkie criticized. "Bend yer arms when ye chop. Ye won't break yer elbows. They'll bend before they'll break. Let me see ye hit another lick."

Did struck another lick.

"That's better," Sparkie said. "Hit another lick."

Did had hacked over the limb and hadn't hit twice in the same place.

"No, that's not the way, Did. Ye're choppin' toward yerself, and if ye larn to chop like that, ye'll split one of yer feet wide open. Ye don't want to chop on yer feet and legs with a double-bitted ax! Square yourself!"

Did didn't know what Sparkie meant. But Sparkie walked over, took him by the shoulders, and squared him around so if he struck an awkward lick, the ax would turn away from him.

"Now take yer time and let yer arms go limber."

Sparkie watched Did chop off the limb.

"The only way ye'll larn to chop is to know how to stand and how to strike with yer ax," Sparkie said. "After ye larn to do this, ye just got to chop a lot and then it'll come to ye. Ye need a lot of practice. The longer ye use an ax, the harder yer muscles'll git. Choppin' white-oak wood is good fer yer arms, good muscle wood."

"Then I want to chop white-oak wood."

"All right, we've got this whole treetop to chop into stove-wood lengths."

Sparkie stood with his hand on his ax handle, looking the situation over. "Watch me hit that knothole," he said, aiming at a knot of a white-oak limb.

Squirt!

"Dead center!"

"Just want to keep in practice."

Sparkie and Did sat down on a limb in the treetop.

"While we wind a minute," Sparkie said, "let's make a few plans fer some teamwork."

"You plan it, Sparkie."

"I've been a-thinkin' it'll be better if ye cut the limbs from the top," Sparkie said. "I can about chop 'em into stovewood sticks as fast as ye can cut 'em from the top and drag 'em over to me."

"That'll suit me."

Sparkie fixed a chop block while Did cut the first limb and dragged it to him. Then Sparkie laid the limb across the block and put his big foot down on it to hold it steady while he swung the ax up and over. Did worked at full speed to get limbs over to the block for Sparkie. Only once did Sparkie stop. He stopped to laugh when Did removed his overall jumper and rolled his sleeves higher. That was when the sun grew warmer and melted the frost that rose in white formless clouds toward the sun. When Arn rang the dinner bell, Sparkie was chopping the last white-oak limb into sticks of stovewood.

"That's some pile of stovewood we've cut from this top," Did said, as he put his jumper on to go to dinner.

"Are yer hands sore, Did?"

"A little."

"I'll try to find ye some old gloves when we go to the shack. Ye don't want to blister yer hands."

"They're already blistered."

62

"Are ye hungry?"

"Hungrier than I thought I could be after that breakfast this morning."

"Well, I feel like my stomach's growed to my backbone and that's real hunger. We'll larn ye!"

The two boys trailed around the path toward the shack. Now the sun had melted the frost and had dried the dampness from the leaves. The dry leaves rustled beneath their feet as they hurried.

After they had lathered their hot faces with homemade wood-ash soap and cold water and had washed away the wood grime and sweat, they rubbed their faces and hands with a cornmeal-sack towel until they were red as September black-gum leaves. Then they walked into the kitchen and dropped into their chairs with their feet under the table.

Did ate hot corn bread, slicing it and spreading it with a layer of yellow butter that melted like frost he had seen melt beneath the sun. He ate hot buttered corn bread and drank buttermilk. His mother had never had corn bread on their table. But Did liked it. He liked soup beans too. Arn had told him to eat them because they would stick to his ribs. He needed something to stick to his ribs if he were to cut white-oak trees into wood. Food had never tasted better to Did. He almost laughed out loud at the table when he thought about how Betty, the maid, used to bring him extras to the table and he'd tell her to take them back. He remembered once she had forgotten and flipped his eggs over and he'd said: "I thought you knew I wanted my breakfast eggs straight up. Take them back!"

Eggs would taste good straight up or over once lightly now, Did thought. What difference would it make? Soup beans taste better than wild honey ever tasted to me. This corn bread is as good a bread as I have ever tasted. Why haven't I had it before? I've missed a lot of things.

Did was almost ashamed of the way he put away beans,

corn bread, fried potatoes, cooked turnips, and apples. He even ate pieces of fat pork swimming in the bean soup, and he tried sauerkraut for the first time in his life.

"If ye cut wood, ye got to eat," Arn said.

Did ate until the skin on his stomach felt as if it had been stretched. He kept on eating after Sparkie and Arn were through. Sparkie looked at Arn with a pleased look on his face, and Arn smiled.

6

"LET'S HAVE A little fresh night air in here," Sparkie told Did. "This air's close after breathin' under the oaks and pines."

With all the cracks between the logs in this barn loft, we get fresh air enough, Did thought, but said nothing.

Sparkie arose and walked over to the gable end of the barn, unfastened a hasp from the staple, and pulled the gable-end door back, giving them an open view of the timbered hill where they had cut and corded wood all week.

"Think it'll be a lot better in here now," Sparkie said, as he walked over and sat down on the hay beside Did. "Didn't you feel a closeness in yer breath?"

"Well, not . . . not exactly," Did stammered.

"I shore was beginnin' to feel it!"

But it is better with the door open, Did thought, as he looked out over the hills where the big wagon-wheel moon was rolling up over the distant rim, flooding the hills with a mellow golden light that shone on the brown leaves still clinging to the white oaks. Did could imagine the many cords of short wood for the stove and long wood for the big fire-place stacked neatly under the trees. And all of this looked good to him since he had helped cut the wood and stack it.

"We've done a good week's work, Did!"

"You think so?"

"I know we have. See, I'd much rather work with ye than Peg. Peg's a good worker if ye work with 'im when the ground is froze. If the ground ain't hard, he jabs the sharp end of his wooden leg in the ground . . . I've seen his wooden leg go down in the ground so deep Peg would spin round and round before he could pull it out. I've often thought if I ever made enough money, I'd get Peg a real leg, one he could wear a shoe on so he wouldn't get stuck in the mud."

"That would be a fine gift," Did said thoughtfully, watching Sparkie take a leaf of burley from his pocket.

"It would be somethin' to give 'im a new leg fer a Christmas present some time," Sparkie continued. "I remember when I ust to hang up my stockin' fer Santie to fill Christmas Eve. In the mornin' my stockin' would be filled with candy and nuts and some little presents."

"If we could capture the barn burners," Did said dreamily. "Looks like somebody could get them. Somebody's barn has been burned down every night this week!"

"But these barn burners are sharp as foxes!"

"They may catch us asleep and burn us up in this hay. Did you ever think of that?"

"Yep, I have. I'm worried to think of it!"

"This hay would go up like a powder keg!"

"I reckon it would."

"There's another thing that worries me as much as the barn burners. I have a feelin' Father is going to find out where I am and come to take me home!"

Did and Sparkie could hear Dick and Dinah eating hay in

the stalls beneath them. They could hear the cattle rustling the fodder stalks, pulling them from their mangers as they stripped the blades. They could hear the cows crunching the corn nubbins and hear the grains dripping from their mouths back to the feed boxes with a sound like acorns falling from the oak trees on the frosted leaves. And they could hear the heavy fattening hogs wheezing when they got their breaths in their little log pen just across from the barn. Now and then they could hear a dog's chain rattle as the hound-dogs cuffed fleas and they could hear the roosters give queer little sounds of warning to their flocks of an approaching owl.

"Did, there's another present I'd like to buy," Sparkie confessed.

Then there was silence while Did and Sparkie looked at each other in the hayloft where the moonlight drifted in at the cracks and through the door.

"It's fer a gal." Sparkie looked away from Did through the door at the hill beyond the barn.

There was silence between the two boys for a minute.

"Do ye like gals, Did?" Sparkie asked.

"I've been to a few high school parties, but I—uh—never had a date with a girl," Did stammered.

"I've been sweet on Lucy Howard ever since I ust to go to school with her," Sparkie said.

"I can't say I'm exactly in love with any girl," Did said, his teeth chattering. "I've always wanted to hunt, to cut trees down, and to wade through deep drifts of snow, and to be able to shoot and use an ax and do things like that . . . I've never, never, well, not exactly. . . ."

"What's the matter, Did?" Sparkie asked. "Is that yer teeth a-rattlin'?"

"I guess it is," Did said, feeling a chill go over his body. "Since that door's open I'm getting too much fresh air."

"I'll shet the door then." Sparkie got up from the hay, shut the door, and fastened the hasp. "Now ye'll get warmer."

Sparkie sat down beside Did.

"When the snows come and the weather gets real raw, do you get cold when you sleep up here?" Did asked.

"Nope, I don't," Sparkie said.

"Do you bring covers out here to spread over you?"

"Nope, I don't," Sparkie said. "I have somethin' better than kivers."

"What?"

"I bring one of my hounds up here to sleep with me," Sparkie said. "Ye talk about somethin' warm! Ye never know what cold is with a hound-dog a-sleepin' with ye."

"Don't you get fleas from the hounds?"

"Now let me tell ye somethin', Did. Ye've heard a lot about dog fleas. I happen to know a hound-dog flea won't hurt ye. They've never bothered me. What's a little flea bite?"

"Maybe it was that bath I took in the creek that's making me chill," Did apologized for his shaking.

"Nope, these October nights are gittin' colder," Sparkie said. "Ye know the first day ye come out here how the smoke was goin' to the ground. That's a good sign of fallen weather! It's been a-gittin' colder every day. Ye better sleep with a hound tonight."

"I'll sleep with Shooting Star."

"Then I'll sleep with old Lightnin'," Sparkie said.

7

"IT'S TIME TO git up, Did," Sparkie said, shaking Did's shoulder. "Hear the roosters crowin'!"

While Sparkie stood over Did, stretching his arms above his head and yawning, Shooting Star whined and kissed Did's face.

"Git up, Did," Sparkie said. "I see Peg comin' with the lantern!"

"Shooting Star, that's enough!"

Did arose from beside the dog, sat up, rubbed his eyes, and yawned.

"Did you sleep warm last night?"

"I dreamed of picking peaches on a hot day in July," Did said. "I must've got awfully warm in the night. Shooting Star's a real bedfellow."

"Now, did the fleas bother you?"

"If they did, I didn't know anything about it!"

"I told ye a dog flea wouldn't bite a body!"

The lantern moved through the morning darkness from the house to the barn. While Did sat on the hay beside Shooting Star, he thought about what Sparkie had told him about his going to get Peg an artificial limb so he could wear a shoe, when he made enough money.

"Are ye boys awake?" Peg yelled up to the barn loft.

When Peg's lantern came to the barn at this hour and his

wooden leg sounded against the frozen ground, every living thing around the barn awakened. Did heard, above the music of the roosters, Dick and Dinah stand up in their stalls and bray. He heard the popping of knee joints as the cattle arose in their stalls. The hungry fattening hogs spoke to Peg with wheezing grunts. Even Shooting Star and Lightning spoke with pleasant whines and Fleet and Thunderbolt answered them from their kennels.

"Roll out," Peg shouted again. "Yer breakfast 'll git cold if ye don't."

"We're up, Peg," Sparkie answered. "We're a-comin' right down!"

Sparkie and Did went down the scuttle-hole with Shooting Star and Lightning following them. They took the dogs to their kennels, snapped their chains in their collars, and left them whining to go free.

"Jest a minute, boys," Peg said.

Peg was on his way to the hog pen with a feed basket of corn in his hand. He came over where Sparkie and Did were caressing the hounds.

"I've jest been thinkin' ye'd better set yer trap line today," Peg said, stopping before them, smoothing down his long, wind-ruffled beard with his free hand. "Won't be long till Christmas, and ye'll be needin' some spare change."

"Ye're right, Peg," Sparkie agreed. "The weather's a-gittin' cold enough fer the pelts to look bright when they cure."

"How much of a trap line do ye plan to set this year?" Peg asked.

"From twenty to twenty-five miles," Sparkie said. "Want to set it from Buzzard Roost to the Reeves Pond, then down with the Little Sandy River to Shackle Run."

"That's a good twenty-five miles. Ye'll have to ride the mules around the circuit."

"That's wonderful, Peg."

"Jest as soon as ye eat yer breakfast, the mules'll be through

69

with their corn and hay," Peg told them. "Saddle and bridle the mules and ride!"

"Ye ever ride a mule, Did?"

"No, I never did, Sparkie."

"Then here's where ye larn."

"Ever set a trap line, Did?"

"No, never."

"Then, here's where ye larn that too."

8

AFTER SPARKIE AND Did had eaten breakfast, they went to the corncrib, where they put a hundred steel traps, of various sizes, in each coffee sack. After they had sacked their steel traps, they went into the barn and Sparkie showed Did how to use a currycomb and brush on Dick, who was more gentle than Dinah. While Did combed and brushed Dick until his hair looked fluffy and bright, Sparkie made impatient Dinah stand long enough to be groomed for the long ride. Then Sparkie showed Did how to bridle and saddle a mule.

"Pull the girth strap as tight as ye can pull it," he told Did. "Ye can't git it too tight. The mule draws in a big breath and expands when ye start tightenin' the girth."

"That's as tight as I can draw it, Sparkie!"

"But it's not tight enough. Let me show ye."

Sparkie took hold of the girth and pulled it two notches tighter.

"See, if ye don't have it tight, yer saddle will roll," Sparkie

70

said. "Ye're liable to roll off. Remember we're ridin' over rough roads!"

They took the mules from their stalls and while Did held their bridle reins, Sparkie carried the sacks of steel traps and tied one behind each saddle to the saddle rings.

"Wait jest a minute longer, Did. There's somethin' else we want to take along!"

Did watched Sparkie go down to the barn and run his hand back into a hollow barn log and bring out a long bright shiny pistol. Then he reached back and fetched out another one. Holding the two pistols in one hand, he brought out two holsters.

"I don't mind ye a-knowin' where I keep my belongin's, Did," Sparkie said. "I keep 'em in that log."

"I've stood beside that log many times, but I never dreamed you used it for a secret hiding place."

"I've used it fer years," Sparkie said, putting the pistols in the leather holsters. "It would be a sight to see the different things I've kept in that log."

"Will the mules be scared if we shoot these pistols?"

"They're ust to my ridin' 'em and shootin'," Sparkie said. "Here's the .25 automatic fer yerself. I'll take the .38 Special."

"Is it safe?"

"When the safety's on," Sparkie said, showing Did the safety. "Now when ye want to shoot, pull this safety back and let go!"

"When must I shoot?"

"Any time ye're ridin' along and feel like it."

Sparkie buckled his holster around him so his pistol would be on his right hip and easy to draw at a second's notice.

"If we see a wildcat, he's a goner," Sparkie said.

"Do we have wildcats around here?"

"Several of 'em around the old coal mines. They plunder the farmers' hen houses and sheep barns. They'll carry off a lamb or a pig."

71

Sparkie held his hand for Did to step on before he mounted the tall mule, filling the seat of the small cowboy saddle. Sparkie pulled a big burley leaf from his pocket and crammed it into his mouth, put his foot into the stirrup, left the ground, flinging his leg over Dinah's back, and landed squarely on the big saddle.

"We're off," Sparkie said. "Let Dick follow Dinah."

A blanket of white frost lay over the land, rock cliffs, and trees. Where the mules' steel shoes hit the frozen earth, they chipped pieces of frozen dirt, leaving little holes in the white carpet of frost. Dinah wanted to run, but Sparkie held her down with a tight rein while they crossed the pasture field. Dick didn't try to run ahead but was content to follow Dinah.

When Sparkie rode to the drawbars enclosing Peg's pasture field, he slackened Dinah's bridle reins and she cleared the drawbars with a wild leap. Did slackened his bridle reins to let Dick follow Dinah. Just as Sparkie looked back, he saw Did bounce high from his saddle, pitch forward over the mule's shoulder, and hit the frozen ground on his face with his legs and arms sprawled.

"Are ye hurt, Did?"

Sparkie reined Dinah back to Did.

"Just knocked the breath from me," Did grunted, getting up.

"Bruised yer face a little is all," Sparkie said.

"I've never done any muleback riding," Did said, walking over where Dick was standing, getting ready to mount him again.

"All ye got to do is sit easy, Did," Sparkie told him. "Jest think ye're a-sittin' in a rockin' chear."

Sparkie helped Did mount, then mounted Dinah and they were off. Now they were on the old coal-wagon road and Sparkie slackened his reins so Dinah could gallop. She leaped the rut-washed ditches and threw back a shower of frozen clumps of dirt from her hind feet. While Sparkie rocked easily

72

in the saddle with one hand on the reins, he pulled his .38 from his hip holster and held it into the air, emptying it. Did pulled his automatic from the holster, turned the safety off, braced himself, and pulled the trigger back.

"Ain't this wonderful, Did?" Sparkie said, turning his head back as Dinah raced on.

"G-great!" Did said, trying to get his smoking pistol back in the holster and stick on the mule at the same time.

They rode full speed along the wagon road until they came to the dilapidated coal tipple of a worked-out mine. Here the wagon road ended.

"We haf to take a path from here," Sparkie said.

Great streams of breath were flying from Dinah's nostrils like clouds of fog when she exhaled. They expanded and thinned to nothingness on the clear blue morning air. Her sides were working in and out like a bee smoker.

"Let's wind the mules a minute," Sparkie said. "Then we'll start up this mountain."

"I thought it would rest me to ride a mule," Did laughed. "But I'm gettin' my breath about as fast as Dick. It was hard for me to stick in the saddle! And I thought Dick was goin' to fall several times."

"Don't worry about Dick a-fallin'," Sparkie said. "Mules are shore-footed things. That's why we use 'em among these hills. Ye watch 'em climb this mountain path!"

Sparkie reined Dinah around the coal tipple, past a slate dump, then he turned left onto a narrow path bordered on each side by scrub pines. Often Sparkie had to stop Dinah and break a wild grapevine between the pines on each side of the road to keep them from jerking him from the saddle. But he rode slowly in front and made a way for Did. They rode along a narrow rim of path, barely room enough for a mule to climb. Did trembled in his saddle when he looked on either side at a deep sunken coal mine.

"It's good country fer wildcats and foxes, Did. When they

73

mined this coal out, it left warm caves fer the animals. The only way a body can git one is by trappin'."

"This is a wild country all right," Did agreed.

"Not wild to me," Sparkie laughed.

When Sparkie reached the ridgetop, he stopped his mule.

"That's the Buzzard Roost country," Sparkie said, pointing down to the valley below.

"Why is it called that?"

"Buzzards ust to roost in these rock cliffs. They laid eggs here and hatched their young."

Did reined Dick up beside Dinah and looked over.

"What a country," he said. "Look at the cliffs."

"Cliffs and coal mines," Sparkie said. "And plenty of fur-bearin' animals!"

"But why didn't we set some traps back at the first coal mines?" Did asked.

"Too close to civil-i-zation," Sparkie said. "Animals like a wild country. Here's where they live! Here's where we'll set the big traps fer foxes and wildcats!"

Sparkie dismounted, unsnapped one side of his bridle rein, and tied it to a tree. Did rolled off Dick, stretched and yawned. He did what he had seen Sparkie do; he fastened his mule to the limb of a nearby white oak while Sparkie untied a sack of steel traps from the saddle.

"Do you know where we're going to set them, Sparkie?"

"I shore do," Sparkie said, starting down a path with the sack of steel traps on his shoulder. "Ye follow me. Remember this path, fer ye may haf to come to the traps by yerself some-time."

When they came to a cliff with a hole worn slick between a split in the rock, Sparkie stopped and threw the sack of traps from his shoulder. He pulled off a few loose hairs from the sides of the rock, held them up, and looked carefully at them.

"Gray foxes," Sparkie said.

Did watched Sparkie take gloves from his pocket, shove his hands into them and scoop out a bit of earth big enough to place a trap at the mouth of the hole so the jaws would be even with the ground. He threw the loose dirt he had scooped up into his gloves over the cliff. Then he took a trap from the sack, mashed the spring with his foot, and set the trigger. He put it in the groove neatly.

"Git some dry leaves from back under the cliff, Did," he said. "Be shore ye have yer gloves on."

While Did went after the leaves, Sparkie took a hatchet from his hunting coat and hacked down a small sapling. He cut a stake and sharpened one end. He drove this down into the solid earth in front of the cliff, put the loop on the trap chain over it, and drove the little spike attached to the chain into the stake.

"It takes somethin' to hold a fox," Sparkie said.

Then he took the dry leaves Did had gathered and covered the trap.

"He can't see the trap now," Did said.

"And he can't smell our hands."

"Won't a dog get in that trap?"

"No, it's set too fur back in the hole! I always see to that. I ust to set deadfalls and I ketched two dogs. That larned me somethin', Did. Larned me how to set traps."

Sparkie picked up the sack of traps, swung it over his shoulder, and they moved on to another cliff where there was a big opening.

"Looks like wildcats dennin' here," Sparkie said. "We'll haf to set eight or ten traps to kiver the hole."

Did carried the leaves while Sparkie set the traps and cut the stakes to hold them. After they had set these traps, they went down to another cliff and set traps for red foxes. Sparkie knew where the different animals denned. He would stop at a cliff, scent the wind from back in the hole like a sniffing hound-dog, and then he would look around until he found a hair on one of the rocks and he would examine it carefully.

"You know a lot about setting traps for different animals, Sparkie!"

"I ought to know a little fer I've trapped enough!"

After they had set over half of the traps among these cliffs at Buzzard Roost, they climbed back up a little fox path to the ridge road, where they untied their mules, mounted, and rode around the ridge path, facing the red ball of an early sunrise.

The ridge road was wide and Did and Sparkie could ride their mules side by side. They could look down to their right and see the valley where their shack was and they could look from their left down into a valley that was a wild country, where there wasn't a shack to be seen but where there were deep wooded hollows and palisades of high cliffs. This country was the home of the foxes and wildcats.

"I've been a-comin' to Buzzard Roost since I've been big enough to follow the hounds. There's not a high knoll along this ridge road where I ain't listened to my hounds drive home the fox!"

"You don't mean you stayed out winter nights along this ridge where the wind blows so cold?"

"See this little ash pile here?" Sparkie asked, pointing to a pile of firebrands with charred ends. "I carried wood up from the slopes and built that fire on a night last January. It was zero weather and I laid by that fire. One side of me burned while the other froze."

"You can hear hound-dogs running here for miles, can't you?"

"Ye shore can. This ridge road is the home of the fox hunters. Here's where we come to hear the chases. Ye can come here at night and listen to the hounds after the fox, ye can listen to horns blowin' all over these mountains. I know about every hunter's fox horn soon as I hear it blow. I know about every rock cliff in this country. I know where to set traps and I know the cliffs where if a fox hunter finds my

76

traps he'll take 'em up and break 'em. I know it 'cause it's my country."

Did noticed that Sparkie never bounced in his saddle. He rode as easily when his mule jumped over the trees that the wind had blown across the ridge road as if he were glued to the saddle. And as he rode along, he took his pistol from his hip holster.

"What do ye say we ride and shoot again," Sparkie said. "I like to ride and shoot when I'm this close to the sky!"

Sparkie started off in a gallop, his pistol high in the air over his head. He began shooting. Did followed him out the straight stretch of ridge road, his pistol barking so fast he couldn't count the times. Now it was a race to see which mule could get ahead. Their mules leaped over entire treetops that lay in their path. Once Dick barely cleared a tree, his hind foot just grazing a limb. He stumbled but didn't fall, and Did held to the saddle horn to keep from pitching forward over his head. Dick kept beside Dinah as they ran toward the morning sun. A cool mountain wind was hitting the boys' faces, a wind so strong they could hardly get their breaths.

"Here's where we stop," Sparkie said, with a grunting breath. "We turn to our right again here! We got to go down a long ridge path!"

"Where are we headin' for now, Sparkie?"

"Polecat country."

"Where's that?"

"It's a lot of fields betwixt here and the Reeves Pond. It's really the polecat country."

Sparkie led the way down the mountain to a broom-sedge-covered field where there were dirt holes under the steep bluffs that fringed these old deserted, worn-out tobacco lands. In each one of these holes they set from one to three small steel traps. They found holes under a few cliffs where they set traps, holes where Sparkie had set traps in other trapping seasons.

"Ye know, Did," Sparkie said, "polecat pelts is where a body makes the money. If we can only git some solid black hides or some narrow stripes! They fetch from seven to nine dollars apiece! That money ain't to be sneezed at!"

They rode across the old deserted fields, Sparkie leading the way. They rode along a cow path through pawpaw and persimmon thickets where the fruit lay in heaps, frost-ripened and mellow, under the trees and under the carpet of leaves.

"See, this is a good possum country too," Sparkie said. "Over in the next hollow the possums den under the cliffs, and we'll set some traps there."

When they reached the next hollow, their mules needed a rest. They reined them to oak trees, took an armload of traps, and went up the hollow to find the cliffs and the slick-worn dirt holes where they set their traps.

After they had set their traps in Possum Hollow, they mounted their mules and rode toward Reeves Pond. It was a long ride over Tunnel Hill and down Nicholl's Hollow and then they came to the Little Sandy River bottoms where they dashed across open corn fields, where often the mules sunk down over their hoofs in the mud. The sun had thawed the frozen ground.

"There are minks and weasels around that pond. Maybe muskrats." Sparkie pointed to a pond out midway of the big bottom.

They rode across the bottom to the pond, dismounted, and tied their mules to clumps of wild snowball bushes. They walked around the pond inspecting the slick-worn holes in the soft bottom earth. Where the holes were used, they set their traps, staking them and placing dead leaves from the wild pond lilies to conceal the jaws and triggers.

"Ye'll see this is the place to git muskrats," Sparkie said as they untied their mules from the wild snowball bushes, mounted them, and rode toward the Little Sandy River.

Where the Reeves Knoll sloped down toward the river

were many cliffs, and here they stopped their tired mules and set more traps. At the Putt Off Ford, where the Sandy River bottoms stretched across Hungry Valley, they found more muskrat holes where they set traps.

"We've only got a few traps left, Sparkie," Did said. "When we started with two hundred traps this morning, I wondered where we'd set 'em all. "

"We could set another hundred traps if we had 'em," Sparkie said. "Shucks, we ain't visited half the rock-cliff dens and the slick-worn holes that I know among the mountains and hollows! We're jest a-comin' into the good possum country now and we don't have over fifteen traps to set!"

They rode along beside the Sandy River where the tall sycamores grew along the river bank and leaned out over the small winding river.

"I'm a-gittin' mighty hungry, Did," Sparkie said. "I'd like to sit down to a table of good grub. I feel as empty as a hollow beech tree. How do you feel?"

"I feel about the same way, Sparkie!"

They reached the Shackle Run valley where the apple orchards were on the south hillside slopes.

"See, right down here along these bluffs next to the creek are the possum holes," Sparkie said. "The groundhogs dug the holes and the possums took 'em. I know where there are a hundred more dens the possums use. We'll set what few traps we have left."

Did reined Dick to a water birch beside Shackle Run and Sparkie tied Dinah to a low branch of a sycamore nearby. They took the last traps they had and set out along the steep bluff alongside the creek. They set them in the slick-worn possum dens and returned to their mules, mounted, and rode up Shackle Run toward home.

"We'll ketch somethin' in some of these traps," Sparkie said.

"How often will we have to look about these traps?"

"One will haf to ride the trap line Monday. Would ye like to?"

"I'd love to!"

"Sunshine, rain, or deep snow?"

"It doesn't matter."

The mules were as wet with sweat as if they had swum Sandy River. They rode past a cold ash heap that had once been Tid Barney's barn. Sparkie and Did whistled as they rode slowly toward home.

PART FOUR

I

IN THE DISTANCE they could hear the hounds on the mountains. They could hear the music of more than seventy hounds barking at once. The music would get loud and then it would fade away.

"Listen, Did," Sparkie said, patting his feet on the planks where Peg had fed the hay. "Ain't that purty music?"

Lightning, Fleet, Thunderbolt, and Shooting Star charged at their chains, barked, howled, growled, and kicked dirt up with their hind feet.

"Listen to our dogs, Did," Sparkie said, as he patted his feet on the hay. "They want to get back to the chase!"

The barking of the hounds faded away again while Sparkie sat on the hay with his hand cupped over his ear.

"Listen, Did, ye'll hear 'em come over the Tunnel Hill in jest a minute. They're a-comin' this way!"

"Whose hound-dog's leadin' the chase, Sparkie?"

"Brier-patch Tom Eversole's War Horse," Sparkie said. "He can always lead when I don't use Lightnin' to burn him out, then Fleet to cut him out! I bet old Brier-patch Tom's happy tonight that my hounds're not loose!"

When the hounds topped the Tunnel Hill, Sparkie patted his feet louder. There was a thunderous roar of fine and coarse barking hounds, hounds with long howling barks and squealing barks, hounds with short barks and long mournful barks —all blended together as they drove the fox toward the Buzzard Roost country.

"They're in Possum Hollow now," Sparkie said, when their barking faded away again. When they reached the old fields, the polecat country, Did never heard such a chase in his life. He remembered how long it had taken him to ride a mule across these fields, but the pack of hounds didn't take three minutes to cross it. Then he heard them reach the mountain. Their barking was plainer than ever now as they climbed. Many of the barks were little short grunts. In a few minutes they were running on the ridge road, and Did could tell just as well as if he had been there by the sound of each hound's barking. They topped over the mountain into the wild Buzzard Roost country, the home of the foxes and wildcats.

"There's nothin' in the world like hound-dog music on these mountains," Sparkie said. "It's the sweetest music under the stars."

Through the gable-end door Did and Sparkie could see Arn and Peg out on the doorstep. They were standing in the moonlight, Peg with a cigar in his mouth and Arn with her pipe, and Peg with his arm around her shoulder, listening to the hounds running the fox on the mountains.

"Do they like hound-dog music?" Did asked Sparkie.

"Shucks, they love it much as I do," Sparkie said proudly. "Arn and Peg's gone with me a many a night and we'd just take my hounds out and start a fox, and they'd stay after midnight beside a fire listenin' to the hounds. Nearly everybody round here loves hounds but a few cranky terbacker raisers!"

When the hounds went beyond the mountain, their barking faded slowly until there wasn't a sound. Sparkie's hounds went back into their kennels and Arn and Peg started back in the house, but they stopped on the doorstep. They were looking toward the barn.

"Listen, Did," Sparkie said, cupping his hand over his ear to catch the sound, "do ye hear strange voices?"

"Yes, I do, Sparkie, and one of the voices I've heard before!"

"Whose voice is it?"

"Father's."

Though the moon was shining, two men came down the path that wound between the pawpaw and persimmon groves, the path that Did had walked over when he first came from Greenwood, and one was lighting the way with a high-powered flashlight. When it was turned toward the barn, it cast a circle of light bright enough within its radius for one to see a rusty nailhead in a weathered barn plank. Once the two men stopped talking and turned the light on the log shack.

"That's where they live," said one.

Then he focused the light on the barn and beams of light flickered through the cracks across Did's and Sparkie's legs.

"That's the barn."

Then he focused the light on the chickens roosting in the trees. The roosters quirked to their hens. Did and Sparkie could see Arn and Peg still standing on the doorstep watching the light and listening to the voices. The flashlight focused on Arn and Peg, and Arn threw her hands before her eyes to keep out the light.

"That's Arn and Peg," the voice said.

"So this is where my son's stayin'," came the harsh tones of another.

"That's Father," Did whispered.

"Do ye want to git out and take to the hills?"

"I want to stay up here and see what happens. Maybe he won't find me here."

When the two men came down beside the barn, they stopped.

"Mr. Hargis, do ye think ye can find your way back all right?"

"Oh, sure," Mr. Hargis said. "Just one path leading all the way back to the wagon road. Can't miss it. But just a minute."

Sparkie and Did watched Mr. Hargis run his hand down in his pocket, pull out his pocketbook.

"I owe you something, young man," he said.

They could see him give the man something.

"Thank ye, Mr. Hargis."

"Which one of the Eversoles did you say your father was?"

"I'm Brier-patch Tom Eversole's boy. Cief Eversole!"

"He's a polecat," Sparkie whispered to Did. "He ust to spy on moonshiners and git twenty-five dollars fer turnin' a man over to the revenooers. Now he makes moonshine hisself."

"You're sure this is the right house?"

"Quite shore, Mr. Hargis!"

When the hound-dogs barked at the strange man, Mr. Hargis shined the flashlight in their eyes until they tucked their tails and ran inside their kennels.

"That'll stop your clatter."

Cief Eversole watched Mr. Hargis for a minute and then he went down the path toward the beech grove holding something in his hand. He stopped a few steps down the road, held it up to the moonlight, looked at it, and then hurried on.

"Hello," Mr. Hargis shouted when he reached the gate.

"Howdy do," Peg said softly from where he and Arn were waiting for their visitor on the doorstep.

"Are you Mr. Sparks?"

"Yep, I'm Peg Sparks."

"I'm Bill Hargis from Greenwood, Peg Sparks."

"This is my wife, Arn, Mr. Hargis," Peg said.

"Good evening, Mrs. Sparks," Bill Hargis said.

"Won't ye come in?" Peg invited him.

"No thank you. I've not come for a social visit. I'll be brief and state my business. Is Didway Hargis here?"

"Yep, he's here," Peg told him.

"Mr. Sparks, just what do you mean by harboring my boy

84

at your home after this outlaw you are raising came to Greenwood and tolled him off to a place like this? We've looked everywhere for Didway."

Mr. Hargis spoke frankly, waving the flashlight with one hand while he talked.

"I'll have ye know, Bill Hargis, I'm not a-harborin' yer boy!"

"Then what would you call it? What do you mean by letting him sleep under your roof?"

"He don't sleep under my roof. But he can sleep under it any time he wants to."

"Ye know I didn't toll you off, Did," Sparkie whispered. "Ye come because ye wanted to."

"But Father's mad, Sparkie," Did whispered. "I know when he's mad. I can tell by the way he talks. Watch him prance around out there in the yard."

"He sleeps in the hayloft," Arn said, drawing a wisp of smoke from her pipe.

"In a hayloft on these cold nights? If his mother only knew this! She's almost crazy now!"

"Yep, he sleeps with one of the hounds on a cold night."

"I can't understand it! Has he lost his mind?"

"It ain't sich a bad place after all, Mr. Hargis," Arn said. "If ye's to live here a while, ye might like it!"

"Like it!" Bill Hargis sputtered. "I had to leave my car over there on a lonely wagon road and walk for miles! You think I'd live in a place like this?"

"Yer boy Did loves it," Arn said. "He likes his bed of hay with a hound fer a bedfeller. He loves th' grub we give 'im. Ye ought to see how he's gone to eatin' since he's been with us and been workin' a little."

"Just what kind of work is he doing here?" Bill Hargis asked.

"He's been heppin' Sparkie cut down white oaks and split 'em into firewood and stovewood."

"You mean he's using an ax and a saw?"

"Yep, that's what we mean," Peg said. "He's a little weak at first, but he's goin' to make a good worker!"

"He's not goin' to make a good worker, I'll have you know," Bill Hargis shouted. "He's going back to school as soon as I can get him back. What right have you to keep my son out here to cut your firewood? He's going back with me."

"Maybe I will," Did whispered to Sparkie.

"Sh-sh," Sparkie whispered. "Don't let 'im hear us up here!"

"I'm not harborin' yer boy," Peg shouted, his temper getting higher, "but I'm not a-goin' to run that boy off! He's a fine boy!"

"Of course, he's a fine boy," Bill Hargis said. "He's been well raised. His mother has seen to that! We never allowed him to associate with a boy like this Sparkie."

"Be keerful what ye say about my boy," Peg warned.

"Your boy?" Bill Hargis laughed. "Your boy, huh? You think I don't know the story. I can tell you plenty. I'll tell you whether you want to hear it or not. He's not any more your boy than he is mine!"

"What's that?" Sparkie whispered to Did. "I'm not Peg's boy?"

"Mr. Hargis, we won't talk about that!"

"Oh, yes, we will," Bill Hargis said. "We'll talk about it in court if you don't give me my boy! You know this Sparkie is not a Sparks. You know your wife there was tramping along the highway with him a little baby in her arms, when you took them in. You lived alone and you took her in to cook for you and married her and now you have this awful boy on your hands!"

"Gosh-old-hemlock," Sparkie whispered. "That ain't true. I'm Peg's boy."

Sparkie put his face in his hands, with his elbows resting on his knees, and he looked at the shafts of moonlight that filtered through the barn cracks on the hay.

"Don't pay any attention to what my father says," Did whispered, trying to look into Sparkie's face. "He ought never to have said it."

"Did ye know it, Did?"

"No, Sparkie, I didn't. But it doesn't matter to me whether you are Peg's boy or not."

"If I had my choice of a father, I'd rather have Peg as any man I know on this earth." There were tears in Sparkie's eyes. "I still want to git 'im a leg fer Christmas so he can wear two shoes like other men."

"You know, Mr. Sparks, that this Sparkie would never go to school," Bill Hargis said. "He started to school a couple of times and dropped out shortly. Then the next thing I found about him he was running over the country with a couple of big pistols strapped on him, shooting at about everything he saw. He's even helped make moonshine and what is more, he has carried it to Greenwood and peddled it on the streets on stock sale days. He's gone into neighbors' pasture fields and got their mules and horses and rode them at night. He's stolen chickens, ducks, geese, and turkeys. All he's ever done has been to pilfer, hunt, steal, and kill. He's even robbed farmers' bee hives at night."

"Jest a minute, Bill Hargis," Peg broke in. "Ye've said about enough. He's my boy. I won't have ye talk about him like that. Ye might get hurt if ye keep it up. All that saves ye now is yer own boy. He's a much better man than his father, and if it wasn't fer Did, I wouldn't let ye leave this place in one piece."

"They're gettin' into it, Sparkie," Did whispered. "Do you suppose we'd better go down there and stop a fight if it starts?"

"It ain't a-goin' to start, Did," Sparkie sobbed. "When hound-dogs do a lot of fussin', they don't fight. They just quarrel. That's what they're a-doin'."

"I don't want my boy in a place like this, I tell you," Bill

87

Hargis continued. "I want him home. That's where he belongs. Not out here with a den of hillbillies sleeping in a barn."

"Don't fergit, Mr. Hargis, if these hillbillies ye don't like would stop tradin' at yer General Merchandise Store, where would ye be? You wouldn't have yer big fine home and yer big car! Ye wouldn't hold yer head so high yer nostrils ketch the rain! Don't fergit we could norrate some of the things ye've said here and yer trade wouldn't be very much!"

"So you would do something like that," Bill Hargis snarled. "Just plain blackmail! But I'd expect that of you!"

"When ye fight and talk about us, remember we'll fight back," Arn said. "And ninety-nine out of every hundred hill people will hep us!"

Sparkie was still holding his face in his hands. Did looked from a crack in the barn at Arn and Peg. They stood on the front doorstep looking down at Did's father, who pranced around like a wild fox in a cage.

"I don't think you'll be able to hurt my trade, Mrs. Sparks," Bill Hargis mocked jeeringly. "You'd better get that notion out of your head. Is my son hiding in that house?"

"No, he's not in this house!"

"Would you give me permission to look inside?"

"Look all ye want to," Peg said, pulling the latchstring.

"Father's said too much, Sparkie," Did said softly, after they'd gone inside the shack. "He's really mad!"

"Do ye aim to leave, Did?"

"No."

"Reckon he'll search the barn loft?"

"I expect he will."

"Then let's go over to the cows' stalls."

When Sparkie and Did started down the scuttle-hole, they saw Bill Hargis come from the front door with his flashlight.

"Yes, Mr. Hargis, ye can look up in the barn loft if ye want to," Arn said. "Ye may find'em up there asleep."

"I can't understand it," Bill Hargis said, as Did and Sparkie

88

ran across the mules' stalls for the cows' stalls. "Why on earth would my son leave a good home to come here?"

"Maybe the Eversoles could tell ye, Mr. Hargis," Arn spoke gently. "They seem to give ye a purty good story about Sparkie! They didn't leave much out."

"How do you know the Eversoles told me, Mrs. Sparks?"

"Didn't Brier-patch Tom Eversole's boy, Cief, fetch ye here?"

"But he didn't tell me."

"You paid him to bring ye here, didn't ye? We heard ye talkin' as ye topped the ridge."

"Don't fergit, Mr. Hargis, Sparkie and Did may be a-fox huntin'," Peg said. "We were standin' on the front steps a-listenin' to the hounds and that's why we heard ye a-talkin' to Cief Eversole when ye crossed the ridge and come down the path."

"It doesn't matter what I've said," Bill Hargis told Arn and Peg as he walked toward the gate. "I don't want you to give my boy another bite of food. I want him home. If he doesn't come home, I'll take this to court!"

"Remember we're not sendin' 'im away. Take it to the court! Remember what ye've said about us! Remember, we've given ye yer profits!"

Peg and Arn stood on the doorstep watching Bill Hargis go toward the barn, focusing his flashlight up and down the front wall looking for the entrance to the barn loft. He focused it on the gable-end door and then he stuck the flashlight in his coat pocket, climbed up the logs like a squirrel, and tried to open the door.

"Open this door, Didway," he shouted. "You're in there! Open up!"

Sparkie and Did were down under a stall. They heard Bill Hargis pound the door and ask Didway again to open it. Then they heard him go back down the logs, walk around to the barn door, open it.

"Whoa, mule," he said to Dick as he flashed his light around until he spied the scuttle-hole. He crossed the stall, climbed up on the manger, and stuck his head up through the scuttle-hole. Then he went up.

Did and Sparkie heard him walking over the hay. They could see the reflections from his flashlight as he searched the hayloft.

Here's where they've slept, he thought. I can't understand it! How can Didway sleep in a place like this? Has he gone wild like a varmint? What's come over him? Where on earth can he take a bath? What's he doing for clothes? Wonder what he has to eat? It's awful to think about him sleeping down in one of these holes with a stinking hound beside him!

Did and Sparkie could hear him jumping up and down on the hay.

"He thinks we're hiding under it," Did whispered softly in Sparkie's ear.

"Sh-sh," Sparkie whispered. "He'll hear ye."

After he'd tramped the hay for several minutes, he came back down the scuttle-hole, flashed his light over the mules' stalls and under the mangers. A sweat broke out on Did's face. When Bill Hargis went out the barn door, slamming it shut behind him, Did and Sparkie breathed sighs of relief.

"He's not gone," Sparkie whispered, as Bill Hargis went out where the dog kennels were.

Bill Hargis called to the dogs and they came from their kennels.

"It doesn't look like they've gone fox hunting to me," he said. "Here's the hounds."

Then he found four empty kennels where Sparkie had kept his hounds that were poisoned.

"Maybe they hunt with four while the other four take a rest," he said, and started back toward the path.

Did and Sparkie lay under the stall. Through one crack of the barn, they could see Arn and Peg standing on the front doorsteps watching Bill's flashlight, listening to the words he muttered for them to hear. Through a crack between the logs in the cows' stall they could see his flashlight in the golden moonlight as he walked up the path, around the pawpaw and the persimmon groves. When he reached the cliffs, near the hilltop, Sparkie and Did got up from under the cows' stall and went through the mules' stalls and out at the barn door. When they stood in the barn lot, they saw his light on the ridge road.

2

"WAIT A MINUTE before you go to bed," Peg called to Did and Sparkie. "We want to talk to you."

Arn and Peg left the doorstep, walked through the gate into the barn lot, out beneath the chicken roost where Sparkie and Did were standing.

"We jest want to talk with ye and have a understandin'," Peg said. "Let's go over here and sit down on this log."

"I'm sorry about the way Father talked to you, Peg," Did said.

"He was riled about ye, Did. When a man's riled, he's liable to say somethin' he's sorry about later."

"But he said some things about Sparkie!"

"Don't worry about that, Did."

Peg, supporting himself with his hand, sat down on the log. Peg took a cigar from his coat while Arn took tobacco from her apron pocket and filled her pipe. Sparkie pulled a match from his cap bill and lit Peg's cigar and Arn's pipe.

"I don't think yer Pap liked the way we blowed terbacker smoke around 'im awhile ago," Peg said. "He kept fightin' the clouds of smoke away from his nose."

"Father has never liked tobacco smoke. He doesn't smoke nor chew, and he's always advised me against the use of tobacco."

"I've never told Sparkie not to use it," Peg said. "How could I tell 'im not to when his Ma and I both use the fragrant weed? But we didn't come over here in the barn lot to talk to ye about terbacker. Ye heard every word yer pappy said and we feel the same way about yer stayin' with us as we did about Sparkie's usin' terbacker! We didn't tell ye to come here and we ain't goin' to tell ye to leave! We want to know how ye feel about it after ye heard what he said tonight!"

"I feel the same way that I've felt since the first day I came," Did said. "I love it here."

Arn wheezed on the stem of her pipe. Peg drew a cloud of smoke from his cigar. The end of his cigar was like a glowworm in the dark.

"But I don't want to get you into any trouble, Peg," Did said, thoughtfully. "If you and Mrs. Sparks think it best for you, I'll leave. But as long as you will keep me, I'll stay!"

"We ain't a-goin' to tell ye to leave, son," Peg said. "I've always liked boys. Even if Sparkie has been called an outlaw and his reputation told over agin to me tonight, I still love him. Since ye've come here, I'm beginnin' to feel the same way about you. We've got a pair of boys now. I wish we had more. Wish I had a house big enough fer ten or twelve."

"I love ye too, Peg," Sparkie said. "Ye're my father too," he said emphatically.

Sparkie moved about restlessly on the log, stirring the dead leaves on the ground with his brogan shoes.

"But yer pappy, I believe, aims to fight us with the Law," Arn said.

"How will ye feel, Did, if we fight 'im back?" Peg asked.

"You don't aim to. . . ."

"We don't aim to harm his body," Peg broke in, "but we'll hurt his trade."

"He didn't have any right to talk about the hill people the way he talked tonight," Did said.

"All I haf to do is put the words yer pappy said about us on the grapevine telephone," Peg said, shaking his head and blowing a cloud of smoke. "It won't take long fer the news to git around. Ye'll be surprised how fast it travels. It goes faster than a foxhound can run down a mountain!"

"I'm not going to tell you what to do," Did said. "I know I want to stay here. I don't want to leave."

"The news will hurt his trade," Peg said. "I like to think what the news will do to 'im when the people sell their terbacker and hides!"

"Ye mean what terbacker there is left in these parts," Arn said. "Don't fergit a barn is burnt down somewhere nearly every night!"

"This means yer pappy will haf to turn away some of his clerks," Peg said. "He won't need 'em. About all the trade he'll git will be from city folks when I put the message on the grapevine."

"Are ye shore the grapevine's in good workin' order, Peg?" Sparkie asked.

"It's been workin' a long time, Sparkie. It worked all through prohibition and it's been workin' ever since. Ye know that. What a quaire question to ask!"

"Reckon yer pappy will be back tomorrow?" Arn asked Did.

"Don't think so, Mrs. Sparks," Did told her. "Sunday's his busiest day."

"He don't run the store on Sunday?"

"No, but Father teaches a Sunday School class in the morning. He plays golf in the afternoon. Then he goes to church in the evening."

"Gosh-old-hemlock, I'd never have thought that," Sparkie said.

Arn laughed and drew on her pipe. "Can't tell who is a Christian anymore."

"I think he'll be back some evening this week," Did said. "He'll wait until his day in the store is done and drive out as far as he can and walk the rest of the way like he did tonight."

"He's a-goin' to bring the Law next time, I fear," Arn said.

"He'll probably bring Mother along to talk to me," Did said.

"Is she a proud woman?" Arn asked.

"Well, I don't know, Mrs. Sparks," Did said.

"Why did ye ast Did that fer, Arn?" Sparkie asked, disgustedly.

"I've heard about what a nice home she has," Arn said. "And I hate fer her to see our shack. She'll think Did stays in an awful place."

"What do you think she'll think of me?" Sparkie said. "Cief Eversole told Mr. Hargis my life story. What'll she think about Did's stayin' with me when Mr. Hargis goes back and tells her what Cief Eversole told him?"

"If she comes and asks me about Sparkie, I'll tell Mother he's a good boy," Did said.

"Cief Eversole told the truth about Sparkie, Did," Peg said. "We want ye to know that!"

"And the truth don't sound too purty," Sparkie said. "It hurts some. First time in my life I've ever felt that way about the truth. I don't know why I feel that way!"

"But I'll tell Mother, Sparkie has never asked me to take a chew of tobacco," Did said. "I'd tell her he never offered me a drink of whisky, that he never tried to get me to do anything wrong. And I'll be tellin' her the truth too."

"Did, ye make me feel good," Sparkie said, squirting ambeer at a tree down near the corner of the barn, splashing it against the bark. "Ye really say some purty things about me."

"Sparkie, you're the first person ever to take my part, except Mother and Father, and they don't know how, really."

"Yer one of us now, Did," Peg said thoughtfully. "I want to know if ye want to stay with us. I want ye to know that Sparkie has done all the things yer pappy said he had. He's done things yer pappy didn't mention."

"Aw shucks," Sparkie said. "Let's don't talk about 'em now, Peg."

"No, let's all go to bed and get a good night's sleep," Peg said, getting up slowly from the log, throwing his cigar butt down and pushing it deep into the earth with the sharp end of his wooden leg.

They got up from the log. Arn knocked the ashes from her pipe and followed Peg toward the house.

3

PEG, ARN, AND Sparkie knew that after the heavy frosts fell on clear cool October nights, the sun melted the frost into white mists that ascended toward the sun if there wasn't a mountain wind. If there was a mountain wind, it blew the vapor through the air, over the earth, and through the tobacco barns. They knew this vapor was carried by the wind among the drying tobacco plants in the wall-less tobacco barns and it moistened them and put them in case. They knew if there was a rainy season, the tobacco would be put in case. They knew if there were not any frosts to be melted into vapor, if there were only dry winds, cold winds, or freeze, the tobacco would remain dry and brittle.

Peg always decided when the tobacco was in case. The brown shriveled tobacco leaves had to be soft and pliable as sun-wilted sassafras leaves in July. Peg examined it carefully to see if any part of a leaf was dry enough to crumble. It was all right if it would hang together like glue. When the tobacco was in case, Peg took the sticks down from the tier poles and removed the plants from the sticks, stripped away the leaves, graded and tied them into hands. Peg, Arn, and Sparkie called this "terbacker season." When the tobacco season was on, while the season was good and the fragrant plants soft and pliable, they worked almost day and night to strip their tobacco, grade it, hand it, and get it ready for market.

"The terbacker's in case," Peg said after he carefully examined it early that October morning. "This means we work day and night. I want to git it to the Standard Warehouse in Maysville before Christmas."

"But what about the trap line, Peg?"

"There is that trap line!" he said. "I'd fergotten it. Varmints can't stay in traps long as terbacker will stay in case."

Sparkie looked at the ground and shuffled his brogan shoes against the frosted leaves.

"I'll have to hep ye, Peg," Sparkie said thoughtfully, looking toward Did.

"But who'll follow the trap line?"

"I'll follow it," Did said, "though I'd like to learn how to work in tobacco too."

"Ye'll git to work with terbacker," Peg said.

"Then I'll follow the trap line today."

"Sparkie, ye'd better tell Did how to kill the game and sack it."

"Reckon you can find all the traps we set, Did?"

"I don't think I've forgotten a hole or cliff where we set one, Sparkie. I can go back to every one of them."

"Then I'll saddle and bridle Dick fer ye," Sparkie said. "Be keerful. Don't ride too fast but keep Dick movin', fer it's a long ride to the traps. Ye may come back with a load of game."

"I'd like to," Did said, catching the excitement. "I'd like to come back with a full sack of game."

Sparkie combed and brushed Dick as if he were taking him to Greenwood. Then he bridled and saddled Dick and led him from the barn.

"I can mount 'im, Sparkie," Did said, putting his foot in the stirrup and swinging his leg over the high mule's back, seating himself squarely in the saddle.

Sparkie went to the hollow barn log, got his .38 Special and a box of cartridges.

"Now if ye git a wildcat, be sure ye shoot him betwixt the eyes," Sparkie cautioned Did. "Cats are mean. Don't git too close to the trap. If ye git a fox, shoot him betwixt the eyes. Shoot the polecats and don't git too close. Ye know what will happen if ye do. Never stick yer head down the hole."

"What about the possums, minks, weasels, and muskrats?" Did asked.

"Don't kill the possums," Sparkie said. "Bear down on the springs of the traps and lift the possum out by the tail and put 'im in the sack. Knock the minks, weasels, and muskrats in the head with a stick."

"You mean knock them in the head with a club?"

"Yep, that's the way to kill 'em."

"Must I put 'em all in the same sack?"

"Now I'm goin' to tell ye about that," Sparkie said, walking toward the corncrib to get the sacks.

"Put the polecats in a sack to themselves," Sparkie told Did when he returned with the sacks. "Put the possums in a sack to themselves and the weasels, minks, and muskrats together. They'll all be dead and can't fight. If ye get one fox, sack 'im like ye do the other game. But if ye get two foxes, tie th' feet together and let one hang down on one side the mule behind yer saddle and one on the other side. Be shore they're tied to the ring in the saddle. If ye git a wildcat, sack 'im just

97

like ye would a fox. Don't fergit to balance the game on the mule's back and be shore all the sacks are tied at the ends and to the saddle."

Sparkie tied four sacks and a bundle of small rope together and fastened them to the rings in the saddle. Then he gave Did a long-bladed hunting knife that went into a tan leather sheath.

"Ye may need this knife," he said, watching the mule prance, wanting to go. Dinah brayed from the barn and Dick answered her.

"Will Dick be afraid of blood?" Did asked. "Will he scare when he smells it?"

"Never did," Sparkie said. "He's carried a lot of game from my trap lines."

"Then I'm on my way," Did said.

"Good luck, hunter," Sparkie said, as Did rode away.

Sparkie watched Dick jump the drawbars with Did and then they were out of sight. Sparkie walked slowly to the tobacco shed to help Peg and Arn.

4

DID LET DICK trot slowly over the rutty road until he came to the coal mine tipple. He went over and over Sparkie's instructions, one at a time. He rode around the tipple, up the path that led to the mountain, along the narrow trail between the sunken mines, and up the mountain between pine groves on each side of the path. He let Dick walk, for the greenbriers and wildgrape vines slapped at his face. With one hand he shoved the briers and vines aside without having his mule stop, and with the other he reined the mule to this or that side of the path until he had reached the mountaintop. When he looked over the cliffs into the Buzzard Roost country, he dismounted and tied his reins to a white-oak limb. With two sacks, rope, his hunting knife, and pistol, he went down the path the way he had gone with Sparkie to set the traps.

When he looked down at the rock cliff where Sparkie had set the steel trap in the groove, he saw what he thought to be a friendly dog sitting out in front of the rock cliff. Did stopped, looked a minute while it looked at him, and then the dog tried to get away, but the trap held it by the left foreleg. When it tried to squeeze back into the groove, Did grabbed it by the hind leg and pulled it out, standing between it and the rock.

It's a pretty fox, Did thought as he pulled his pistol and waited to get a chance to shoot it between the eyes. But the fox wouldn't turn its head toward him. Then he aimed at the side of its head, behind the ear, fired, and the fox fell over, its body quivering, a little red stream of blood trickling from the bullet hole in its head to the slick-worn ground. Did stood watching its gaunt sides work up and down, a little less each time as it inhaled and exhaled, for its life was quickly going.

"First thing I've ever killed," he mumbled to himself, looking proudly at the fox. Then he looked at the trap hanging to its foot. It didn't have a chance, he thought. I shot it with its foot held in a trap.

He put the big fox, warm and limber, into a coffee sack and threw it across his shoulder. But something disturbed him when he looked at the rugged hills where the fox had run free at night and had outwitted a pack of hounds, where it had chased across these mountains with its mate, maybe with its young, enjoying this wild country as he, Did, was enjoying

99

it now. He thought how much the fox had wanted to live and how it had struggled to get away and how it had feared man and death.

Then he walked down to the cliff where Sparkie had set the cluster of traps. Before he reached the traps, something looked up at him and snarled. It showed its teeth like a wolf and snapped and snarled. But it couldn't move, for three of its feet were in traps.

"Another fox," Did mumbled to himself. "It's in pain. I want to get it out of its misery as soon as I can."

While the helpless fox snarled, barked, and looked at Did with its wild beady eyes squinting at the light, Did aimed at the center of its forehead, squeezed the trigger, and it toppled over on the leaves Sparkie had spread over the traps.

It's an unfair way to kill, but it's out of its misery, he thought, looking at its feet that were cut by trap jaws. Did watched the fox's beautiful gray body quiver while its life slowly ebbed away. He wondered what was wrong with himself when he wished that he had not had to kill this fox, he who had always wanted to be a hunter. A few dollars for this hide that some woman would wear. The hide is worth more to the fox, he thought.

When he got the trap loose, he found that one of its legs was broken. He put the big gray fox into the coffee sack, swung the sack over his shoulder, and walked slowly up the fox path toward the other traps.

I hope I don't find anything more, he thought, pulling up the path by holding to sassafras sprouts with his free hand.

He was glad when he came to the cliff where Sparkie had told him he caught something every time he set traps here. Did threw down his sack and walked up under the roof of the cliff. The traps were just as they had been set; they hadn't been molested. Then he walked happily away, picked up his foxes, and went to the next cliff. The traps were empty. He was under the ridge road, walking toward the mule, and had only one more cluster of traps to inspect in a cliff just above him. This was the cliff where Sparkie had told him he never had any luck trapping. Did wasn't thinking about these traps. He was thinking about the foxes he had killed and the way he had stood at close range and blasted their life forever from them.

Gr-r-r- . . .

The cat jumped the length of the trap chain, its mouth open, showing long yellowish teeth, its wild eyes wide and glaring and filled with madness. Its long claws on its front foot sliced Did's overall pants leg as if it had been sliced with a razor. Did jumped back, losing his balance, and tumbled down the steep hill, losing his sack that rolled against a clump of sourwood sprouts. He rolled into a greenbrier cluster that tangled in his overall jumper and hair, and he lay there until he was able to regain his breath. He lay there, untangled the greenbriers from his hair, pulled a few briers from his hands; then he unwrapped them from about his legs, got up, and put his cap back on his head. He drew his pistol from the holster and his hunting knife from the sheath. He went toward the cliff, watching for the wildcat to charge again.

When the cat dashed again, Did fired at it without taking aim, hitting its shoulder. He stopped the cat's advance. It pulled wildly against the trap trying to free itself to get to him, and Did thought he saw the stake give under its weight. Before the cat could do much pulling at the chain, he fired again at its ribs thinking he might hit its heart. This time the cat quivered . . . but didn't go down. It stood facing him, snarling, showing its long yellow teeth. Then Did aimed and hit it squarely between the eyes. It toppled over as the foxes had done. Its long ugly body lay there quivering as its feet moved up and down and its toes contracted. It struggled for breath. Did watched the last breath go as the cat straightened its long body and lay perfectly still. Its unexpected attack had angered him at first. Now he wasn't angry. He didn't blame the cat for fighting for its life. Maybe the jaws of the trap were paining its right hind leg, for they had cut deeply, burying the trap jaws in its flesh.

Did put the hunting knife back in the sheath and refilled the chamber of his .38 while a thin stream of cold smoke slowly oozed from its long barrel. Soon as he'd reloaded his pistol, he put it in the holster and walked up to the cat. He pushed down the trap spring with his foot, pulled the buried jaws from the flesh, and released its leg. Then he held it up by the hind legs and its nose came to his ankles. It was much bigger than either of the foxes. It was almost as large as Did. And it was heavy to lift. Did laid it back on the ground, looked at its dangerous claws, felt its muscled legs, and opened its mouth wider to look at its long sharp teeth. He carried the cat up to his mule and stretched it on the ground; then he went back down the mountain and fetched the sack with the foxes.

He wondered how he would carry them on the mule at first. After thinking it over, he roped the foxes' hind legs together, then he roped the cat's legs together, weaving the rope between the wildcat's legs and the foxes' legs until they were tied securely. He used the sack for a pad across Dick's back and laid the wildcat on one side of the saddle, the foxes on the other to balance the cat. Then he tied them tight to the saddle. He untied the mule, fastened the rein, mounted and rode away, looking back at the game across his mule as it trotted along the ridge path.

He rode until he came to the knoll, where he turned to his right down the long path to the polecat country, the old worn-out tobacco fields now dotted with persimmon and pawpaw groves. Did tied his sweaty mule to a persimmon tree and set out across the broom sedge wasteland to the cliff that skirted the field where the traps were set.

When Did came to one of the holes, he got down, stuck his face up to the hole to look. One of the trap chains was twisted and he pulled it out with his hand. There was a leg in it.

"Poor polecat," Did said to himself. "He must have wanted his freedom awful bad to gnaw his leg off."

When Did stuck his face up to another hole, a big possum, with his leg in the trap, was lying there asleep. He did what Sparkie told him. He caught the possum by the tail, pressed his foot on the trap spring and freed the possum and put him down into a coffee sack. He had the feeling that he had rescued a living possum from the steel jaws of a trap and he felt good about it. Did found a rabbit in another trap before he reached the end of the bluff and he hit it across the head with a little stick, killing it easily. He put it down in the sack with the possum. Now that he had looked at all the traps along this bluff, he crossed a ravine to the little hill where they had set traps along some rock cliffs.

At the first one Did stopped and put his face down to look in the hole. Something hit him . . . his face and eyes . . . stinging his eyes like a wasp sting planted in each one. . . . He fell backward, dropped his sacks, and rolled to the ground as he had heard hound-dogs did when they attacked a skunk. Did never had butterflies walking in the pit of his stomach before, but they were there now as he rolled, wiped his eyes with his hands, and cried. He sat down and waited for the spell to wear off. He would never stick his head in a hole again. When he got up, he approached the hole carefully.

When the polecat backed from the hole toward Did, he stepped sidewise and shot it through the side of the head. Now that he was already covered with the scent, he didn't mind picking it up by the leg and dropping it into the empty sack.

With much caution he approached the remaining traps set in the polecat country, finding two more polecats and another possum. He shot the polecats when they started backing toward him. He freed the possum and put it in the possum sack. He tied more game behind his saddle and, mounting the mule, rode across the sedge grass land toward Possum Hollow.

Where the path forded the creek, Did looked down to see

something black beside the water. Dismounting, he found a dead polecat with three legs.

Thirst from the loss of blood after it lost its leg, Did thought. It came down here and gorged on water. Sparkie had told him about this sort of thing.

It was black as midnight. Did untied the polecat sack and dropped it inside. He retied the sack and fastened it securely to the saddle ring. Then he mounted his sweaty mule and rode to Possum Hollow, where again he tied Dick to a pawpaw bush.

He felt a tiredness in his legs as he hurried from trap to trap. The bright carpet of autumn leaves rustled under his feet now that the sun directly overhead had melted the frost and dried away the mists. Did took three more possums from the traps, two large ones and a small midnight possum. He sacked them, hurried to his mule, and was soon on his way over Tunnel Hill, then down Nicholl's Hollow, and across the open river bottoms to Reeves Pond.

Did found two muskrats' legs in the first two traps. He killed a weasel by hitting it over the head with a wild snowball stick. When he examined the last trap, he found a big animal with pretty brown fur with dark rings across it. It was much larger than the kind of mink Sparkie had told him about and when he went near the trap, it stood on its hind feet, lifting the trap that held its front paw. It was a pretty animal and Did hated to kill it. But I'm a hunter now, and I have to, he thought.

While the animal stood looking Did over, Did's right hand fumbled to his hip for his revolver. At close range he leveled at a spot between its eyes, but the animal remained on its hind feet looking at him curiously. At the crack of the revolver, it slumped over, blood trickling from the tiny hole in its head. Did couldn't pick it up as long as it drew its hind legs up and down and as long as it struggled for breath. He waited for its body to become still while the wind played across the open Sandy River, rustling the fine fur, bending it up and down. When it had ceased to move, he freed its foreleg from the trap.

He examined this animal and found a collar around its neck. Wonder what it is I've killed? he thought, as he sacked it in the last empty sack.

Did rode along the river until he came to the Reeves Knoll. Here he picked up three more possums and a skunk from the traps. He'd bagged so many skunks he had forgotten how much he smelled of that first one. At Putt Off Ford were six more muskrat legs in the traps. At the last trap he found a rabbit, tapped it on the head with his pistol barrel, and put it in the sack with the strange animal he could not identify. Then he moved on toward Shackle Run, the last lap of his journey. The sun was moving over toward the west and Did felt hunger gnawing at his stomach as he rode the sweaty mule across the soft bottom loaded with the game he'd trapped.

It's a good thing I didn't get all the muskrats that lost their legs in the traps, he tried to make himself believe, as he thought about the polecat that had lost its leg in a trap. He couldn't stop thinking about how hard a time a four-legged animal had making its way in the woods, and how much harder it would be with three legs.

He tied his mule to an apple tree when he went along the Shackle Run line of traps set in the groundhog holes that possums had taken over. He took four more possums, a weasel, skunk, and rabbit from these traps and he was glad when he had sacked them. He had a load on Dick, and his mule was tired and sweaty. Did loosened his bridle reins, and Dick moved rapidly toward home despite his load. Since Did was tired, he sat in the saddle as if he had grown there, relaxed, and let Dick choose the parts of the road he liked best as he bore him and the game toward the shack. He remembered the way the animals looked at him with their legs held in the vise of steel jaws, with hurt and pain in their eyes, and how he had shot them when they didn't have a chance. The only one he couldn't feel sad about was the wildcat that had fought back. Yet that was something he would have done, he thought, if he had been trapped. He sat thinking, while Dick trotted up the creek, splashing blue water up in sprays that shone like silver in the sun.

5

WHEN DID RODE Dick into the barn lot, Sparkie came from the barn stretching his tobacco-glued hands and arms above his head.

"Gosh-old-hemlock," Sparkie shouted, his face beaming. "Come here, Peg, Arn. Look what Did got!" Then he stopped and his hand went to his nose. "Phew! And a polecat got him!" Sparkie danced back and forth, laughing and holding his nose. With his hand still in front of his face, he ran up to the mule's side where the wildcat was hanging.

"Have any trouble killin' him, Did?"

"Look where he cut these overalls with his claws," Did said, pointing to the rip. "He jumped at me before I reached the trap!"

Arn and Peg walked from the barn with their sleeves rolled and their hands and arms dirty with tobacco glue. They looked at the wildcat.

"A biggen," Peg said. "He's killed many a calf, chicken, and pig! It's the biggest wildcat I've ever seen among these hills! Phew, polecat, polecat," Peg laughed as he put his hand over his nose.

"Did, I can't believe ye've done this," Arn said. "Ye're such a small pale-faced boy with city ways! An' all that polecat smell on ye! Ye'll never smell the same again!"

Then they walked to the other side of the mule, holding their hands to their noses and looking at the foxes.

"Ye shore have a load on the mule," Sparkie said. "I didn't dream ye'd bring two foxes, a wildcat and. . . ."

"Five polecats, twelve possums, two weasels, three rabbits, and a funny-looking mink with a collar around its neck," Did said proudly. "Caught it at the Reeves Pond."

"Ye never ketched a mink with a collar around its neck," Sparkie said. "Where is it?"

"In one of the sacks!"

Sparkie started taking the sacks from behind the saddle. He couldn't wait to untie them, so he cut the ropes with the hunting knife he took from Did's sheath. He dumped the polecats from the sack on the ground.

"Look, Peg," Sparkie shouted happily. "Not a broad stripe among 'em. All narrow stripes and black!"

"I'm not a-gettin' near them polecats, Sparkie," Peg laughed. "Ye and Did can have 'em!"

Sparkie opened the possum sack, for they were fighting and growling.

"What about this polecat smell on me?" Did asked. "Won't soap and water wash it off me?"

"Soap can't take all the scent from ye," Arn said. "Ye'll haf to bury yer clothes deep in the ground fer three days to kill the scent."

"Shucks, fergit about a little polecat scent, Did," Sparkie said, holding the sack open for Arn and Peg to see the possums. "Only one midnighter among 'em."

"Did is a lucky hunter," Arn said.

"Did is a good hunter." Sparkie was happy as he carried the sack of possums down to the pen while Did opened the sack and showed Arn and Peg the weasels.

"Weasels ain't no good," Peg said. "All they're fit fer is to cut the throats of chickens and rabbits and drink their blood. Hides ain't worth much, but I'm glad ye got 'em."

Then Did opened the sack with the animal in it he took to be a mink.

"Look what a coon!" Peg shouted. "He's a buster!"

"A coon?" Did said. "Sparkie never told me about 'em!"

"They're a-gettin' scarce around here, anymore!"

Sparkie brought back a rabbit from the possum sack. He threw it down by the two Arn had taken from the sack the coon was in.

"Gosh-old-hemlock, what a coon, Did!" Sparkie said, feeling the collar around his neck. "He's been somebody's pet coon!"

"We have rabbit and coon meat now," Arn smiled, filling her pipe.

"We'll have to send Did again fer luck," Sparkie bragged. "That's the biggest haul we've ever trapped at one time!"

"Sparkie, I love to hunt," Did said. "I love to hear the hounds run the fox and I like to see Shooting Star put a possum up a tree. I like to shake a possum from the tree. I can wear off the polecat smell. I can bury these clothes if you've got more for me to wear. But I don't like to kill. I thought it over as I rode the mule home. I don't want to follow the trap line again. I'll stay here and help strip the tobacco and let you go in my place."

"I'LL CARRY THE wood and water to the house," Did told Sparkie. "I'll help feed the cattle, the mules and I'll learn to milk the cows. I'll do anything but help skin these animals! It does something to me. It makes butterflies flap wings in my stomach. I can't stand it!"

"Then I'll do the skinnin', Did," Sparkie said, honing his long hunting knife to a razor's edge. "Ye hep Peg and Arn with the terbacker."

Sparkie's eyes followed Did as he walked toward the tobacco shed.

"I'll follow the trap line from now on too," Sparkie called after him.

The smell of cured tobacco was not a bad smell. Did didn't mind reaching up overhead to take the sticks down from the tierpoles. Peg couldn't climb up to get them on one good leg. And Arn couldn't climb very well.

"Ye're just like a squirrel," Peg told Did. "Ye can beat Sparkie climbin'."

Did climbed up among the tierpoles, lifted the sticks, loaded with cured tobacco plants, and handed them down to Peg, who stacked them carefully on the dirt floor. When Did had removed all the sticks in his reach, he walked out the pole like a chicken on a limb until he got within reach of more sticks and then he handed them, one at a time, down to Peg. Arn sat on a hickory bark-bottomed stool, smoked her pipe, stripped the tobacco leaves, and sorted them into different grades of tobacco. Did watched her rough hands move quickly and steadily.

I'd like to see *my* mother do that, Did thought.

After he had handed many sticks of tobacco down to Peg, Did dropped down from one tierpole to another, swinging with his hands until he reached the ground floor. Then he got himself a stool and sat down close to Arn. She showed him how to strip the leaves and grade them into neat little piles.

"Ye're fast with yer hands, Did," she told him. "Ye'll make a good farm hand. I've never seen a boy take to work like ye have!"

"And just fer the few weeks ye've been here," Peg said, "I can see a new color comin' in yer face. Can't ye see it, Arn?"

"Ye're not as pale as ye were, Did. Ye're gettin' sunshine, rain, and wind in yer face!"

"I've got an appetite," Did said, laughing. "I eat so much I'm ashamed of myself! Do you know, my hands are gettin' hard!"

"That's caused by a-usin' the ax and crosscut," Peg said. "That will make yer hands hard as rocks."

Did liked to work with Arn and Peg. They were kind to him. They showed him what to do, but they never told him to do a thing as they did it. They never gave him advice unless he asked for it. Did was doing skilled labor when he graded tobacco. Peg told him he was doing it all right. Arn told him he was doing it better than Sparkie.

"Ye see, Did, we've got to work while we got a season," Peg said. "That's the reason we're workin' early and late hours to get this done."

While they stripped tobacco, they heard Sparkie's hammer driving tacks into boards to hold the pelts after he had stretched them on boards. When they didn't talk, they heard Sparkie's hunting knife rip the skin around the animals' forelegs, and up and down the fore and hind legs and sometimes up the belly, depending on the animal he was skinning. When Did heard this, he started talking to drown the sound.

One day while they all worked stripping tobacco, Brier-patch Tom Eversole walked into the tobacco shed.

"Good mornin', folks," he said friendly like, rubbing one of his big gnarled hands over his beardy face. "Looks like ye got some mighty fine terbacker here!"

Then Brier-patch Tom laughed a wild laugh at his own words, as he fondled a piece of dirty rag he always carried between his index finger and his thumb.

"Purty good, Brier-patch Tom," Peg said. Peg worked on and did not look up.

Arn sat on her stool and stripped tobacco as if Brier-patch Tom hadn't come inside the shed. Sparkie stood upon a tier-pole with a tobacco stick in his hand that Did had handed down to him from the topmost tierpole in the shed. Sparkie had been relaying them on to Peg. Now Sparkie stood looking at Brier-patch Tom but did not speak. Did viewed the scene from above.

"I guess ye heard about Fond Short's terbacker barn a-goin' up in smoke last night?"

"Nope, hadn't heard a word about it," Peg grunted. "But I know one thing. I'd like to shoot the men betwixt the eyes that's a-burnin' these barns!"

"Yeah, and a-pizenin' all these dogs too," Sparkie said.

"Poor old Fond had all his terbacker stripped and ready fer the market," Brier-patch Tom talked on. "I've been afraid somethin' was a-goin' to happen to my barn. I've been ex-pectin' to see flames start poppin' from it some midnight. That would about ruin me too. Ain't ye worried none about yer terbacker, Peg?"

"Why don't ye git the man that's burnin' 'em?" Arn asked.

"I've been thinkin' about that reward," Brier-patch Tom said.

"Think I'll put out a reward fer the man that pizened my hounds," Sparkie said.

"Too many strange people have moved among the Plum Grove hills," Brier-patch Tom said. "Jest what I told Tid Barney when he lost his barn. Ye know about us old-timers, but ye don't know about these strangers! A man can't have hounds and terbacker among these hills any more, and they're two of the finest things in a man's life."

Then Tom laughed hysterically at his own words. Arn and Peg and Sparkie didn't even smile.

"This ain't what I come to see ye about, Peg," Brier-patch Tom said. "I'd better state my business and move on."

"I didn't send fer ye," Peg said, looking him straight in the eye. "When ye state yer business, ye had better move on."

"I just wanted to tell ye, I've been to Greenwood and the city folks are riled against ye, Peg," he said. "Thar's a lot of talk about sickin' the Law on ye! Bill Hargis has told the people how ye're-a-keepin' his boy! It's even gittin' dangerous fer a Plum Grove man to go to Greenwood. The Greenwood people are riled. They're beatin' up the Plum Grove men in the streets. Jest come to warn ye, Peg. They're lookin' fer ye and Sparkie."

"Just what did yer son Cief tell Bill Hargis about Sparkie last Saturday night?" Arn asked. "What do ye folks mean by stickin' yer noses into other people's affairs! All the Ever-soles've ever done is to spy on people! Now ye're a-goin' over to the Greenwood side and spyin' on the Plum Grove people. Ye've turned against yer own kin."

"When ye went into Bill Hargis' store, did ye see many people?" Peg asked.

"Come to think about it, I didn't," Brier-patch Tom said. "What made ye ast me that?"

"Never mind the reason. That's none of yer business no-how. Our grapevine telephone don't reach yer shack."

"I thought I was yer friend by comin' in to tell ye," Tom

said. "Don't git mad at me about it! I can't hep it if he does sick the Law on ye! I can't hep it if they do lay fer ye and Sparkie in Greenwood. I've come as a friend to warn ye."

"Ye're not a friend to me," Peg said. "I know yer son Cief told the truth about Sparkie. But why did he tell anything about Sparkie? Yer Cief's done worse things than my Sparkie."

"Ye'd better clear out, Brier-patch," Sparkie said. "Ye've packed enough tales fer one day!"

"Who are ye, young man, to order me from this shed?" he asked, rolling up his wild eyes at Sparkie.

Squirt!

"Oh, oh, oh." Brier-patch Tom screamed, clasping his hand over his eye. "Ye've put my eye out!"

Arn laughed aloud. Did turned his head so Tom Eversole with his one good eye couldn't see that Did was laughing too.

"Git out, Brier-patch!" Peg shouted. "I'd hate to lambast ye with a terbacker stick."

"I'm gittin' out, Peg," he answered. "Don't ye worry."

"I say ye are!" Sparkie said.

"But I'll remember ye," he said, looking up at Sparkie as he started to leave. "Ye won't be able to sell yer possums in Greenwood now. Peg won't be able to trade his baskets of eggs fer groceries at the stores either."

Squirt!

The ambeer splashed just below Brier-patch Tom's good eye.

"That was a poor shot, Sparkie," Arn said.

"But he jerked his head, Arn."

Brier-patch Tom Eversole ran from the tobacco shed with his hand clasped over his eye. In the other hand he still clutched the little piece of dirty rag between his thumb and index finger.

P A R T F I V E

I

THE BIG DOUBLE-LOG shack, with a dogtrot running between the two log pens, was just beyond the coal tipple of the worn-out coal mine. When Sparkie and Did arrived walking, they saw mules with saddles and mules without saddles tied to the paling fence and the low trunks of the shade trees. Hitched among the mules were a few horses that whinnied and fought with the mules. They reared up and tried to get to one another. They saw more mules and horses coming through the moonlight, a few with only one rider but many with two. Sometimes the girl would ride behind the boy. But more often the girl was in the saddle and the boy sat behind her with his arms around her.

Sparkie and Did heard the strains of fiddle music above the roar of talk and laughter and above the mad brays of the mules and the shrill whinnies of the horses. They could hear Tim Gilbert calling the sets. They could hear the brogan shoes and the low-heeled slippers cracking on the broad-plank floor.

"My feet feel the music, Did," Sparkie said. "I know Lucy's a-waitin'. Why are we late?"

Sparkie did a few steps to the music as they crossed the yard. His brogan shoes rustled the dead October leaves while his long body, in his tight-fitting blue serge pants, swayed to the rhythm. When his gray coattail bounced up, Did could see the .38 Special handle sticking from the holster on Sparkie's hip.

"Will you be safe carryin' that pistol to a dance, Sparkie?"

"It's part of a man's dress around here," Sparkie said. "We don't carry 'em to use; they're only fer ornaments. Wait until ye see how the other boys are dressed."

Did wondered if he were properly dressed since he didn't carry a pistol.

"Ye ought to make a good dancer, Did," Sparkie said, as they walked up the big stone steps to the dogtrot. "Ye've got plenty of action. Don't be bashful now! Git right in there and dance! People here are as friendly a people as ye've ever seen! They believe in dancin' and havin' a good time."

"But I don't know many people around here," Did said. "And I never danced in my life!"

"Won't be long until ye'll be a-knowin' the people," Sparkie said. "They'll be a-knowin' ye too! They'll be yer friends! Wait and see!"

Sparkie didn't knock on the door that went from the long dogtrot into the room where the music was playing, where Tim Gilbert was singing his dance calls, and where the fiddles, banjos, and guitars were playing a lively tune. Sparkie just opened the door and walked in.

"Sparkie, ye're late," said a girl with blond curly hair. "I've been a-waitin' fer you."

"All right, Lucy," Sparkie said. "We'll haf to wait now to ketch the next set. Lucy, here's my friend, Did Hargis."

"Oh, I've been a-wantin' to meet ye," Lucy said. "Ye're the city boy, ain't ye? Everybody among these hills has heard about ye."

Now the set had ended. The music ceased, and the dancers stood about over the floor with their mouths open getting all the breath they could, for the dance had been fast and furious. Did saw old men and women, young men and women, boys and girls not over twelve years of age, all on the floor dancing together. He saw the pistol handles sticking above the holsters on men's hips and he saw the outlines of pistols in their pockets. He had never seen anything like this before in his life. Only the small boys and a few of the old men didn't carry pistols. Did knew he wasn't properly dressed.

"Before ye start the next set," Sparkie announced above the bee-loud hum of voices, "I got somethin' I want to say."

Everybody stopped talking and turned around to face Sparkie.

"There's so many here, I can't take my friend and yer friend around and interduce 'im to ye. But I've got with me Did Hargis, who's as good a hill man as we have here tonight!"

There was a roar of voices went up to the low ceiling and a clapping of hands as everybody looked at Did standing there in his wrinkled gray suit. Color came to Did's pale face.

"We've heard of ye, Did," said a beardy-faced man. "Ye're the young fellar that's started a war between Greenwood and Plum Grove. Ye're smaller than I thought ye'd be!"

"We've heard of ye on the grapevine telphone," said another man with a high collar around his long neck and a bow tie beneath his Adam's apple, that worked up and down when he talked. "We heard of ye the first day you came to these hills."

"I'm glad to meet all of you," Did stammered. "I'm glad—uh. . . ."

"My name is Sandy Braiden, son," said a tall sandy-haired man who emerged from a group of dancers and took Did by the hand. "I was a-thinkin' ye's a big man after all I'd heard about ye over the grapevine. Ye're jest a boy and not properly dressed at that. Here," he said, as he mopped his brown sweaty face with a big bandanna with one hand while with the other he unbuckled the holster from his narrow waist, "take my pistol fer the night."

Did choked. He stood looking at the tall skinny man whose tight-fitting pants legs clung to his long skinny legs.

"But I . . . I . . . don't especially. . . . Well, I never. . . ." Did couldn't finish. There was silence in the room while the mountaineers looked on.

"Did ain't took to all our ways yit," Sparkie said, as he walked over where Did was standing. "He'll soon be a-dressin' properly fer these dances."

Everybody laughed. Did tried to smile.

"He's shore welcome to my decoration," said Sandy Braiden. "If he's one of us, he's perfectly welcome to my favorite pistol."

"Thank you, sir," Did stammered.

The mountaineers walked up slowly and quietly to meet Did. Even the musicians left their places and came to meet him. Sparkie introduced him to the old and young who shook his hand and looked over the boy from Greenwood, whose arrival in the hills had started trouble between the hill and city people. Sparkie introduced Did to several mountain girls, who were as shy as Did. Among them was Pollie Porter, a girl of sixteen, with blue eyes and black curly hair.

"Now everybody git his partner and git ready fer the next set," Tim Gilbert shouted. "Every man git his partner."

"Don't be bashful, girls," Sparkie said. "One of ye will haf to take Did through this set. Did's never danced."

"I'll dance with 'im," Pollie Porter volunteered.

Pollie, standing the closest to Did, had been silently looking him over. The other young girls he had met stood back and watched. For the first time in Did's life, a lot of girls seemed to take notice of him. But their silence made him squirm. He wondered if it wouldn't be difficult dancing with one since he had never danced in his life.

When the partners started pairing off for the dance, Did still stood there bewildered. He had met all of these people. They had shaken his hand warmly and each had said a kind word. One had even tried to lend him his pistol. Did knew that he was among friends. I wonder if I can go through with this dance, he thought. His face grew suddenly warm and his heart pounded. Pollie Porter stood near him, waiting. Did felt frozen to the floor. Finally she walked over beside him and smiled. He felt better.

As the mountain musicians tuned their instruments for the dance and the couples moved out on the floor to their places, Did's eyes roved about the big dance room and the dancers. He had not said a word to Pollie. Not yet. And she had not spoken another word to him. The musicians returned to their places at the end of the room. Not all of them sat down. Lacie Howard didn't. He stood behind his big bull fiddle and looked down it. He was one of the mountaineers it would take a long time to forget. Long Lacie Howard had hands a foot long, long thin fingers, and a long red chicken neck. His fingers, like sticks of brown kindling, were playing with the bull fiddle strings.

All of the household furniture had been moved so the dancers would have plenty of room. Did could see, in the yellow glow of the four kerosene lamps, lighter places on the newspapered walls where a piece of furniture had sat and protected the paper. Overhead the big rough-hewn oak beams supported a ceiling that was circled with dark stains in many places, where the upstairs roof had leaked. If Mother could see this, Did thought. She'd never stand for roof-leak stains on her ceiling. If these people could see my home. . . .

But the laughter and the talking of the couples broke up Did's thoughts. He had never heard laughter like this in his home. He glanced over the floor at the couples of old men and women he thought were too ancient to dance. He saw boys and girls not any older than he was standing on the floor eager and ready. There were young men too, with sun-tanned faces, wearing tight-legged pants with pistols showing from their holsters, standing with tall, straight girls. They are a tall people, all right, Did thought, and Pollie Porter took him by the arm.

The band finished tuning their fiddles, guitars, and banjos, and the couples got ready for four dancing sets. Jeff and Ephriam Potters played their fiddles, Willie Hampton and John Snowden played Spanish guitars. Arville Short played a steel guitar. Ebb Barney played a five-string banjo and Long Lacie Howard plucked the strings of his big bull fiddle.

"All ready for the grapevine twist," Tim Gilbert shouted. "Every man git his partner."

When the music was in full swing, Did felt something run through his blood. Pollie Porter led him through the dance. All Did had to do at first was to follow her and soon he found his feet marking time to the wild music while the dust came up from the floor and down from the ceiling. He gave his right hand to this girl, his left hand to that. They swung in a circle. Then in and out, over and under. Did could see the holsters on the men's hips as they swung their partners high in the air. The girls' skirts filled with wind and their feet stuck straight out as the men lifted them from the floor. Did had never seen anything like this in his life. He heard Tim Gilbert calling the set. He stamped to the wild music, he was aware of the thunder of heels on the wooden floor. If the boys didn't swing the girls, the girls would swing the boys. Everybody shouted, laughed, talked, and gasped for breath.

Then Long Lacie Howard, with the skinny neck and the fingers, ran from the end of the room with his big bull fiddle and rushed into the middle of the floor. The other musicians left their places too, only more slowly, playing their instruments as they walked over the floor, scattering among the dancers.

"Come on, pet," Did heard Lacie say to his fiddle. "Talk to 'em, pet!"

Lacie played the tune on the fiddle. He played it with the twitch of his lips and the movement of his body. Drops of sweat ran from his radish-red face, but he didn't have time to mop it. Not now, when the fiddles cried and the guitars sang and the banjos laughed and the dancers' feet shook the walls.

Did remembered how the city people had gathered about the mountain dancers on the Fourth of July and Labor Day celebrations in Greenwood and how they had laughed at their dancing, not taking part in it themselves but looking upon it as something that belonged to the crude world of pistol-toting, moonshine-drinking and fist-fighting mountaineers. Did remembered how his mother and father made fun of such dancing. His father had called it "frolicking." They just didn't know what they were missing. Pollie Porter swung him high, her soft curly black hair swishing across his hot face. The mad tempo of the music, the rhythm of Pollie's dancing excited him. Sweat broke out and streamed down his face, but instead of minding it, he liked it.

2

WHEN A CIRCLE of light played on the windowpanes, the mules began to bray and the dogs barked. Did felt a lump come to his throat. Sparkie's face looked troubled as he watched the light on the windowpanes and then looked at Did. Did saw others looking at the light as it flashed on and off. Even Tim Gilbert was troubled by it.

When the set ended and the music stopped, everybody stood silently, for they heard the coarse voice of a man screaming at the gate.

"Hello! Hello! Hello! Sounds like everybody's at home!"

"I'll go down and see what he wants," Tim Gilbert said. "That's a quaire way to act!"

Everybody laughed but Did and Sparkie. Tim Gilbert opened the door and Sparkie went outside with him. The hum of talking started again. Sparkie returned and stood beside Lucy.

"Do ye like to dance, Did?" Pollie asked him.

"I love to dance," Did told her.

"But ye've got so still all of a sudden," she said.

The door opened and in walked Mr. and Mrs. Hargis with Tim Gilbert behind them. They were a good-looking couple dressed very differently from the mountain people.

"Didway," Mrs. Hargis screamed as soon as she saw Did. She ran to him, threw her arms about him, and kissed his face. "Didway! What are you doing here?"

Did looked around in embarrassment.

"Dancin', Mother," he mumbled.

Mrs. Hargis took a handkerchief from her purse and wiped her eyes.

"Didway, what's happened to you?" she asked, standing before him and looking him up and down. "Your face is so brown! What has tanned you so? Your hands are even calloused!"

Did felt the lump grow bigger in his throat. He knew everybody at the dance was looking at him.

"Mother, this is Poll-Poll-ie Porter," Did said, half choking.

"Who is Pollie Porter, Didway?"

"Just Poll-Poll-ie Porter, Mother."

"How do you do, Pollie!" Mrs. Hargis said coldly, staring at the girl. "How long have you known Didway?"

"Jest tonight," she said. "Jest about an hour."

"Jest a minute, folks," Tim Gilbert said. "I want to introduce to ye Mr. and Mrs. Bill Hargis of Greenwood! Many of ye know 'em already."

"Howdy do, Mr. and Mrs. Hargis," the dancers nodded, speaking in low tones. Then they talked to each other in whispers.

"I've seen most of your faces," Bill Hargis said. "You've been in my store in Greenwood some time or other."

"There's been more of us in yer store than'll ever be there again," shouted the man with the stiff collar.

"Yes, Mr. Hargis," said one of the dancers, "we know about ye!"

"We've heard about ye on the grapevine telephone," said the tall man with the beardy face.

"What's the grapevine telephone, may I ask?" Bill Hargis said.

"It's the way we get quick messages to one another," said the tall man. "Say, for instance, I was makin' myself some herbs and Brier-patch Tom, Turkey Tom, Jest Tom, or Cief Eversole spied on me and told the revenooers. I'd get the word over the grapevine telephone in plenty of time so when they came to get me, the only thing they'd find was where my still had been!"

Everybody laughed.

"Have I had the pleasure of being on your grapevine telephone?"

"Ye shore have!"

"May I ask what the message was about me?"

"The message was fer us not to trade in yer store."

"The grapevine telephone," Mrs. Hargis said, laughing. "I've never heard of a grapevine telephone!"

"Blackmail," Bill Hargis shouted. "Plain blackmail! Who started it?"

"Well, have you heard that your son has killed the biggest wildcat that's ever been found among the Plum Grove hills?" Tim Gilbert tried to change the subject.

"Oh, horrors, no!" Mrs. Hargis screamed. "Didway! Didway! Did you kill a wildcat?"

"Yes, Mother," Did shuffled his feet and looked at the floor, "but the wildcat was in a trap."

"Oh, I've been almost crazy," she wept. "If I'd known that, I would've died! How did you kill it?"

"With a pistol."

"Didway, have you gone to carrying a pistol?" his father asked.

"When I follow the trap lines," Did said.

"Didn't it fight you?" Mrs. Hargis broke in.

"It tore a hole in my overall legs. But it was helpless, caught in the trap." Did looked painfully embarrassed.

"Oh, horrors," she exclaimed.

"Here, Mrs. Hargis," Tim Gilbert said. "Sit down in this chair."

"Thank you so much!" she said. "I'm very tired."

Her stockings had been torn by briers, and there were a few scratches on her legs.

Sparkie carried another chair from the corner of the room for Mr. Hargis.

"Thank you, young man," Bill Hargis said gruffly, eyeing Sparkie. "I'll be very glad to sit down. I'm ready for a little rest after this trip."

"That's Sparkie, Mother," Bill Hargis whispered to his wife. "That's the young outlaw Did's taken up with!"

"He's not a bad-lookin' boy," Mrs. Hargis said weakly.

"Ye wouldn't join in a dance with us, would ye?" Tim Gilbert asked.

"Dance," Mrs. Hargis repeated, waving her hand over her face. "I don't feel like dancing. I've been over a rough road. I've swung on a grapevine!"

"I don't dance, I'll have you to know, Mr. Gilbert," Bill Hargis said. "We'll just sit back here in the corner, if you don't mind, and observe one of your dances. It will be amusing, if not educational."

"Thank ye, Mr. Hargis, if that's the way ye feel about our

dances," Tim Gilbert said. "Strike up the band, fellers! We'll show 'em a real old mountain hotfoot. We'll make this dance eddicational!"

"Didway, are you going to dance with Miss Porter?"

"Yes, I am, Mother."

Did didn't look at his mother or father when the music began. Tim Gilbert began singing his dance calls for the grapevine twist, and Mr. and Mrs. Hargis watched Did and Pollie move swiftly to the rhythm of the mountain music. They saw the pistol handles sticking above the holsters on men's hips when their coats flew up, and on some of the men who danced without coats, they saw the holsters hanging in plain view.

"I've never seen anything like this, Mother," Bill Hargis said to his wife. "This is brazen lawlessness."

"I think it's amusing, Bill," she said. "I think I could sit here and watch all night!"

"You don't mean you're coming under this mountain spell that has caught Didway?"

"Not exactly that, but I can understand why he likes it," she answered him quickly.

"Why would he like it?" he asked her.

"He was never noticed in Greenwood," she said. "You know his health was never good! The boys called him a sissy. They called him a poor little rich boy. Now look at him! These people notice him! I believe they like him!"

"Well, what's this got to do with? . . . Why are you talking like this?"

"Sh-sh," she said. "Listen to the music, Bill! It's—it's catching. I rather like it!"

"Nonsense!"

"Didway looks as though he's been fed well enough," Mrs. Hargis said. "I've never seen him look better! That Pollie Porter he's dancing with is a beautiful girl, if she had some nice clothes and knew how to dress! But I can't say that I like her!"

"Naturally you wouldn't like her. But let's not waste any more time. Let's get Didway home!"

"I want to sit here and rest, and listen to the music. I want to watch Didway dance. Look, he's going to swing her!"

Bill Hargis looked down at the floor and saw his wife's feet keeping time to the music while she sat there contentedly watching her son swing his mountaineer partner high in the air. Pollie's feet were toward Bill Hargis and her black hair was flying loose.

"I'm glad I've come, Bill," Mrs. Hargis told her husband, not taking her eyes from Did. "I'll feel better. You painted an awful picture!"

"I'll tell you, Lydia, this boy they call Sparkie is an outlaw," Bill Hargis told her. "I've got enough information on him to send him to the reformatory. I wouldn't allow him to step foot inside my house!"

"Look, Bill," Lydia Hargis said. "Did you ever see such dancing? Isn't it wonderful! Look how happy our Didway is! I've never seen him so happy! Look at his eyes when he swings his girl. It's—why it's romantic, Bill!"

Bill Hargis sat sulled like a possum while his wife smiled, tapping her feet to the music. The men and women nodded and smiled back at her when they danced nearby. But Bill Hargis's feet didn't move.

"This is terrible," Bill Hargis said, slapping his hand on his knee. "It's perfectly terrible! It's the wildest frolickin' I've ever seen in all my life!"

Mrs. Hargis watched the dance as if she didn't hear what her husband had said.

"And you call that music!"

"When people enjoy it like they do, I call it music," she said. "It makes my feet move."

"The only thing I find interesting about it is it amuses me to know how primitive people can live," Bill Hargis said. "Just a few miles from us and they live this way and we didn't

125

know it. I've seen these same people in the store, and you'd never dream they can dance like this when they mope around the story buyin' traps and shells and tools."

"They are not moping now."

"Too full of rotten licker," Bill Hargis said. "You know sober people couldn't frolic like this!"

"I wouldn't say they're full of moonshine, Bill," Mrs. Hargis said. "If they were, I wouldn't call it 'rotten licker.' You don't know!"

"I've had enough of this. It's time we got hold of Didway."

"We'd better wait until this dance ends, then talk to him. It's bad manners to take Did from the dance."

"Do you mean you're enjoying this madness?"

"I can't say that I thoroughly dislike it."

"I can't see one thing I like about it."

"All circle and promenade home," Tim Gilbert shouted, as the couples danced away together and the music came to a stop.

"Was that eddicational, Mr. Hargis?" Tim Gilbert asked, sticking his face up close to Bill Hargis's face, mopping sweat from his brow with a big red bandanna.

"Very educational and exceptionally amusing," Bill Hargis snapped.

"I thought the dance was quite lovely, Mr. Gilbert," Mrs. Hargis said. "I have enjoyed every minute of it."

"Thank ye, Mrs. Hargis," Tim answered softly.

"Didway, your mother and I must see you a few minutes," Bill Hargis said, getting up and walking over to Did while everybody on the dance floor stood mopping their brows.

"Why do you want to see me?"

"You know why, Didway! Don't question me here! Come outside with us and we will do our talking with you there!"

"We think it's best to do yer talkin' in here, Mr. Hargis," said the tall man with the beardy face. "Did Hargis is our friend now."

"But remember I am his father and here's his mother," Bill Hargis replied. "He's our son and we'll take him outside and talk to him if we want to!"

"Only if he wants to go," said Tim Gilbert quietly.

"Ye can do yer talkin' before us," said the man with the long neck, his bow tie working up and down with his Adam's apple when he talked.

"Did's not a-goin' outside, Mr. Hargis!"

"But he's my son!" Bill Hargis said, as he looked around at the different eyes focused on him and his wife, eyes that seemed to be inching toward him as he looked at them. "It's strange when a man can't control his own son without other people's interference!"

"It's not strange, Mr. Hargis!"

"Come on, Bill," Mrs. Hargis pleaded with her dumbfounded husband as he stood looking at the mountain faces and the cool mountain eyes. "We've got a long walk ahead of us! We'd better be going!"

"Remember the people in Greenwood are plenty mad about this thing," Bill Hargis spoke so everybody could hear him.

"We're a-gettin' plenty riled too," said the man with the bow tie.

Did stood beside Pollie Porter and held her hand and looked at his mother and father.

"Didway will be well taken care of," Mrs. Hargis said. "I don't worry one bit about him. He's in good hands. There won't be any bullies hiding along the streets to beat him up here!"

"I'll see to that, Mrs. Hargis," Sparkie raised his voice.

"No harm will come to yer son," said the man with the beardy face. "The message over the grapevine telephone about Did was good. We'll stand by him."

"Then the Law will settle this," Bill Hargis said. "Good night."

"Good night, Mr. Hargis," many pleased voices echoed.

"Good night, Mrs. Hargis," said Pollie Porter.

"Good night, my dear."

3

PEG AND ARN were sitting before the log fire smoking when someone knocked loudly on the door.

"Pull the latchstring and come in!" Peg shouted.

"I'm back," Bill Hargis said. "I've brought company with me this time!"

"Howdy, Sheriff!"

"Howdy, Mr. Sparks," Sheriff Willie Watkins said. "How are you?"

"As well as common."

"I told you I'd be coming back if you didn't send Didway home! Where is he?"

"He's fox huntin' on the mountain!"

"Well, well," Bill Hargis said, snapping his lips like a turtle. "That's funny!"

"No, it's not funny," Arn said. "The boys kept their hounds tied fer some time now on account of the pizened fried taters along the ridges. They thought it was safe to take the hounds to the mountain again."

"Ye know, Sheriff, ye can't keep hound-dogs tied up too long," Peg said. "Ye've got to give 'em exercise!"

"We've not come here to discuss hound-dogs," Bill Hargis said, his heel clicking as he pranced up and down on the barren floor. "We've come here to take Didway home. Are you right sure he's not around this house or out in the hayloft sleepin' with a hound?"

"Take it a little easier, Bill," Sheriff Watkins pleaded. "Leave this to me."

"But I was here the other night and he wasn't here," Bill said. "And I've heard since that he was hidin' in a cow's stall. I thought he was huntin' *that* night, since I found four empty kennels."

"Did yer good friend Cief Eversole or his pappy tell ye all that," Arn asked, never looking at Bill.

"That is none of your business, Mrs. Sparks."

"Be keerful how ye talk to my wife, Bill Hargis!"

"Take it easy, Bill," Sheriff Watkins warned.

"I tell ye they've gone to the mountain to fox hunt," Peg said. "Go to the kennels to see fer yerselves. There's not but one hound here tonight. That's old Shootin' Star, the possum hound. The fox hounds are on the mountain!"

"I'd like to take a look around here in the house if you don't mind, Mrs. Sparks." Sheriff Watkins spoke softly.

"I don't mind. Look all you please!"

"Go to the barn and look too," Peg said. "We want ye to know we're a-tellin' the truth!"

Peg and Arn sat silently before the fire as if nothing were happening while Sheriff Watkins and Bill Hargis searched the shack. They looked under the bed, under the floor, on the roof; they looked everyplace.

"I'm telling you again, Peg and Arn Sparks," Bill Hargis affirmed, "there's going to be plenty of trouble over this kidnaping business. I'll have you know I'm a respected citizen of Greenwood. I've been spreading this injustice to the people. They're against you! They will be waiting for you and your outlaw stepson to come to Greenwood."

"Ye know how the people out here feel toward you," Arn said. "Ye found that out when ye tried to take Did away from Tim Gilbert's dance."

"This has caused a bad situation between you people from the hills and the town people," Sheriff Watkins said. "I had to make several arrests when fights broke out over it last Saturday!"

"You're not only trying to steal my son, Peg Sparks," Bill Hargis shouted, "but you are trying to blackmail my business! And you've been very successful!"

"Ye're seein' now, Bill Hargis, what the grapevine telephone will do," Peg warned. "This is jest the beginnin' of what will happen. Yer business will be ruint if you don't behave yerself."

"I happen to know a little about these grapevine telephones," Sheriff Watkins said. "I've been workin' against them for years!"

"Any kind of stealing is bad," Bill Hargis said, "but your stealing my son in broad daylight is the worst kind of stealing I ever heard of."

"We didn't steal yer son, Bill Hargis," Arn retorted. "Ye know we didn't! He took up with us like a stray hound-dog! And we're not a-goin' to turn him away from our door any more than we would a stray hound."

"Don't compare my son to a hound-dog," Bill Hargis shouted. "That's why you live like you do! I never saw anybody amount to anything in my life with a pack of hounds stuck around them."

"Take it easy, Bill," Sheriff Watkins said. "Don't get rash! Everything's goin' to work out all right!"

"But when, Sheriff? I want my son home!"

"When yer son wants to go home, it will be all right with us," Peg said.

"But we're not a-goin' to run him off," Arn shouted, stomping her foot against the hearth.

"I know you're not goin' to run him off," Bill Hargis said. "I know this from the experiences I've had trying to get him home."

"Listen," Peg said, holding his hand cupped over his ear.

"What do you hear, Peg?" the Sheriff asked.

"I hear our hounds after the fox," Peg said. Peg walked over to the door and opened it.

"Listen to that hound-dog music, won't you," he said while the Sheriff, Bill Hargis, and Arn listened. "I hear Thunderbolt and Fleet! They're a-leadin' the pack! I'll bet old Brierpatch Tom's somewhere a-listenin' with sweat a-poppin' out all over 'im. He can't take it when his dogs lose."

They listened to more than fifty hounds driving the fox from Shackle Run toward the Buzzard Roost country.

"I used to fox hunt some," Sheriff Watkins smiled. "That's good music to my ears!"

"Where would Didway be just now?" Bill Hargis asked Peg.

"He'd be on the Buzzard Roost Ridge."

"How do you know?"

"Just a minute and I'll show ye!"

While Arn, Bill, and the Sheriff listened to the barking hounds, Peg walked over to the wall and lifted his fox horn strap from over a rusty nail. He walked out on the doorstep, put the long horn to his lips, and blew three times. From the distant mountain came four short toots for an answer.

"That's Sparkie," Peg said. "He answered me. Now will ye believe me! If ye don't, go look in the kennels; go search the barn loft, cow stalls, mule stalls, hog pen, woods . . . anywhere ye like."

"I believe you, Peg," Sheriff Watkins said. "We'll go to the mountain."

"Do ye know the way, Sheriff?" Arn asked.

"I know every path over that mountain," Sheriff Watkins said. "I've raided it nearly a hundred times for moonshine stills."

"I'm not so sure," Bill Hargis said. "I think we'd better

131

take a look in the barn, Sheriff, before we go to the mountain!"

"Just as you say, Bill," the Sheriff said, following Bill Hargis out the door.

"Good night, Sheriff."

"Good night."

Peg and Arn stood on their doorstep and watched the flashlight flicker over the mules' stalls, cows' stalls, and up in the barn loft. They watched Bill Hargis look behind the hog pen. After they were through with their search, they watched them follow the path toward the mountain.

Peg waited until the flashlight was out of sight, then he put his fox horn to his lips and blew four long mournful sounds. And now that the hounds were across the Buzzard Roost Ridge, he got Sparkie's answer that rang sweet and clear through the still mountain night.

"They'll never find 'em," Peg said to Arn. "They've got the message."

4

DID WALKED DOWN among the trees to gather a load of dry deadwood while Sparkie whittled slivers of kindling from a pine stump rich with resin. While Did uprooted little dead locust poles, dry and well seasoned for burning, he heard Thunderbolt strike a cold trail and bark a few times. By the time Did had gathered enough wood to start the fire, Thunderbolt was barking faster.

"He'll have that fox a-movin' in a few minutes," Sparkie said, as he placed more pine kindling on the leaping flames. "This is a real night fer a chase."

Then Sparkie placed the wood that Did had gathered across the fire. He laid the little dry locust poles across the fire so the flames could leap up between them. Did stood by watching Sparkie.

The October sky above them was cold and blue. The bright stars were far apart. On their right and left were two deep valleys of darkness where wild life was astir. This was a night when only the high wind hit the ridgetops, stirring the needles on the tall ridge pines, making strange and mournful sounds. Did listened to the high winds stir the pine tops on the mountain while Sparkie finished with the fire and Thunderbolt trailed the fox to a red-hot track.

Toot. Toot.

"Peg's horn," Sparkie said. "He's askin' where we are. Wonder if it's yer pappy and Sheriff Watkins again?"

"Hope not," Did retorted, as Sparkie put his horn to his mouth to answer. "But I do know that Father will be back after me. He doesn't give up very easily."

Did and Sparkie waited in silence for the second message.

Toot. Toot. Toot. Toot. Toot.

"Peg's a-comin' to us," Did said. "Wonder what's up?"

Sparkie put his horn to his lips and blew four short notes.

"Peg knows I've got his message," Sparkie said, dropping his horn to his side and looking into the blazing fire.

Toot. Toot. Toot. Toot. Toot. Toot. Toot.

"That's good news. It couldn't be yer pappy and Sheriff Watkins again!"

"Wonder who is coming out here?"

"Don't know."

The wind blew from the west bending the bright flames toward Buzzard Roost Hollow. Sparkie and Did stood with their backs to the fire in the direction the wind blew so the

133

flames wouldn't leap out to burn their pants legs. They looked into the darkness and up at the bright stars in the moonless sky while Thunderbolt moved swiftly on the track. Lightning and Fleet pulled at their chains and whined to get to him.

"Be quiet," Sparkie told them, "I'll let ye in the chase soon as Peg gets here. I want him to see yer teamwork."

Thunderbolt was driving the fox toward Tunnel Hill when he was joined by other hounds.

"By the time the fox circles back to the Buzzard Roost mountain," Sparkie said, "every hound among the Plum Grove hills 'll be in the chase with Thunderbolt. Listen to that music."

Sparkie and Did walked over to sit on the big log and listen to the chase. While they sat listening, more hounds joined the chase. Thunderbolt, leading the pack of hounds, drove the fox farther away, as Sparkie sat patting his foot to the music of the barking hounds. His foot rustled the wind-dried carpet of leaves that had drifted against the log. When the hounds were out of hearing, Did and Sparkie heard Peg's voice, and women's voices, on Buzzard Roost Ridge.

"Peg and Arn's voices," Sparkie said. "Wonder who's with 'em?"

"Don't you know the other voices?" Did laughed. "You ought to know them."

"That sounds like Lucy and Pollie!" Sparkie was surprised. "Wonder why they're a-comin' up here?"

Four people walked around the ridge bend into full view. Did and Sparkie sat silently and watched the four of them. When they came into the reflections of the firelight, Lucy was carrying a basket and Pollie a thermos jug.

"We're here," Peg said.

"Hi, Sparkie! Hi, Did!" Lucy said with a smile.

"How's this fer a surprise?" Pollie said.

"It's a wonderful surprise all right," Sparkie chuckled, "but we were skeered to death when we got Peg's first message."

"Thought it was Bill Hargis and the Sheriff, I'll bet!"

"That's exactly what we thought, Lucy," Did answered.

"I'll bet we don't git hungry tonight." Sparkie spoke with enthusiasm. "Put the basket down and come and sit beside me."

"Oh, isn't it wonderful to be up here! I never thought I'd go fox huntin' since Sparkie wouldn't invite me."

"Gosh-old-hemlock, I never thought you'd want to go a-fox huntin'! Anyway, since the barn burnin' started, we haven't been goin' much."

"It's my first time too," Pollie said.

"Well," Did started, "I'd have asked you, but you see I'm not really a fox hunter yet, only the friend of a fox hunter." Everybody laughed.

"Where's the hounds?" Pollie asked. "Invited ourselves to go fox huntin' and we've not heard a dog bark."

"Ye'll hear the hounds in a few minutes," Sparkie told her. "They've taken old Hot Foot outten hearin' down the Little Sandy River. They'll be back."

Arn and Peg sat down side by side. "It's a long walk up here, and my leg got a little tired," Peg said. "It feels awfully good to sit down."

"I see ye've got a couple of dogs tied up over there," Lucy said. "Are ye a-goin' to put 'em in the chase?"

"If ye'll only stay out here with us until after midnight, we'll show ye what we aim to do with 'em," Sparkie explained.

"They're our burn-out and our cutting dogs," Did said. "Wait until you see what they can do!"

"Might as well tell ye now before I forget," Pollie said to Did. "Brother Porkie was in Greenwood yesterday. He was a-standin' on the street with his hands in his pockets a-listenin' to men a-talkin'. They're a-gettin' a small army of men together to raid these hills and take ye back."

"Let 'em come," Sparkie said.

"That's a lot of talk," Peg interrupted. "They won't come. If they do come, they won't have more'n a dozen men!"

"Porkie was a-standin' there on the street with his hands in his pockets a-doin' no one any harm, so he said," Pollie continued, "when Sheriff Willie Watkins came along and took him by the arm. All Porkie was a-doin' was a-listenin' to the talk. Brother Porkie was tried before a jury of six Greenwood men, charged with loiterin', and found guilty. He was fined twenty-five dollars and costs. Lucky that he had the money. He got back to warn us."

"It's a-gittin' to the place a hill man ain't safe in Greenwood," Peg said. "Bill Hargis has riled the people against us. And we've riled our people against him."

"Porkie said he went in Bill Hargis' General Merchandise Store yesterday and the clerks were a-sittin' in chairs and on the show cases," Pollie went on. "Porkie said he didn't see a customer in the store all the time he was a-walkin' around with his hands in his pockets a-lookin' and a-listenin'."

"What do ye think of that, Peg?" Sparkie asked.

"That's good news," Peg said. "It goes to show we got a real grapevine telephone. We got one they can't unravel. It'll stand the test."

"But they arrested brother Lacie fer whittlin' on a telephone post on the courthouse square," Lucy said. "So many people have whittled on it that they had to drive tacks in it to keep the people from a-whittlin' it down. They arrested Lacie and locked 'im up in jail. They tried him and fined 'im ten dollars and costs fer destroyin' public property."

"What do ye think of that, Arn?" Sparkie asked.

"When I read the coffee grounds in my saucer this mornin', I could see nothin' but trouble and misery," Arn answered. Did looked up at her quickly to see if she smiled when she said it. Her face was serious.

"Lacie Howard went down to Greenwood," Sparkie sang mournfully, as he looked up at the stars in the blue sky over

Buzzard Roost. All the others stopped talking and looked at each other while he sang:

> Lacie wasn't a-doin' no harm
> When along came Sheriff Willie Watkins
> And took poor Lacie by the arm.
>
> Lacie didn't dream of bars across the winders
> And a bolt across the door
> When he whittled on the telephone post
> Where men had whittled before.
>
> Sheriff Willie put him in the jailhouse
> Where he had been just twice before.
> Lacie hung his hat on a rusty nail
> And he throwed his coat on the floor.
>
> "Don't be afraid, Sheriff Willie,"
> Said Lacie as his hat did fall,
> And Willie trembled in his boots,
> "Bill Hargis caused it all."

Everybody laughed and clapped.

"Ain't that purty, Peg?" Arn said.

"Sparkie, where did you hear that song before?" Did asked.

"Jest made it up," Sparkie answered.

"And all because I won't go home," Did said. "This is the life. Out here singing with you beneath the stars, waiting for the hounds to bring back the fox!"

"Maybe, there won't be any more trouble, Did," Pollie said. "Maybe yer father won't be back after ye. He might decide to let ye stay and be one of us."

"No, not Father," Did told her. "I know he'll be back. Father will come the next time prepared to grab me and take me home."

5

"WHILE THE HOUNDS are after old Hot Foot, I'd like to sample some of what's in that basket." Sparkie looked hungry. "It's nigh on to midnight and the sickle moon is risin'. It's time to eat."

"I feel like I could fight my face too," Peg said. "Gives a body a-hankerin' fer grub to walk up here."

"How do ye feel, Did?" Arn asked.

"I'm always hungry," he said. "These mountains have done it to me."

Pollie walked over to the thermos jug and Lucy lifted the tall basket from the leaves. It was made of white-oak splits. There were two semicircle lids that fastened on little hinges under the handle.

Lucy raised the lids. She lifted a large dish of fried chicken from the basket.

"Well, don't that look good," Sparkie said, all eyes for the chicken.

Lucy lifted a paper sack from the basket and gave it to Arn.

"Biscuits, light and fluffy and brown," Arn said.

Then Lucy took deviled eggs and sweet pickles from the basket. Pollie poured hot coffee into cups and then went to the basket and brought back a bottle of milk. "Knowin' ye don't drink coffee, I brought this to ye," she said and gave Did the milk.

"I'm just wonderin' how a basket can hold so much," Arn said.

"One more thing in it," Lucy said. "Now we'll put Sparkie and Did to work."

Lucy lifted a paper sack filled with small yellow sweet potatoes, the right size for roasting in wood ashes.

While everybody was eating fried chicken, biscuits, deviled eggs and drinking hot coffee, Sparkie stopped eating suddenly.

"Listen, I hear the hounds," he shouted.

"What dog's a-leadin'?" Peg asked.

"Can't tell. Not yet. Must be seventy hounds after Hot Foot!"

The hounds were getting nearer as they streaked across the polecat country heading for the mountain.

Did held a pulleybone in one hand and a biscuit in the other as he listened.

"Brier-patch Tom's War Horse is a-leadin'," Sparkie admitted. "We'll see what can be done about that."

When the hounds reached the mountain slope, Sparkie turned Lightning loose. Like a shot from a gun, he took around the ridge road to join the pack as they came pouring from the woods over the mountaintop. Everybody could hear Lightning's feet hitting the leaves and frozen dirt.

"Ye'll hear something in a minute," Sparkie bragged. "War Horse will lead until Lightnin' gits there. Old Thunderbolt knows what Lightnin' 'll do."

"I told ye it was fun," Arn said to the two girls. "Fox hunters' wives a-talkin' about their men a-goin' out in the winter and a-layin' around on the cold ground and a-ketchin' a death of cold fer nothin'. When I hear 'em talk like that, I tell 'em they ought to go out with the men and fox hunt and they wouldn't talk that way. I tell 'em they don't know what they're a-missin'."

"There's old Lightnin'," Sparkie said. "Hear 'im?"

"Hear that short barkin' dog a-takin' the lead?" Peg said. "That's old Lightnin'!"

Peg patted his foot on the dry leaves beneath the log to the music of the barking hounds.

"Lightning won't be in there but a couple of circles," Did said to Pollie, "then he'll come out."

"Is he the burn-out dog?"

"That's right."

"Sparkie, I want to hear yer cuttin' dog before the chase is over," Lucy said. "I've heard brother Lacie talk so much about 'er."

"Ye'll git to hear her. Soon as old Lightnin' comes out, I'll put her in."

When the hounds had crossed the valley and started up the mountain on the other side of Buzzard Roost Creek, the short barking hound, Lightning, was far in the lead.

"Listen to old Lightnin'!" Peg was patting his foot. "He's a-settin' the woods on fire tonight!"

The hounds crossed the distant mountain and Lightning was nearly a mile in the lead. Fleet charged at her chain to get loose.

"There they go, outten hearin'," Peg said.

"Fleet knows where that fox is a-goin' to cross," Sparkie said. "She'd like to git loose and go meet old Hot Foot and take 'im a sight chase. She knows the nature of old Hot Foot but she ain't been able to figure old Gray Beard out yit. Not any of the hounds can figure 'im out. He's a cheater. He even backtracks himself and throws all the hounds off. He's a bigger cheater than old Fleet."

"Have you got yer foxes named?" Lucy asked.

"Got all named that we know real well," Sparkie said. "We've never seen these foxes, but we can tell the one the dogs are after by the way he runs and the circles he takes. Old Hot Foot is the best of all the foxes. He's the greatest fox that's ever been among these hills. All the fox hunters that will never agree on the hounds agree old Hot Foot is the greatest fox of all times. Wince Leffard saw 'im once and he said old Hot Foot was bigger than a collie dog and that he had a tail as bushy as Lottie Bates' old sorrel mare."

"Everybody be shore he throws his chicken bones in the fire," Peg said. "Don't let the hounds find 'em. Bones in their stummicks give 'em the shivers!"

"It's about time, Sparkie, ye put the sweet taters in the ashes," Arn said. "We'll go hungry by the time they're baked good and done."

Sparkie gave Lucy his piece of chicken to hold while he took a pole of the locust to rake the ashes. He used one hand and held his cup of hot coffee with the other. Sparkie made a big nest in the gray ashes with the end of his stick and tossed the sweet potatoes into it. He covered these potatoes with the gray ash and raked the living embers on top.

"That'll roast 'em," Sparkie said to Lucy. "If I can do anything in this world, Honey, I can roast a tater!"

"Ye've roasted enough of 'em, Sparkie, until ye ought to be good at it!" Peg laughed. "I'll bet ye've roasted sweet taters from more patches than any man among the Plum Grove hills!"

"Spect I have," Sparkie admitted. "I know where everybody's sweet tater patch is."

After everybody had eaten, Arn filled her pipe with burley tobacco crumbs from her apron pocket. Then she got up from the log, walked over to the fire, picked up a firebrand, and held the flame over her pipe. Peg pulled a cigar from his pocket, and Arn carried the firebrand over and lit his cigar. Sparkie pulled a light burley leaf from his pocket, crammed it into his mouth.

"There ain't no pleasure like fox huntin'," Sparkie said. "If I didn't git to fox hunt three or four nights a week from the beginnin' to the endin' of the year, I believe to my soul I'd die. That's one reason I've always been afraid of the Green-wood jail."

"It's not a safe town fer ye now, Sparkie," Peg warned, as he blew a cloud of smoke from his cigar. "They might get ye fer loiterin' or whittlin' on the telephone post."

"Listen," Sparkie held up his hand, "I hear 'em comin'."

The hounds broke into music as they came around the east point of the mountain toward Buzzard Roost Ridge. Brier-patch Tom's War Horse was back in the lead. Thunderbolt was back in the pack and Lightning was no longer in the chase.

"Lightnin' ran only one circle tonight," Did apologized to Pollie.

"One long or two short circles is all old Lightnin' ever runs," Sparkie interrupted. "That's enough to bust the hounds that try to stay with 'im. Thunderbolt understands. He waits until Lightnin' is out of the chase. Lightnin' is on his way to the fire now and Thunderbolt is pullin' up to take the lead. Hear 'im! Hear his bark!"

"Think of hounds runnin' all night fightin' just to lead the chase," Lucy said. "And then they never do ketch the fox!"

"But how about the music, Lucy," Arn reminded. "Ye must like fox huntin' fer that."

Sparkie turned Fleet loose, and with a howl the dog bounded into the dark woods.

"Why is she a-goin' the other way?" Pollie asked, as Fleet took off in the direction opposite the way the hounds were going.

"She's goin' to meet Hot Foot," Sparkie said. "She knows where he crosses the ridge on his way to the polecat country."

"What if she beats the fox there?" Lucy asked.

"Fleet will sit down and wait fer the fox. Then she'll give 'im a sight chase."

"Think of a hound-dog a-havin' that much sense," Arn said. "It's hard to believe."

"Old Thunderbolt's not a cutter or a quitter," Sparkie bragged. "He hangs to the scent and stays with the pack until he gits the lead. In two more hours he'll be a mile ahead of all the hounds."

"I like that kind of a dog," Lucy said.

"Listen to that chase, won't ye!" Sparkie shouted. "Fleet's in the lead!"

Fleet was chasing the fox by sight across the polecat country. When the pack of hounds heard Fleet's barking, they took after her hard as they could go.

"When they git close to 'er, she stops barkin'," Sparkie said. "Old Fleet's smart."

"She's there to win any way she can," Did said.

"Outten hearin' already," Peg laughed. "They're really a-drivin' old Hot Foot tonight. He won't have time to stop ahead of the hounds and find himself a quail or a rabbit!"

"They're a-headin' fer the Nellievale hills," Sparkie said. "Maybe on to the Reeves Pond and down Little Sandy to Shackle Run. Old Hot Foot might take a nigh cut and go down Sleepy Hollow to the Putt Off Ford and down Little Sandy to Shackle Run since the hounds are a-crowdin' 'im tonight."

"How about the roasted sweet taters, Sparkie?"

Sparkie got up from the log, picked up his stick, and started uncovering the potatoes. Then he rolled the potatoes from the ashes over on the leaves to let them cool.

"How long do we aim to stay, Peg?" Arn asked.

"We'll stay as long as Hot Foot is able to stand it," Peg said. "Just so we git home in time to feed the fambly breakfast."

Sparkie picked up one of the sweet potatoes. He tossed it in his hand. Then he broke the skin. "Smells good," he said.

He walked along the log and laid a roasted sweet potato in everybody's hand.

"Listen! Listen," Did said. "Do you hear that! Thunderbolt is coming up Shackle Run with the fox. He's in the lead!"

"That's the dog," Peg bragged. "He gits 'em on the long circles!"

"Come on, Thunderbolt," Sparkie shouted.

Lucy laughed. "Well, if this isn't the funniest fox hunt! The hounds chase a fox they never catch, and we jest sit here a-listenin' and a-eatin' sweet taters. Shore is better than scramblin' through the brush after those dawgs. Pass me another tater, Sparkie."

PART SIX

I

IT WAS CORN-SHUCKING time and the moon rose over the Buzzard Roost Ridge flooding the rugged Plum Grove hills with shafts of golden light. In the moonlight, which was not quite so bright as day, the October wind rustled the cured-tobacco-brown oak leaves, the geranium-red sassafras, black-gum, and sourwood leaves and the October pawpaw, yellow hickory, and poplar leaves. This night was quiet except for the slow rustle of the drowsy wind among the multicolored leaves still hanging to the autumn trees.

Occasionally there was the hoot of an owl from one hilltop. Then there was an answer from its mate across the valley. On a night like this the owls spoke to each other in their own language. These love hoots of the owls and the drowsy murmurs of the autumn wind among the ripe-clinging leaves were seldom disturbed by the shrill barking of the fox. This was the night for the young and the old of the Plum Grove hills to dance and work and have fun. There was not one little white cloud in the sky. Not a single cloud to float across the moon and dim its great shafts of mellow light on valley, mountain, tree, and field.

Did and Pollie rode old Dick along the path over which Sparkie and Did had ridden so often. Pollie sat in the little cowboy saddle and Did sat behind her. She laid her head back on Did's shoulder and leaned against Did's body while his arms reached around her to hold the bridle reins. There wasn't much guiding to do, for old Dinah was in front and old Dick would always follow her.

Pollie didn't need Did's arms around her, for she could ride a mule anywhere one would go. She had broken young mule colts to ride and had jogged a mule over every path and road among the Plum Grove hills. She had driven a mule hitched to a cart and two mules hitched to a jolt-wagon. She had plowed a mule single and she had plowed mules double. But on this night she didn't want to rein the mule. She just wanted to sit and lean against Did and watch the moon through the trees. A few yards ahead rode Sparkie and Lucy on Dinah.

"Smell that smoke," Did and Pollie heard Sparkie say to Lucy. "It's cigar smoke and pipe smoke mixed. I could follow Arn and Peg like a hound-dog follows a fox. I could track 'em by the smoke any night or day, unless there's a brisk wind to blow the smoke away. I'd know that smoke if I smelled it in Heaven, or in the world below." Sparkie let out a wild laugh. "Giddup, Dinah, we're goin' to be late. We've been a-foolin' along."

Pollie, Did, Sparkie, and Lucy were on their way to Peg and Arn's corn shucking. Peg never shucked one ear of corn from the big Buzzard Roost cornfield. He left the corn in the shocks to be shucked by his neighbors on a bright moonlight night in October. Everybody was invited to attend this corn shucking. This was an easy way for Peg to get his corn shucked; besides, each corn shucking was a social event to be talked about and remembered by the Plum Grove people for years to come.

Bert Hoskins and Grace Newberry were riding a horse slowly along the path. Grace was in the saddle and Bert was riding behind on the horse's bare back.

"What's yer hurry, Sparkie?" Bert asked.

"I want to see Peg git his field of corn shucked tonight," Sparkie answered.

"Then ye and Did won't have so much shuckin' to do," Bert said, as he leaned forward against Grace and laughed.

"That's it," Sparkie agreed. "Did and me will have more time to follow the trap lines, fox hunt, and square dance."

"There's plenty just ahead of us to hep shuck the corn," Bert said to Sparkie. "The road is filled with people on horseback and muleback. Some even walking. But what do we keer, Sparkie," Bert added with a laugh, "the longest way and the slowest way there is the sweetest."

In front of Bert Hoskins' horse Tim Gilbert rode his mule. Tim was sitting in the saddle while Doshia, his wife, rode behind him with her arms around his waist. Tim was riding in a springy saddle, but Doshia rode the mule's bony back.

"Look at that, won't ye, Lucy," Sparkie pointed at Tim and Doshia.

"Shucks, that's not anything, Sparkie," Lucy retorted. "That's the way they ride at Plum Grove after they git married. Before they git married they ride like we're ridin' now. The woman has the saddle. That's why I'm enjoyin' the saddle tonight. I want to take advantage of it while I can."

On the path ahead of them was a continuous stream of human traffic on foot, muleback, and horseback. Young lovers walked with their arms around each other. Married men and women walked, not with their arms around each other, but with the man a few steps ahead. This was the old custom for a Plum Grove married man to walk ahead of his wife and carry a stick in his hand for protection against snakes and anything that would do them bodily harm. But the young lovers never thought of snakes.

Friends and neighbors were pouring from the path into the cornfield where Peg and Arn already were waiting to greet them. Behind Did and Sparkie the people were still coming. They could hear the clicking of the steel shoes of the horses and mules on the rocks along the path. They could hear the merry shouts of the young people as they met and greeted each other on their way to Peg and Arn's corn shucking.

2

THE VALLEY, WHERE the wigwamed shocks of corn stood in neat pretty rows around the slopes, was in the shape of a mule shoe. The steel shoe was the ridge's rim where the moon, big as a wagon wheel, yellow as the middle of a ripe October pawpaw, first peeped over between the barren twigs of the wind-swept oaks. The corks on the steel shoe were the rocky bluffs that dropped straight down into deep and dark Buzzard Roost Valley. Even with the bright wagon-wheel moon above the cornfield, flooding it with soft yellow light, this deep valley lay in shadows. It was too deep and dark and sheltered with rock cliffs for the moon to reach with its floods of yellow light. This was the land of the fox, the wildcat, the raccoon, possum, mink, weasel, polecat, groundhog, and rabbit. This was the last outpost of Plum Grove's hunting grounds. But above these cliffs was the semicircle of land, where the sure-footed mules could brace their little hoofs and pull the plow. This was the land where Sparkie had walked behind the plow and turned the dirt over for many spring and summer seasons.

"Howdy, folks," Peg greeted them as they came down the path into the cornfield. "Glad to see ye. Glad to have ye. Welcome to the corn shuckin'."

Peg lifted his cigar from his mouth with one hand while he talked to his guests. Soon as he was through welcoming an old Plum Grove neighbor or a young couple, he would put the cigar back in his mouth and draw a cloud of smoke. It was hard for him to keep fire in his cigar, for so many people came down the path. Married men got down from their saddles and let their wives get down the best they could to greet Peg and Arn. They hitched the bridle reins to swaying oak limbs at the edge of the cornfield. Young men leaped down from the bare backs of their horses and mules and lifted their girls down from the saddles while Arn stood beside Peg smoking her pipe and silently watching the ways of the people of the Plum Grove hills.

Beneath, where the corn shuckers were greeting each other, lay the vast cornfield, the largest in the Plum Grove hills. There were not many places where fifteen acres of slope, not too steep for the sure-footed mule, could be found. But Peg and Arn Sparks had this field, and each October, on a night when the moon was full, Peg and Arn had the greatest corn shucking among the Plum Grove hills. This was the biggest social event of the season.

If this cornfield could be called a mule's hoof, the big dance platform was built down on the frog. The dance platform was down in the middle, on a small level spot in the ravine where a tiny creek flowed through the center and poured over the rocks to the deep valley below. The platform remained standing from year to year. Peg, Sparkie, and Did replaced some of the planks and examined the sills. For this platform had to be strong. Each year, after its exposure to the weather, it had to be rebraced and a few of the planks replaced.

"Glad to see so many of ye folks," Peg said, as he greeted more and more people. "It's a great night fer the occasion."

The men hitched their mules and horses to the trees along the edge of the cornfield until there was a small cavalry. They were careful to hitch them far enough apart so that the horses and mules couldn't get to each other to kick and bite. At many of these corn shuckings a mule had kicked a horse and a horse had bitten off a mule's ear.

"Horses and mules think about as much of one another as the people from Plum Grove and the city dudes," Peg laughed as Tim Gilbert and Bert Hoskins ran to separate their mule and horse.

Sparkie rode down the path, jumped down from old Dinah's back, and lifted Lucy Howard from the saddle. Then Dick followed after Dinah, and Did jumped down and lifted Pollie from the saddle. Did was so little beside the big mule that Pollie had to jump from the saddle down into his arms. But that was the way they did it at Plum Grove. That was right and proper among the young people.

For this corn shucking Did was properly dressed. He was dressed like all the young single men and many of the older married men. He wore one of Sparkie's big shirts with gray checks and red stripes, a big red bandanna around his neck, and a pistol in a holster on his hip. The bright handle of his pistol stuck above the holster and gleamed in the moonlight.

There was laughter to drown the barking of the fox or the hooting of the owl. More people kept coming down the path until a small army of corn shuckers stood on the brown carpet of soft crab grass among the corn stubbles. Jeff and Ephriam Potters, Willie Hampton, John Snowden, Arville Short, Ebb Barney, and Lacie Howard—the orchestra—were among the first to arrive. They stacked their musical instruments under a big oak at the edge of the cornfield.

"Friends and neighbors from these Plum Grove hills," Peg shouted, holding his hands high, "may I have yer attention jest a minute. See that big bright moon up there in the sky! It's not a-goin' to stay that high and bright all night. We must git to shuckin' corn while we have plenty of light. We can dance when the moon goes down . . . but my corn, folks, I want it shucked while we have light!"

"We'll shuck it, Peg," Jim Braiden shouted. "Enough here to shuck three times this much corn."

"Ye bet we'll shuck it, Peg."

"Let's be off with our partners to the fodder shocks," Lacie Howard shouted.

"Jest a minute, folks," Peg said, waving his arms above the crowd. "We can never trust that purty moon! I'll tell ye the reason ye can't trust it. I've heard my pappy say many a time, there was an Eversole put in that moon fer burnin' brush on Sunday!"

The laughter was loud. Not an Eversole had come to Peg's corn shucking. Glenn Shelton, Jimmie Dennis, and Ivan Nicholls, Did and Sparkie's fox hunting friends, hadn't come either. Everybody among the Plum Grove hills had a standing invitation to come. It had always been this way. Anybody could come that wanted to help Peg get his corn shucked and dance the rest of the night on his great platform down on the frog of the mule's hoof.

"Is the man in the moon any blood-kin to old Brier-patch Tom?" Wince Leffard asked.

"His great-grandpappy," Peg shouted. "He was put there fer burnin' brush on Sunday."

They laughed again.

"Now each man with his wife and each young man git his partner," Peg shouted. "Young couples, ye'll go to the bottom of the slope and shuck the bottom shocks. Yer legs are young and powerful. We older folks have climbed too many mountains."

"Okay, Peg, we're ready," Slim Winters said as he took Olive Kilgore by the hand. "We're ready and a-rarin' to go!"

"Just one thing more before ye go," Peg said; "this corn is white corn. It don't have too many red ears!" When a man found a red ear, he was bound to kiss the girl who was his partner.

"Oh, we know ye, Peg," Slim Winters laughed. "We'll

151

watch to see how many red ears ye and Arn find in yer fodder shock."

"Won't be any in our fodder shock," Arn said, with a chuckle. "Peg and I ust to find several red ears. But we don't any more."

The young men and girls, hand in hand, ran into the corn-field.

"Everybody to his shock of fodder," Peg shouted. "Everybody to work before the moon is down. No one knows what old man Eversole will do to the moon! Everybody, everybody to work while we have the light."

3

THE YOUNG COUPLES walked down the slope amid the cornstubble that shone brightly in the moonlight. Peg and Arn walked toward the first fodder shock in the top row. It was hard walking for Peg, for his sharp-ended wooden leg sank deep into the brown carpet of dead crab grass. Arn walked beside Peg on the side of his wooden leg. He laid his big hand on her shoulder for support.

As the men walked, ran, and jumped over the cornfield, holding to their wives' and their lovers' hands, the handles of their pistols above the holsters on their hips shone like polished silver in the moonlight. The red bandannas around their necks, their red, brown, and gray shirts with stripes and checks, and the gay colors of the women's dresses were autumn colors like the leaves still clinging to the trees. It was a night filled with brightness from the floor of the rugged earth to the tops of the trees.

There was music too, in the moon-drenched blue of the night. There was the drowsy rustle of the wind in the fodder blades and through the fine silk-hair of carpet crab grass. There were laughter and music in the loud voices of the young people as they raced toward the fodder shocks. It was a night that made Peg and Arn, Bert, Grace, Tim, and Doshia stand beside their fodder shocks in the top row and watch the sturdy young, with living red blood in their young veins, take off in a race toward the wigwams of fodder. Those with the good years behind them, with the stiff legs and the hair on their heads turned white as the first snow, looked on with tears coming to their eyes. This was the night of play-work, the great autumn night that would be talked about for years to come.

"Everybody to his shock of corn," Sparkie shouted. He lifted Lucy in his arms and leaped over the cornstubble rows to the bottom of the slope to beat everybody else. Did couldn't very well pick Pollie up and carry her. She was as large as he.

Soon there was a great rustle of cornstalks beneath the moon, out in the evening air of autumn. Out where the dim stars looked down from the sky of Wedgwood blue. Young men ran against the fodder shocks, throwing the weight of their bodies against them to push them over. Then they ripped away the top band and the middle band that tied the fodder shock. Though the men had fancy revolvers down in the shined and waxed holsters on their hips, they didn't have fancy store-bought shucking pegs. Each man had made his peg from a piece of seasoned hickory wood. He had whittled and sharpened the end to his own liking for himself and his partner and had put a little leather or groundhog-skin strap on it that fit neatly over the back of his hand. The man pulled the shucking pegs from his pocket for his girl and for himself and they went to work.

"A red ear," Sparkie shouted. "Look," he screamed as he held it up in the moonlight for everybody to see. "First ear I tore the shuck from was red!"

"Ye lucky boy," Tom Moore shouted.

"I don't believe it," Lacie Howard said.

It was an honor to get the first ear of red corn. Everybody stopped shucking corn long enough to watch Sparkie kiss Lucy.

"Did, ye see if old Sparkie's a-tellin' the truth," Peg shouted down the hill.

"Yes, it's red all right, Peg," Did yelled back up the mountain.

"It's redder than a sourwood leaf, Peg," Tom Moore shouted.

Everybody stood cornstubble-still as tall Sparkie leaned over the fodder shock that lay on the ground and held Lucy tenderly in his arms and kissed her slowly.

"That's enough, Sparkie," Rube Conley shouted from the far end of the cornfield.

There was laughter and there was the ring of happy voices that sounded far across the deep valley below that was filled with shadow and darkness. There, too, was the rustle of the dry fodder and the rip-rip of the tight husk from the ear as the men and women went to work.

"A red ear," Tom Moore screamed with excitement.

Then everybody stood still to watch Tom kiss Lucretia Quisenberry.

"Ye're a-takin' too long," Finnis Pratt yelled down from the top row. "Peg won't git his corn shucked tonight. Not before old great-grandpappy Eversole does something to the moon. Remember he's the light fixture on this night, and we don't know what he thinks of Peg!"

"Found a red ear," Peg shouted. Then he laughed as his friends had never heard him laugh. His rich laughter carried across the valley on the wind and echoed back to him.

"All right, Peg," Tim Gilbert said, "let me see if ye're a-kiddin' us!"

"Pon my word and honor, it's red," Peg said, laughing again.

"It's a red ear all right," Tim Gilbert shouted to the corn shuckers.

"All right, Peg, ye know what comes after ye find a red ear."

"Ye're the lucky woman, Arn."

Though it was customary for everybody to stop shucking only when the first red ear was found and to watch the finder and his partner kiss, everybody stopped to watch Peg lean over the fodder and kiss Arn. As he embraced her, Tom Moore pulled his revolver and fired a salute toward Grandpa Eversole.

The corn shuckers shucked fast through the medium-sized shocks of corn. For the corn did not grow tall on this mountain where the soil was thin and where the land was farmed year after year. There were approximately four shocks of corn for each couple to shuck.

The moon was high and bright. When a rabbit or a mouse ran from a shock of fodder, the shuckers could see him take off in the moonlight. This was the night of all nights, when there was the rustle of the dry fodder blade, and the ears of white and red corn were constantly in the air sailing to little heaps, while lovers' lips met across the buff-colored fodder blades. This was a night of love and October mellowness, when the ears of corn, fodder blade, and leaf were ripened by the frosts, and the pumpkins yellow, brown, and golden lay over the big cornfield. The harvesters, dressed in colors as rich as those in the autumn woods, worked in unison to finish the field so they could dance until the morning hours

4

"HERE, SHEP, HERE Shep," Lonnie Johnson called to the big animal with the bushy tail as it ran helter-skelter between the fodder shocks. "Don't be afraid, Shep," Lonnie stood with an ear of corn in his hand, "we're not a-goin' to hurt ye!"

"That's not a shepherd," Tom Moore shouted as the animal ran past the shock he and Lucretia Quisenberry were shucking. "That's a big gray fox!"

"What's a fox a-doin' in here?" Tim Gilbert shouted. "A wild fox wouldn't run to us of its own accord."

"And I don't hear any hounds," Did said. "Wonder where that fox came from?"

"Gray fox in the cornfield," Mort Higgins shouted.

"Did ye say a gray fox was in the cornfield?" Peg asked. "If ye did, we'll have bad luck. There's always bad luck when a gray fox visits ye at night! It's a bad sign."

"I don't believe in them signs, Peg," Willie Abrahams said.

"Then ye jest wait and see," Peg stood beside his fodder shock and warned his guests. "I know I'm right. We'll have bad luck before mornin'. Dance floor will fall or old Eversole will turn the moon upon its corner and cause a downpour of rain! Something will happen. I've lived long enough to observe the signs. Signs will appear before the real thing comes along."

The young corn shuckers did not listen to Peg. They were hurrying to finish Peg's cornfield and get down to the platform and start the dance.

When the shadow of widespread wings passed directly over Arn, she looked up toward the sky. "Look, Peg," she shouted, taking her pipe from her mouth and holding it in her hand. "Did ye ever see a hoot owl big as that one? It's shore a bad sign fer a hoot owl to fly over ye at night!"

Peg and Arn stood quietly beside the fodder shock and watched the silent bird, on its great outstretched wings, fly across the valley and drop down into the deep dark shadows which the moonlight didn't reach.

"That shore is a bad omen, Arn," Peg agreed.

A mule ran across the cornfield with a saddle on its back but no bridle.

"Whose mule is that?" Slim Winters asked. "He's slipped the bridle!"

"Somebody ketch 'im," Bert Hoskins shouted.

But the mule was running, braying, kicking as if he were trying to kick the saddle from his back. Then a horse without a bridle and saddle ran across the carpet of brown fine tooth-comb crab grass, whinnying as he ran. His head was high and his flaxen mane and tail rode freely on the wind.

"I warned ye," Peg said. "I told ye when that fox crossed this cornfield somethin' would happen!"

"I told ye the owl was a bad omen too, a-flyin' directly over a body's head in the night," Arn said. "That shadow skeered me till I have the weak trembles!"

"Something is a-goin' to happen," Lucille Dodderidge said.

"Look, there goes another horse, another mule a-carryin' empty saddles," Peg shouted in a trembling voice. "Am I dreamin' or am I awake?"

"Ye're awake, Peg," Arn told him. "It's the truth. Horses and mules without bridles are a-runnin' all over the cornfield a-carryin' empty saddles!"

"How are they a-gettin' loose?" Lacie Howard asked. The corn shuckers stood frozen beside their fodder shocks. "What's a-goin' on here?"

"That gray fox was a warnin'," Lydia Mobley said.

"The owl was the greatest warnin'," Arn said. Now that the laughter and the merriment had been hushed into a strange silence, her voice could be heard all over the cornfield. "Ye laughed at the signs but ye will see!"

"I thought I saw a tree without leaves betwixt me and the moon," Lucretia Quisenberry said. "But I didn't say anything. Bein' a woman I thought ye'd think I had fears. Bein' a mountain woman I have only fears of the signs and the things that slip upon me. Not things I can see. But the silent tree, shaped like a man," she added, "had slim branches without leaves, the sides bent down like a man's arms dropped down to rest. The tree had been broken off by a ridge wind, I thought, so I didn't say anything lest ye would laugh at my fears! But I saw something that was either a silent man or a tree trunk betwixt me and the moon!"

"Hadn't we better search these woods?" young Annias Pratt asked.

"Stay in the cornfield," Peg answered.

The women moved over on the other side of the fodder shocks beside the men. All eyes were turned toward the ridge's rim, from where the gray fox had come down the mountain and the great owl had flown. Restless, calloused fingers played with the bright handles of revolvers that stuck above the holsters. But along the upper row of fodder shocks, now lying in fodder bundles on the ground with heaps of corn beside them, horses and mules with empty saddles ran after each other, squealing, kicking, and biting. Their steel-shod hoofs sank deep into the soft cornfield earth and pounded fire from the loose rocks. The corn shuckers stood silently and watched and waited. They knew the throat latches had been unsnapped and the bridles had been pulled from over the horses' and mules' heads. They knew that whoever had done it knew about this corn shucking, where the cornfield was, and where the horses and mules were hitched. Did and Pollie, who had

158

just finished their third shock of corn, walked over and stood beside Sparkie and Lucy. They looked for the man between them and the moon, the man Lucretia Quisenberry thought she had seen.

"It's trouble, Did," Sparkie whispered. "I smell it. I can taste it."

Sparkie instinctively pulled a long dry leaf of homegrown burley from the hip pocket of his tight-fitting pants. He crammed the leaf into his mouth with one hand, swelling his jaw to a knot large as a duck egg while the other hand played with the handle of his pistol.

"Do you suppose they've come to get me?" Did said in a low tone, while the horses and mules ran helter-skelter across the field. Many of the horses and mules found the path, the way they had come, and the corn shuckers could hear the sounds of their pounding hoofs.

"It could be that, Did," Sparkie said.

"But I'm not goin', Sparkie."

They stood in the cornfield like frozen cloud statues in dark troubled skies.

"If it's trouble," Peg shouted to his guests, "do not shoot until they shoot at ye. Then lie down behind yer fodder shocks. Do be keerful of the people in front of ye. Don't shoot yer own people!"

"We hear ye, Peg," Slim Winters shouted. "Let anybody come!"

5

"THEN I HAVE come," shouted a shrill familiar voice. "Hold your fire until I have said what I have to say!"

"Oh, it's Father," Did said to Sparkie. "It's trouble. He's come to get me this time."

"Take it easy, Did," Sparkie said. "He ain't a-goin' to git ye!"

"So it is you, Bill Hargis," Peg shouted. "Back here again."

"I told you, Peg Sparks, that I would return to get my son. I am here and I have brought force enough to get him! I'll take him home tonight."

"If yer son wants to go, ye can have 'im," Peg said, as Bill Hargis walked toward him.

"Somebody led him to us," Sparkie whispered to Did. "He couldn't have found this cornfield 'less somebody showed 'im the way. The Eversoles, I'll bet. They told him where we would be tonight!"

"My men and I have this cornfield surrounded," Bill Hargis warned. "We have been watching you and your antics. We watched the path for my son and that outlaw of yours. But we missed them. Since we didn't get them on the ridge, we have been here listening to all of your blabber while you got your winter work done with free labor! You make me laugh! And about the red ear of corn and the lustful love-making," Bill Hargis added with a sarcastic laugh, "how an old buzzard like you can promote such nonsense is more than decent people can understand. You are the head of all this, you old kidnaper!"

"Bill Hargis, ye've said enough," Lacie Howard shouted up the slope.

"Glad ye've come," Porkie Porter shouted from the west end of the field.

"I'm glad ye're here too," Tim Gilbert added, as he walked slowly toward Bill Hargis. "A hill man can't go to Greenwood without he's beaten up! A fight is picked with him. He's arrested, throwed in jail, and fined. Ye have yer Law on yer side. We have our Law on our side!"

"Don't you come a step farther," Bill Hargis warned. "My men are just waiting for the signal. I have two hundred men in these woods! We're not afraid of all your pistols. We have guns too. We have good guns. We have come to get my son tonight. We are goin' to have him! You bring that boy up here, turn him over to me, and there will not be any trouble. Don't you come a step farther, I'm warning you," Bill Hargis added, pointing a trembling finger at Tim Gilbert. "I remember how you talked to me at that lawless brazen frolic a few nights ago!"

"I don't keer what ye remember," Tim said. "Ye had my brother Alf arrested in Greenwood and he's in jail now. He can't pay that hundred-dollar fine! That's the only way ye've got of capturing our men!"

"Stand back, Tim," Peg interceded. "Let us see what Did wants to do!"

"I'm not goin'," Did shouted from down under the slope. "I'm not goin' one step!"

"What's come over you, son?" Bill Hargis asked. "Do you like sleeping with a hound-dog in the hayloft? Is that nicer than a decent bed? What magic do these hillbillies hold for you?"

"Yer friends beat me up in Greenwood, Bill Hargis," Lonnie Johnson shouted. "But you didn't git to throw me in jail. I outran yer damned Law!"

"Ye fined me fifty bucks in your lousy town, Bill Hargis," Tom Moore shouted. "But I had the money I'd got from the starvation poles I'd sold yer lumber dealer. I paid my fine and shook the dust from my feet on yer streets."

"How's yer trade now, Mr. Hargis?" came Olive Peyton's soft voice from down under the slope.

"You have not only kidnaped my son but you have blackmailed my business," Bill Hargis admitted. "You can ruin my business, but I'll have my son."

"Go away in peace, Father!" Did shouted. "Leave me alone. Why do you come to get me every time we are having the time of our life?"

"Because one of his paid spies lets 'im know where we are and what we're a-doin'," Doshia Gilbert broke in. "We know the enemies among us, Mr. Hargis!"

"I heard that crazy talk about the moon too," Bill Hargis said. "I heard that superstitious talk about the fox and the owl. Only a crazy person would believe that stuff. When we circled this field, all but the cliffs down below, we drove that fox across the field. He got in our circle. We scared the owl from his tree! Then old Peg and old Arn said it was a bad omen!"

"It is a bad omen," Arn shouted. "Look what's happened."

"Not half has happened that will happen before this night is over," Bill Hargis warned. "Didway, walk up this hill right now. It will save trouble and, perhaps, bloodshed! Get out of that Sparkie's old clothes you are wearing."

"Don't do it, Did," Sparkie shouted. "There's not a better place than this cornfield fer Plum Grove and Greenwood to tangle."

"This is the place to fight," shouted others. "If we have to fight, let it begin right here. Not one of us is safe in Greenwood now."

"But our wives and our womenfolk are with us," Hester Thombs warned. "We can't fight with guns. A bullet will find one of them same as it would find one of us!"

"We have not fired a shot at anybody yet," Bill Hargis said. "We have you surrounded. Now let's get this over with, once and for all! I don't want to have to take my son by force."

"I'm a-standin' by Peg, guns or no guns," Arn said, as she stooped over the cornpile and picked up the largest ear of corn.

The mixed cavalry of horses and mules that had first run toward the west side of the cornfield now circled down toward the cliffs. They sniffed the air from the deep valley below; then they ran along the south side of the field, up past the dance platform toward the east side. When they started for the line of trees on the east end of the field, a shot rang out from the woods. The horses and mules turned toward the path, the way they had come. One horse found it and the others followed. The steel-shod hoofs of the scared animals thundered a retreat over the same path they had come. More shots were fired from the woods hitting the branches of the trees above them to scare and scatter them into the wildest wooded section among the Plum Grove hills.

"One thing is sure," Bill Hargis said, as the fleeing hoofs pounded the hard path, "you will not be able to get to your saddles and ride away. You cannot get over the cliffs at the south wall. We have the rim of this horseshoe ridge fortified. Not one place is left unguarded! Now, come out and have some sense and surrender while you are able!"

"How'd ye know about the south wall and the cliffs, Bill Hargis?" Peg asked. "Ye've never been down there in yer life!"

"That's my business, Peg Sparks," Bill Hargis snapped. "Now will you surrender my boy to me?"

"I will not surrender him," Peg said. "He don't want to go. He is one of us by his own choice."

"Very well, my men are getting restless."

"Remember, Bill Hargis, our men are armed too," Peg warned. "They shoot squirrels from the tall hickories and black walnuts with pistols. We're not afraid of all the fancy firearms ye brought from yer store! We just want to know how ye aim to fight. Remember we have our unarmed women with us."

"Any way that suits you," Bill Hargis said. "We can take care of you anyway we fight! You have your choice!"

"Without guns and knives," Hester Thombs shouted.

"That suits us," Bill Hargis agreed.

"All right, men, you that brought guns leave them at the edge of the field," Hargis shouted his command to attack. "Tear up their fiddles first. Let's go!"

6

THE GREENWOOD MEN came down from the woods around the entire semicircle of the mule-shoe-shaped ridge. The moon was still high and bright. It was almost as bright as day. A scared rabbit came down in front of them and zigzagged across the field toward the south wall of cliffs. Three men rushed down to the oak. They smashed the guitars, fiddles, and banjos. One jumped upon Lacie Howard's bull fiddle with his feet.

"That will end the dancing," Bill Hargis shouted. "Now you people look to see that we are approaching you without guns!"

"My fiddle," Lacie Howard shouted in a rage.

"My steel guitar," Arville Short cried.

The men followed Bill Hargis's order. They held their rifles, Winchesters, and pistols up so the Plum Grove men could see them. Then they laid them in piles around the border where the cornfield met the trees.

"Now show us that you are of the same faith," Bill Hargis shouted.

Down at the foot of the hill, the young corn shuckers unfastened their holsters, held them high for the Greenwood men to see, then laid them beside their fodder shocks. The few married men in the fodder-shock rows upon the slope unfastened their holsters and laid down their ornaments that they had worn. The old men were quite active now as they were first in line to be attacked. They were at a great disadvantage too, for they had to fight uphill. They forgot about the mountains they had climbed and the stiffness in their knee joints as they faced the long, long line of silent men emerging from the woods.

The Plum Grove men formed a line at the bottom of their slope. Their wives and women marched beside them.

"You will be the first casualty, Peg Sparks," Bill Hargis shouted. "Here is where the fight begins. I've been wanting to get hold of you since the first time I ever laid eyes on you!"

"Don't ye come a step further, old Bill Hargis," Arn shouted. "Don't ye tech my man. I don't like ye nohow!"

"Come on, Bill Hargis," Peg shouted as he braced himself with his good foot down the hill and his wooden leg up the hill, "I'm ready fer ye!"

"Stay where ye are, Bill Hargis," Arn warned, as Bill stepped forward slowly with his eyes on Peg and his fists clenched.

"Stop before I lambast ye," Arn shouted, as the lone line of Greenwood men walked slowly down the steep slope.

"Oh, I'm shot," Bill Hargis screamed as the big ear of corn broke against his ribs. He stopped in his tracks.

"I told ye I'd lambast the daylights outten ye if you teched Peg," Arn shouted, as she picked up another ear of corn. Arn was puffing furiously on her pipe. Little clouds of smoke were rising up and thinning to nothingness on the blue night wind. "Stay where ye are before I finish ye!"

Bill Hargis stood still in his tracks.

"Attack, men," he shouted with a half breath.

"I think I about busted a panel of yer old ribs," Arn laughed.

Then came the first clash. The Greenwood men went into action against the Plum Grove men. There was only a thin line of old men with their wives beside them to meet the Greenwood men as they came over the slope. But up the hill came another line of young men and women.

When the Greenwood men attacked, fists flew. Men hit the soft carpet of crab grass. When Tim Gilbert hit the ground, Doshia Gilbert pulled up a cornstubble with dirt still clinging to the old roots and she came overhand on top of the head of the man who had knocked Tim down. Down went the man that hit Tim, with his knees buckling beneath him. She came overhand on another man and he went down. She hit another man and most of the dirt was knocked from the old cornroot, but she brought him to his knees. Then she pulled another cornstubble and went back to work.

"Brain 'em with pumpkins," Jeff Potters shouted. "They busted our fiddles."

Now the second Plum Grove line of men and women had reached the first thin and battered line. Both men and women were lying on the ground. "These women fight like men," shouted a Greenwood man. "Upend 'em same as you do the men!"

The Plum Grove men went into action with their fists.

"Oh, oh, I'm struck in the eye," a Greenwood man shouted, as he dropped to his knees with his hand over his eye, face toward the ground.

Lucy Howard pulled up a cornstubble and ran up and broke

166

it over his head. He lay still. Did Hargis was flattened on the ground, but Pollie Porter hit the man that she thought knocked Did down. She caught him in the face and eyes with the full force of the dirt on the end of a cornstubble. He lay sprawled and moaning on the crab grass.

A man screamed that something was in his eye. Another screamed that his eye was out. Sparkie never used his fists. He just ran up and fronted a man, stuck his face out like he was bannering the man to strike it, and squirt! It was all over. He always got one eye. Sometimes he got both.

"Why did we bring firearms, Bill Hargis?" a man shouted. "We're tricked."

Then Lucille Dodderidge hit this man over the head with a big pumpkin. It broke into pieces and pumpkin seeds covered the man as he dropped to his knees.

There was fighting the entire length of the field. Men on both sides went down. Many lay there without stirring. Men and women swung cornstubbles, cornstalks, and pumpkins and watched the Greenwood men go down to their knees. When the fight started, because of their superior number, the Greenwood men went into action with all confidence. There were fifty more Greenwood men than Plum Grove men and women.

"Vengeance," screamed Lacie Howard. "Remember our music boxes! Remember my fiddle!" He was weeping and swinging.

"Go to it, my men," Bill Hargis shouted with a half breath. He stood frozen in his tracks, afraid to move.

"Ye keep quiet, Bill Hargis," Arn warned as she held another ear of corn ready for him.

Peg ran up the hill. His wooden leg sank deep in the ground. He spun around twice before he finally pulled it out. Then he reached Tim Gilbert and helped him to his feet.

"We need our firearms, Hargis," someone shouted from down under the hill.

"But ye won't get 'em," Peg shouted, as he and Tim Gilbert

hobbled up where the cornfield edged against the timber line.

Peg and Tim started gathering their firearms and carrying them back into the woods.

"Leave our guns alone," Bill Hargis shouted. He started toward them.

"Not another step, Bill Hargis."

He stopped dead in his tracks when Arn raised her throwing arm.

"If ye take another step, I'll larrup ye with this ear of corn right betwixt the eyes."

"They're gettin' our guns, men," Bill Hargis shouted.

"You messed up the works by letting them fight on their own terms, Bill Hargis," someone shouted from down under the hill.

Hargis took one step toward Peg and Tim. When he did, Arn let drive with her ear of corn. She upended Bill Hargis. He fell moaning and groaning among the cornstubble. Then Arn rushed to help Peg and Tim collect the guns and carry them into the woods.

Down below on the steep slope men fell and rolled among the cornstubble. Men swore as the fighting became more intense and the lines thinned. Pumpkins came down on men's heads, breaking into hundreds of pieces. Men were hit over the heads with butt ends of water-soaked cornstalks. They were hit with clods of dirt in the ends of cornstubbles. Men moaned and rolled on the soft brown carpet of crab grass. Men and women uttered unintelligible, crazy words. More than a score of Greenwood men were screaming they had been blinded.

"Get that Sparkie," somebody cried. "Hargis told us about this outlaw."

"Yeah, come and git me," Sparkie bannered them. "Here I am. Come and git me."

Squirt. Squirt.

Another man let out a scream and slapped a hand over each

eye. Lucy ran in with her cornstubble. One lick over the head and he lay sprawled on the grass same as the other men that had tried to get Sparkie.

"Are ye Greenwood smart alecks a-gittin' enough?" John Snowden screamed.

"Come on, they're thinnin' out. Let's finish the job," Hester Thombs shouted.

Did Hargis had not come to his senses. He lay across a shock of loose fodder. Pollie Porter was knocked down twice. But each time she rose to fight again.

"If you Plum Grove women fight with the men, using corn-stubble and pumpkins," shouted a Greenwood man with little grunts of breath, "you'll have to take what we give the m—." He never finished. A woman hit him in the head with a root.

"What do you say now, Bill Hargis?" one of the Green-wood men shouted.

"He can't answer ye," Arn told him, as she looked at the writhing bodies lying in a curved line around the steep slope in the moonlight. Many were lying kicking on the loose fodder.

"Chase 'em back to town."

"Brain 'em with pumpkins!"

Squirt. Squirt.

"Oh, oh, my eyes!"

Squirt.

"Eiii-i! I'm blind!"

"Upend 'im, Tim."

"We've about got 'em!"

The lines did not extend from one end of the field to the other now. Many fighters limped away. Many writhed on the crab grass and the fodder with their hands over their eyes. Sparkie and Lucy fought on. They fought harder now among the weakened and disabled Greenwood men than they had fought in the beginning.

"Greenwood, will ye give up?" Peg asked. "If ye don't, we'll finish ye."

"I'm willing," a man shouted with hands over his eyes. "Who are we fightin' for? Bill Hargis?"

"He's still dead to the world."

"How will we ever get out of here?"

"What about our wounded?"

"I say we surrender."

"What else can we do?"

"All right, we stop fightin'." Peg gave the order.

Only a few wouldn't stop.

"Break it up, Plum Grove," Peg shouted. "Turn 'em loose."

The tired men sat down on the grass. The Plum Grove men had lost the red bandannas from around their necks. Their shirts were ripped off. The Greenwood men were scratched and bruised. Their eyes had been blackened. Their lips were broken and bleeding. Many had missing front teeth.

"Now each group take keer of his wounded," Peg said. "Let's git our men and git 'em home."

"How will we ever get our men back to the Plum Grove turnpike?" asked a tired Greenwood man, whose clothes had been torn off down to his underwear. He stood shivering in the chill of the October night.

"That's yer problem," Peg said. "Ye jumped on us. Ye'd better be a-gatherin' yer wounded before the moon goes down."

"Let's gather our men," Sparkie said. "Let 'em take keer of their own."

The men and women from Plum Grove went over the cornfield gathering their own. The women bandaged the cuts and bruises with their handkerchiefs and picked up men's bandannas here and there amid the cornfield debris. Four Plum Grove men, one to each leg and each arm, started carrying the disabled up the hill to the path and toward home. Greenwood men found their wounded and started for the path. Peg, Sparkie, Lucy, and Pollie carried Did up the hill.

They followed behind four men who were carrying Bill Hargis.

"Don't fergit our bridles," Tim Gilbert shouted. "Let's git them from the trees."

"And our new supply of guns," Peg said. "Our men that didn't have guns will have 'em now."

While the Greenwood men gathered their wounded and unconscious together, before the long march to the Plum Grove turnpike, the Plum Grove procession moved slowly around the ridge the way they had come a few hours before when the moon first peeped over the Buzzard Roost Ridge. They carried their wounded, their bridles and new supply of guns. Now the moon was going down and the Greenwood men they had left behind would have to find their way along the winding narrow path in the semidarkness. But Did was going home, although he knew nothing about it, with the people he had chosen to live among.

7

"SPARKIE, ARE YE awake?"

"Not wide awake, Peg!"

"Is Did awake?"

"Don't know, Peg!"

"I'm awake, Peg," Did muttered. "But why are we gittin' up so early?"

"Early? Listen out there in the barnyard, won't ye? Everything is a-wantin' to be fed. The sun is high in the sky! It's nigh onto ten o'clock!"

Peg was sitting up in bed looking at the notches he had cut on the window to tell time by the sun. The rays of the morning sun had reached the ten o'clock notch.

"I don't see the sun, Peg," Did said. "It's still night time for me!"

"Gosh-old-hemlock, Peg, Did's eyes are swelled shet," Sparkie said.

"He was too little to be in that battle," Arn spoke softly.

Peg lifted his shirt from the chair where he left his clothes at night. Then he reached over and got his pants from the chair. He put his good leg down through the leg of his pants, pulled them as far as he could while he sat on the side of the bed. He put the sock and shoe on his foot. Doubling the loose pants leg over the end of his half leg, he put his knee down onto the pad of his wooden leg. Then he pulled his pants up around him and fastened the big leather belt around his waist. The leather belt served two purposes: it held up his pants and it held his wooden leg in place. By the time Peg was dressed, Arn was standing by waiting to lace his shoe. This was the morning routine ever since they had been married.

"Peg, ye put a fire in the cookstove and in the fireplace," Arn said. "I aim to do what I can fer Did."

Arn walked over to the pallet they had spread for Did. They had put a quilt on the floor and laid a feather pillow on it for his head. Sparkie had lain beside Did without a feather pillow. There were only three feather pillows in the Sparks' shack.

"Don't reckon he's blind as a bat?" Peg said, as he put kindling in the cookstove and struck a match.

"Shucks, no, it ain't that," Sparkie answered. "Remember four years ago when I fought Cief Eversole in the fox huntin' woods when he kicked old Thunderbolt? He closed my eyes. Later," Sparkie chuckled, "when I found a better way to

172

fight, I closed his eyes. Did's all right. Put the cold spring-water poultices to his eyes, Arn! Remember how they took the swellin' from mine."

"Ye'll have to fetch me a bucket of fresh water from the spring," she said.

"Then throw me my pants," Sparkie said.

Peg picked up Sparkie's pants from the floor and tossed them to his outstretched hands. Sparkie sat up under the quilt, put his feet down his pants legs, and pulled them up. Then he got out from under the quilt, and ran down the hill to the rock-walled spring under the giant beech trees. He didn't take time to snap the short rope onto the bucket bails but lay down flat on his stomach on the damp cool beech leaves from which the sun had just melted the frost. He reached over and dipped the bucket into the clear cool spring water. Then he hurried to the house.

Arn was standing inside with a pan and a clean towel. Sparkie poured water from the bucket into the pan and Arn went to work. She wet the towel in cold water and laid it gently over Did's eyes that were swollen to narrow slits. The flesh around his eye sockets was dark as mushrooms on old rotting oak stumps.

"Gee, that feels good," Did said.

He put his swollen hand to his mouth and felt a tooth.

"One of my front teeth is loose and I hate to lose it," he said.

"Don't work with it, Did," Sparkie advised. "Leave it alone. Shucks, it'll settle back in place if ye don't fool with it. Cief knocked three of mine loose. All as tight as wedges in a hickory log now."

Did took his hand away from the tooth. Arn spread the cool water-soaked towel over Did's lips.

"I'd like to know the man that closed Did's eyes." The color rose in Sparkie's face. "Just two squirts and I'd close his'n."

"I would too," Arn said, as she lifted the towel from Did's face and put it in the pan to soak up more cool water.

"Wasn't a man hit me," Did explained. "I remember that. A woman hit me in the face with a cornstubble. I think it was Lucretia Quisenberry! That's the last thing I remember. Don't tell her about it," he added. "She just made a mistake! She thought she was getting a Greenwood man."

Arn applied the cool wet towel again to Did's face.

"That feels so good, Arn," he said.

Arn passed the towel gently over his swollen eyes.

"That was an awful fight last night," Peg said. "It devilish nigh ruint me. We'll haf to finish shuckin' that corn and clean up the cornfield before we can plow that ground."

"But I hated to miss that dance more than anything," Sparkie said.

Did said, "I hated to have to be carried home."

"Yer pappy was carried home, too," Peg said.

"What happened to him?"

"He was hit with a ear of corn."

"Was he hurt?"

"No, he'll come to his senses all right," Arn said.

"He won't come to his senses until he quits a-bringin' the Law and armies of city dudes out here to fight us," Peg said, as he laid kindling in the big fireplace.

Arn lifted the towel from Did's face while the hungry hounds, hogs, cattle, and chickens called for their breakfasts.

"I can see the light," Did shouted through his thick swollen lips. "I can see out of my left eye! You look all right, Sparkie."

"I'm in purty good shape, Did."

"You look all right too, Arn."

"My neck's a little sore," she said. "Somebody throwed a pumpkin at somebody else, and it hit me in the side of the head and jarred my neck."

Sparkie, Did, and Peg laughed.

"That laughin' helped my lips," Did said. "I just had to laugh."

"Ye're all right, Did," Sparkie said. "Can ye stand up?"

174

"Well, not now . . . not quite," he said.

"Throw his pants over here, Peg," Sparkie said.

Sparkie caught his pants and gave them to Did.

"Reach down there under the quilt and put 'em on," Sparkie said.

"I'd never thought of that," Did said.

"That's the way to dress when wimmen folks sleep in the same room with ye," Sparkie said.

It was easy for Did to pull the big pants over his legs. They were Sparkie's old pants that Did had worn threadbare.

"We couldn't put ye up through the scuttle-hole to the hay last night," Peg said. "We done mighty well to git ye here. Had to git our wind several times as we toted ye around the path last night. Ye're a-gainin' weight."

"Here's yer shoes and yer shirt," Sparkie said. "Git these on and git out in the cool mornin' air while there is still the smell of frost. It will hep ye. Ye ain't ust to a room with a fire in it. This room will hurt ye, Did."

"Gee, I'm so sore all over I can hardly move," Did grunted as he put his arms into his shirt sleeves. "When I think about what that cornstubble did to me, I wonder about a lot of the Greenwood men!"

Sparkie and Peg laughed.

"Don't make me laugh," Did said. "It hurts my lips."

That started them laughing again.

"Come, let's go do the feedin' while Arn gits breakfast," Sparkie said. "Did needs this cool mornin' wind before the sun gits too high."

"I've put on a pone of corndodger fer the hounds," Arn said. "I'll soon have breakfast fer ye. Don't be gone too long."

When Peg's wooden leg hit the planks on the little porch, there was a great noise in the barnyard. The fattening hogs told Peg they were hungry. The cows told him to throw hay into their mangers. The hens cackled in the barn lot and the roosters crowed. The hounds charged against their chains.

"How I miss my mules," Peg said. "They're always the first to speak when I step on the porch! Place is not the same without 'em. I miss their mornin' brays. They speak to me and I speak to them!"

"Throw down hay to the cattle, Sparkie," Peg said. "I'll feed the hogs and shell corn fer the chickens."

"Did, ye walk around out here in the fresh air," Sparkie advised. "This mornin' wind will be a help to yer eyes."

Sparkie climbed up the log wall like a cat and went in the barn loft at the gable-end door. Peg went to the corncrib and filled a basket of corn for the hogs. When he threw the corn over to the big hogs, they stopped their squealing. Did walked up beside the pen and watched them eat contentedly while Peg stood nearby and shelled corn for the chickens.

The cattle stopped bawling in the barn.

"Everything around here is a part of the fambly." The chickens picked up the bright grains of corn as fast as Peg could shell them from the cob. "Everything's so hungry. We're a-feedin' about five hours late! It hurts me to keep cattle, dogs, hogs, and varmints and let 'em starve. They look to us fer help."

"I'm as hungry as anything around this barn," Sparkie shouted, as he went to get the dogs' breakfast from Arn.

While Sparkie divided the pone of hot corn bread among his hounds, Did poured two gallons of buttermilk into the trough for the possums. Did watched the possums come from the hollow log to the trough and drink buttermilk.

"Sparkie," Did shouted, "my other eye is comin' open. I can see with it."

"What's the matter, Did?" Lacie Howard said, as he came riding up from toward the beech trees by the spring. "Is one of yer eyes closed too?"

"Both of 'em were closed this mornin' when I got up," Did told him.

"I got one closed," Lacie said, turning his face for Did to

176

see. "But this ain't as bad as losin' my fiddle. I've cried over my fiddle this mornin' until I couldn't sleep."

"Lacie, ye got a shiner," Sparkie said. "Who hit you?"

"One of the Plum Grove girls," he said. "Can't tell you which one. Hit me with a cornstubble. In the last minutes of the fight so many Greenwood men were on the ground knocked out that we got to fightin' one another."

"Where did ye find yer mule, Lacie?" Peg asked.

"Down nearly to Cedar Riffle," Lacie said. "I saw men out everywhere a-huntin' their mules!"

"See my mules anyplace?"

"Never saw hide ner hair of Dinah and Dick," he said. "I rode up here to tell you about Pap's terbacker barn. It went up in flames last night."

"Ye don't mean that." Peg stepped back. "Lose everything?"

"All but this mule, and I rode him to the corn shuckin'."

"Come to breakfast before the coffee's cold," Arn shouted from the porch.

"That's too bad about Greene Howard's barn," Peg said thoughtfully.

"Ye'd better watch yer barn," Lacie said. "Can happen to ye."

Then Lacie was off in a gallop toward home.

"Let's get to our own breakfast," Peg said. "Afterwards we got to find the mules."

PART SEVEN

I

"WHAT ARE YOU a-goin' to do this mornin', Sparkie?" Peg asked.

"We're a-ridin' to Nellievale." Sparkie took the currycomb and brush down from a crack betwen the logs. "We're a-goin' to ship our hides! Did has to have clothes. I've not got too many clothes myself," Sparkie added, as he raked the currycomb down old Dinah's flank with one hand and with the other used the big brush to sleek Dinah's hair until it was bright and fluffy.

"We've been rough on clothes," Did chuckled, as he waxed the cowboy saddle. "I got plenty of clothes at home but I'll never go there after them!"

"If I had the money, boys, I'd let ye have it," Peg said. "I won't have any money until I sell my terbacker!"

"We know that, Peg. I've told Did ye'd buy clothes and shoes fer us if ye could. I told him that I'd trapped, sold hides and possums since I was twelve and bought my own clothes!"

"That's right, Sparkie," Peg admitted. "Ye've had to scratch fer yerself! I've not been too good a father to ye when it come to providin' clothes. I've not been able to raise enough terbacker."

"We'd rather help you, Peg, than have you help us," Did said.

"Stand still, old gal," Sparkie told Dinah. "Just a-tryin' to make ye look purty. Never like to see a mule that didn't look purty! When a mule is ugly, he's the sorriest sight ever!"

"Boy, look at this saddle," Did said, as he shined it with a rag. "You can see yourself in it, Sparkie!"

Did laid his cowboy saddle to one side. Then he lifted Sparkie's big saddle from across the partition that separated the log barn into two big stalls for the mules. This was the place they kept the saddles, mule collars, and harness.

"I hope ye get a good price fer yer hides," Peg said as he turned to look at Did.

Did was spreading wax over the big saddle. Peg could see Did's leg through holes in his pants leg below the knee. The right pants leg was split from the knee to the thigh.

"Ye sartainly do need some clothes, Did," Peg said, as he looked at Did's small brown legs that had been tanned by the sun, exposed to the wind, rain, and frost. "Ye'll haf to have some clothes, fer winter is not far away."

"We'll have 'em!" Sparkie spoke with confidence. "We've got some good hides this year. Best hides we've ever had. These cool nights and white frosts have cured the pelts as purty as they ripen the pawpaw and the cimmon!"

"Where are ye a-sendin' yer hides this year, Sparkie?"

"To the Good Fur Company, Peg. They've always give me the best price fer my hides."

Sparkie finished with Dinah and walked around on the other side of the partition to apply the currycomb and brush to Dick.

"Got the hides off the boards, separated, and sacked?" Peg asked.

"Got 'em off the boards and separated," Sparkie said. "Got the sacks ready too. But we don't aim to sack the hides until we git to Nellievale. We want people along the road to see the purty hides we got this year! Whoa, Dick!" Sparkie scolded. "Stand still! I ain't a-goin' to hurt ye. Peg," Sparkie continued, "Did fixed the tags in fancy handwritin'. Gosh-old-hemlock, he can write purty. Somebody at the Good Fur Company will know there's one trapper with a good eddica-tion!"

"Ye keep on a-goin', son, like ye have been," Peg said, as he watched Did pull on the girth until he fastened it in the right hole, "and ye'll be a man someday."

"Reckon I'll ever be as strong as Sparkie?"

"I 'speck ye will, and a lot smarter too," Peg said, laughing louder than the morning wind.

Did carried the cowboy saddle and the blanket over to Dick's stall. While Sparkie combed the brush of Dick's tail, Did spread the blanket over Dick's back and put his saddle on.

"Good teamwork," Peg said, as Sparkie led old Dinah and Did led old Dick from their stalls through the barn door into the brisk morning air. Peg followed them to the corncrib, where they threw the bridle reins over the mules' necks and let them stand while they went inside the corncrib.

"Look at this, Peg," Sparkie said.

"That's a whopper crop of possum hides," Peg admitted, as he looked at the big hides with the good fur stacked by themselves, the little midnight-blue possum hides in another pile, and the medium-sized hides in a third stack.

"Three sacks of possum hides," Sparkie said. "This means we'll order from the *Wish Book*. Polecat hides," Sparkie continued. "Solid black, narrow stripes, and broad stripes. There's the money."

"I 'spect they'll average ye four dollars apiece," Peg said.

"More than that," Sparkie broke in.

"Red fox hides will bring money too," Did said. "I've been looking up the prices! Eight to ten dollars apiece! The price of a gray fox is low!"

"Wait a minute, boys. I want Arn to see this!"

Peg went to the house to get Arn while Did and Sparkie

tied the bundles of possum, polecat, fox, coon, weasel, mink, and the muskrat hides to their saddles. They were roping the coffee sacks behind their saddles when Arn walked back across the frosted yard grass with Peg.

"They're ready fer Nellievale, Arn," Peg said. "Look what a shipment of hides!"

"That will buy 'em clothes," Arn said between clouds of smoke. "Mostest hides I've ever seen leave this place!"

"We'd a-had more," Sparkie said, "but Did didn't like to trap wild animals. That's why we took up the trap line."

"I know it, Sparkie," Did said. "These hides are pretty. But I think of the animals that were in these pelts and how I shot them in the traps. I think of the ones that lost their legs in the traps and died. I even think of that wildcat I killed there. Look at his hide now!"

Sparkie eyed the great bundles of pretty pelts tied to the saddles, but he just couldn't look sad.

"Guess I'm soft-hearted when it comes to animals," Did said. "I can't be any other way!"

"But ye're a good hunter, Did," Sparkie bragged. "Never a better hunter in these woods!"

Then Sparkie put his foot into the stirrup and lifted himself into the saddle.

"It's as purty a batch of hides as I've ever seen," Peg bragged. "These hides will fetch ye some money."

"I hope they fetch ye a good price," Arn said, holding her pipe in her hand.

Did climbed into his cowboy saddle. The brisk morning wind of October had brought color to his face and to the places on his legs his pants didn't cover.

"Giddup," Sparkie said, giving Dinah the rein.

"Good luck to ye," Peg shouted, waving his big calloused hand.

"Hie to the hunters," Arn shouted. She stood beside Peg and watched them gallop away.

2

DID AND SPARKIE rode back to the barn in a rush that Saturday evening. They didn't take time to put the mules in the barn but looped the bridle reins over the sharp palings, opened the gate, and ran toward the door. When Peg heard the plowpoints jingling and the rusty gate hinges screeching, he looked out the window and saw Sparkie and Did running toward the shack.

"Wonder what's wrong now?" Peg said to Arn, jumping up from his chair.

Arn had time to get up from her chair and look out the window just as Sparkie made a wild leap for the little back porch.

"What's the matter, son?" Peg shouted, limping to the door to meet Sparkie and Did. "What's happened?"

"Plenty has happened," Sparkie said. "We got something to show ye!"

"It's good news," Did said.

"Ye skeered me," Arn said, feeling into her apron pocket for light burley crumbs. "I thought somethin' might 've happened as ye rode from Nellievale."

"I thought another barn had burned," Peg said.

"We'll show ye what happened," Sparkie said. "Sit back down."

Sparkie had trouble getting his big hand down into his tight hip overall pocket.

"That's a good tight pocket," Sparkie said. "The only safe one I got."

Sparkie didn't carry the money in a billfold. He had never owned one. He carried the money loose in his pocket. When Peg saw the handful of bills, his eyes got big. Arn didn't show any excitement.

"Look at this, won't ye?" Sparkie said, as he counted out five twenty-dollar bills and laid them in a little stack on Peg and Arn's bed.

"One hundred dollars," he said.

Then he laid down five more twenty-dollar bills.

"Another hundred dollars," he said. "That makes two hundred."

Then Arn looked over at Peg, but Peg's eyes followed Sparkie's hand as it went from the money in his hand to the bed ten times.

"Another hundred dollars. That makes three!"

"That's more money than I git fer a terbacker crop," Peg said. "Where'd ye git all that money, Sparkie?"

"From the Good Fur Company," Sparkie said, as he laid down two twenties and twelve ones. On top of the paper money he laid down a dime.

"Three hundred fifty-two dollars and ten cents," he said proudly. "Can ye believe it?"

"Tom Flannigan's eyes got big when we asked him to cash this check," Did laughed. "He said, 'Boys, you must 've sold a good batch of hides. Best fur check I've had this year. Don't know whether I can cash it or not. But maybe I can,' he said when he looked in his cash register. 'This place is like a bank. It's a sight at the checks I cash.' I'll bet twenty-five people were in the store. Hester Thombs was there and he said, 'You are real hunters. That's some check.' Everybody was looking at us."

"What are ye a-goin' to do with all that money, Sparkie?" Arn asked as she blew a cloud of smoke toward the news-papered wall.

"Clothes fer Did," Sparkie said. "Clothes fer me. I'll pay Peg's taxes too."

"No, ye won't either, Sparkie," Peg said. "Not unless my barn burns. Soon as we git another season we'll strip the rest of my terbacker and take it to Nellievale. I'll pay my taxes then. I'll pay my store accounts and buy some little things fer Christmas."

"That's yer and Did's money," Arn said. "Buy yerselves some purty clothes."

"That'll make Lucy and Pollie love 'em more," Peg said. Then he laughed and whetted the sharp end of his wooden leg on the rough floor. "I think it's wonderful to see ye and Did in love—a-trappin', a-huntin', and a-sellin' hides jest to buy yerselves clothes!"

"Ye'll use the *Wish Book* now," Arn said, as she eyed the catalogue from a mail-order house.

"I say we'll use the *Wish Book*," Sparkie said. "We've been a-turnin' through the pages a-lookin' at the things we plan to buy! Did will write our orders tonight."

"We want to order before the Christmas buying starts," Did said.

"We've not got enough work clothes between us to last two more weeks," Sparkie said. "We've got to have clothes."

"You want to see how the prices of the hides ran, Peg?" Did said, giving him the statement.

"Ye read it fer us, Did," Peg said. "I don't know the letters."

"Oh, excuse me," Did said, forgetting that Peg, Arn, and Sparkie didn't read.

"The thirty-nine possum hides brought fifty-nine dollars and sixty cents," Did said. "The highest priced hide was two dollars and eighty cents. The lowest priced hide was sixteen cents."

"The good hide come from that possum we ketched in that little cimmon tree the night Shootin' Star got shot," Sparkie said. "That little sixteen-cent hide come from that little blue midnighter ye climbed the grapevine in the sycamore to git on the same night. Body ought'n to fool with the little midnighters."

"Six black polecat hides, seventy-one dollars and forty cents," Did read from the statement. "Seven narrow stripes, thirty-five dollars and thirty-one cents. Eight broad stripes, twenty-seven dollars and sixteen cents. Total for our polecat hides, one hundred thirty-three dollars and eighty-seven cents."

"That's the big money," Peg said. "It's in the polecat hides! Think of that!"

"Funny about the polecats," Sparkie said. "We got the black ones in around Possum Hollow. Trapped most of the narrow stripes around Buzzard Roost Ridge. Got the broad stripes down in Shackle Run Valley."

"Listen to this," Did said. "Eight red fox hides, ninety-two dollars and fifty cents. Seven gray fox hides, twenty-eight dollars and six cents. Total for the fox hides, one hundred twenty dollars and fifty-six cents."

"That's good money, too," Peg said.

"But I don't like to kill a red fox," Sparkie said. "When a body traps fer the gray foxes, he will ketch a red one. One thing I never understood," he added. "Why is it a red fox hide is worth so much more than a gray one?"

"Two coon hides, eight dollars. One wildcat hide, three dollars."

"I'd a-thought that big hide would have brought more than that," Sparkie said. "Hide would have been worth more to the wildcat than it was to us."

"Nine muskrat hides, twelve dollars and fifty cents. Six weasel hides, three dollars and seventy-five cents."

"Too cheap to fool with," Sparkie said. "But weasels are

bloodsuckers and ought to be kilt. One will cut the juglar vein of any animal he can and drink its warm blood."

"Two mink hides, ten dollars and eighty-two cents."

"That's the most money I've ever seen in this shack," Peg said.

"It's the most money I've ever seen in my life in one pile," Arn said.

"That's one hundred seventy-six dollars and five cents fer Did and fer me," Sparkie said. "Did counted it up. That will buy clothes, won't it?"

"I know why ye come a-runnin' in here now," Peg said. "If I had that much money, guess I'd a-run to have showed it too."

"Be keerful with yer money," Arn said. "When ye're fightin' like at the corn shuckin' the other night, somebody might git his hand in yer pocket."

"Clothes fer Sparkie and Did," Peg said. "New clothes fer Sunday. Work clothes to wear in the fields."

"A new suit," Sparkie shouted. "New shirts, socks, new shoes fer my feet and bandannas fer my neck."

"New clothes fer Did," Arn said. "Look at them old rags he's a-wearin' now!"

"Do be keerful with that money, Sparkie," Arn cautioned.

"I've got a good safe place to keep this money, Arn," he told her.

"After supper we'll order from the *Wish Book!* Gosh-old-hemlock," Sparkie shouted excitedly as he picked up Arn's catalogue from the floor, and he and Did ran jubilantly to feed the mules, "three hundred and fifty-two dollars!"

3

"OLD DINAH IS the near mule when ye have 'em in the britchen," Sparkie instructed Did, who stood between the handles of the hillside turning plow. "Let 'er walk along the lower edge of the field until ye strike the first furrow. When ye go to yan end of the field and start to turn, pay no mind to the plow but keep yer eyes on the mules. Watch that the trace chain don't come loose and swarp old Dinah on the leg. She's techy about things like that. After ye turn at yan end, be shore to hold Dinah up on the hard ground and let old Dick walk down in the furrow."

Did put the leather check lines over his left shoulder and under his right arm. Sparkie showed him how to arrange his check lines.

"Dick and Dinah are powerful mules," Sparkie said, as he looked over the check lines to see if there were any breaks in the leather. "If Dinah gits skeered at a fodder blade or a piece of pumpkin, ye should have the check lines behind yer shoulder and not all the way around yer neck. Yer shoulder is more powerful than yer neck when ye start heavin' on the check lines to hold a skeered mule team as big as Dick and Dinah. And when yer a-plowin' peacefully along and ye want to rein old Dick or Dinah, all ye haf to do is take one hand from the plow handle and pull on the line the way ye want the mule to go. Ye know how to turn the plow. Ye know

187

how to shift the moldboard and let the mules swing the plow around. Did, ye ain't big enough to lift it!"

"I think I can do it all right," Did said proudly. "This is something I've always wanted to do. Walk between the handles of a big plow with a mule team in front of me and turn the dark land over. Not a boy in Greenwood has ever done this. I believe," Did smiled, "that this will put muscles on my arms and make my shoulders broad like yours, Sparkie."

"If ye do enough of it," Peg said, "it will make yer shoulders broad as an ax handle is long."

Peg laughed and slapped his thighs with his big calloused hands as he looked at little Did Hargis standing between the plow handles ready to go.

"Never slap Dick and Dinah with the lines," Sparkie warned. "They 're high-lifed mules. Ye know that, Did. Ye know the nature of Dinah. She's like a stick of dynamite, ready anytime to explode. Ye don't ever haf to slap one of these mules with a line. Just follow 'em all day and ye won't have any trouble sleepin' at night. It used to take Peg twenty days to plow this field. That was before I started plowin'. I started plowin' when I was twelve years old. It took me twenty days the first year I plowed it. Next year it took me sixteen days. The third year I plowed it in fourteen days. Last year I plowed it in twelve days."

"I've never plowed a furrow in my life," Did said. "I'm ready to begin. See that I do it right. Let's go, Dick and Dinah!"

They were off, stepping lively around the steep slope. Did held stubbornly to the handles of the turning plow while Sparkie and Peg looked on. The dark loam rolled over from the moldboard as the mules went around the mountains.

4

LONG BEFORE DID ever stepped between the handles of a plow, Sparkie had shown him how to harness the mule team, how to put the padded collars on the mules, how to lay the britchen over their backs, fasten the hame string, and buckle the bellybands. He taught Did the near and off sides and carefully instructed Did always to put Dinah on the *near side* and Dick on the *off side*. Once he put each on the wrong side to show Did what would happen. They kicked at the doubletree, squealed, bit at each other, and went backward. Dinah even bit at Sparkie's ear, she was so mad. Sparkie showed Did the right link in each of the four trace chains to hook to the singletrees. He taught him the use of the clevis, singletree, doubletree and open-links. He let Did drive the mules when they were hitched to the sled loads of corn so he would know their teamwork and how they pulled together. Now Did was through with practicing. Now, for the first time, he was plowing.

"Did'll tackle anything," Peg was watching intently. "I like his nature. He's willin' to larn. He'll do more than his body can stand."

"He ain't afraid to tackle and to fight," Sparkie said, as he looked at the first furrow Did was making. "He's got the lay of the land all right. His furrow runs true to the bend in the slope."

When Did plowed Dick and Dinah to the far end of the field, Sparkie and Peg watched him carefully at this crucial moment while he turned his team for the first time on a steep mountain slope. They watched him kick the trigger on his moldboard as the big mules turned in unison. While they were still moving, little Did righted his plow and pushed the trigger back in place to hold the moldboard.

"That's the way," Sparkie said with a smile. "He can do it."

Did kept Dick down in the furrow and Dinah up on the unplowed ground.

"Dick and Dinah know they've got a real plowboy behind 'em," Sparkie said. "That was perfect, Did. All 'cept one thing. Remember what I told ye when ye first started usin' an ax? Ye chopped with stiff arms. Let yer arms be limber as a willow in the wind. It will be easier on ye and the mules if ye do."

"Thank you, Sparkie," Did beamed as he turned the team perfectly and tripped the moldboard of his plow.

He was off again to the other end of the field while Sparkie and Peg looked on to see if he made any mistakes.

"As nigh perfect as a plowboy can be," Peg said. "Wish I had two good legs and could git around like Did. I wouldn't ast no man the odds of work to do."

Peg picked up his sprouting hoe and started cutting cornstubbles and sprouts.

"We'll haf to move, Sparkie, to keep this field cleaned ahead of the plow," Peg said. "But one thing," he laughed, "many of the cornstubbles have been pulled up! Look over this field!"

"I'll git the fodder shocked, Peg," Sparkie said. "I can walk over the plowed ground better than ye!"

While Peg cut the remaining cornstubbles and sprouts, Sparkie carried the bundles of fodder down onto the strip of earth that Did had plowed. He stood the bundles up into big fodder shocks until he had a row of fodder shocks all the way around the mountain. Then he went into the woods and cut wild grapevines. He tied these big fodder shocks with the grapevines. He tied them tight and securely against the constant blow of wind on this high hill, a cleared space of mountain land too big for the timber and the cliffs to serve as windbreaks. While Did plowed and Peg cut the sprouts and cornstubble ahead of the plow, Sparkie not only shocked the fodder, but he gathered the pumpkins that had not been smashed the night of the corn shucking. Sparkie left the smashed pumpkins for Did to turn under with his plow.

Did was turning his team at the end of the cornfield when he saw Sparkie pick up his first pumpkin. Sparkie held the pumpkin in his big hand, braced his feet, aimed at the fodder shock down the hill with his free hand, and then heaved the pumpkin toward the shock. It hit the center of the shock. It went inside the fodder, safe from the freezes to come. When Did saw Sparkie do this, he stopped the mule team in the furrow and watched him heave another pumpkin. Did thought the accuracy of the first heave had been accidental. The second pumpkin hit the fodder shock dead center. He watched him heave a third and a fourth pumpkin and each heave was dead center. He was throwing the big and little pumpkins, from anywhere above the top furrow dead center into the fodder shocks below.

"How on earth can you do that, Sparkie?" Did asked.

"I've always throwed 'em in the shocks," he said. "It's much faster. Saves a lot of walkin' and work!"

"Say, there's a big one you've got now," Did said. "Can you heave it to the shock from where you're standin'?"

"Think so," he said, aiming his free hand at the fodder shock thirty yards down the steep slope, drawing back over his shoulder with his other arm until he had the right aim, and then letting go. This pumpkin went end over end—boom—into the middle of the big fodder shock, shaking it to its foundations.

"What a football passer you'd make, Sparkie," Did said. "You could play basketball too!"

"What kind of games are they?" Sparkie asked.

Did rested between the handles of his plow and explained the games to Sparkie.

"I never saw a basketball," Sparkie said. "But I 'spect I've seen boys a-playin' with footballs on the Greenwood streets along about September. Ain't a football shaped like a blowed-up hog bladder?"

"That's right," Did said, starting his team after a little rest.

Over Did's head the big yellow, light-yellow, creamy-white, and green-striped pumpkins sailed through the air, plumping the fodder shocks like wild birds on a winter evening seeking shelter for the night. Did had never seen anything like this. This is what made Sparkie what he is, plowing and chopping wood and working with his hands and his back, Did thought. What I am doing made Sparkie, and it will make me too.

Did felt a new strength come to his body as he breathed the fresh November wind in the morning and mellow mountain wind of the bright afternoon. Did Hargis kept the plow moving up near the sky, behind the mighty mules.

"Shucks, one mule will pull that plow all day," Sparkie told him. "They'll ask no quarters and give none. All they want is plenty of fodder, corn, hay, and water. Ye don't have to worry about the mules. Worry about yerself. Can ye take it like they can?"

I can take it, Did thought. I can plow this field in twelve days if Sparkie can. I can walk as fast as Sparkie. I can work as hard.

On the fifth day Did looked out over the great dark bread-loaf mountains with tall upturned teacup-shaped peaks that jotted the ridge line against the sky. The great sweeps of bright brisk wind that blew through the pine needles on the mountains and the teacup-peaks swept over the dark upturned loam that Did Hargis had plowed. Did walked between the handles

192

of his plow and breathed this wind. He swelled his chest as he breathed the good wind more deeply than he had ever breathed before. The beauty of this world he had adopted had become his own. The rugged beauty of this earth and the kindness of these people of the earth had done something to him. He didn't know exactly what it was. Whatever it was caused him to work, grow, play; whatever it was caused him to love life more than ever before; caused him to want to live forever. He felt like a man, doing the work of a man, working with men.

The cool wind seethed through the holes in his pants leg and touched his bare flesh. It felt good. The sun on his face and arms felt good. His face was getting as brown as an oak leaf. When he lay down and drank from the big spring at the lower edge of the field, he could see his color change from day to day.

Did thought as he plowed: These are the words that Father never heard. These are the words the world has never heard. These are the soft mellow earth words that the men of Greenwood and the boys in Greenwood High School have never heard. These are my words.

Above the elbow roll of one of his shirt sleeves, he felt the coolness of the wind against his flesh. His shirt sleeves were split. Did stopped Dick and Dinah and saw a long row of cowbirds in the furrow behind him, picking up worms and bugs from the mellow dirt.

Muscles, muscles in my arms, Did thought. He drew his arm back and looked at the muscle, larger than a duck egg, hard as the brown hickory nuts falling from the Plum Grove hickory trees. Peg was working near the upper edge of the cornfield cutting sprouts and stubbles, and Sparkie was cocking his arm back, aiming at a fodder shock for a long throw with a big moon-colored pumpkin.

This earth is a great living body, Did thought as he stretched his body on the plowed ground and put his ear against the earth. There must be great rivers running underground that are its veins and arteries and it must have a heart. Not anything so rugged yet so beautiful could be so alive unless it had veins, arteries, and a heart.

He lay there with his ear against the ground and listened for the pounding of the earth's heart. He knew the pounding of the earth's big heart would be as loud as thunder. Even the sun-caressed mellowness of his earth were soothing to the flesh where his pants legs were torn and threadbare. I hear the earth's heart, he thought. It almost lifts me up. I will shout to Peg and Sparkie and tell them what I have found! As he raised his body up, the pounding of the earth's heart stopped. He couldn't feel it with his hands. He lay down again and felt it again. Then he realized that the pounding was his own heart and the surge of blood that he thought he had felt running through the earth he had plowed was the blood in his own veins. His heart was the heart beating for the world, his blood was the blood of the world, his words were the dirt words speaking for the world.

When he arose from the plowed ground, Sparkie was standing still with one hand aiming at the fodder shock below and his other arm drawn back holding a pumpkin. Peg was leaning on his hoe handle too. They were looking at him. When Did stepped between the handles of his plow and the mules were off on another furrow, Sparkie threw the pumpkin dead center to the fodder shock below. Peg lifted his shop hoe high and its worn edge shone like polished silver in the sun.

5

IT WAS NINE o'clock in the morning. Sparkie and Did stood by Thunderbolt's empty kennel. Sparkie got down on his knees and looked inside. There was the bed of dry leaves where Thunderbolt had last slept. The leaves were loose and fluffy around the inside walls of the little room that had been Thunderbolt's home for six years. Thunderbolt had slept here from the time he was a puppy.

"It shore seems strange to look in here and not see Thunderbolt," Sparkie said, rising to his feet. "Thunderbolt always comes home when the chase is over."

"I thought something was strange when the hounds stopped runnin' old Hot Foot at three this morning," Did said. "Hot Foot always runs until daylight. When he's feelin' right, he'll run until nine and ten in the morning. Remember once he ran until three in the afternoon."

"I believe he's pizened," Sparkie said. "I know Thunderbolt as well as I know you and Arn and Peg. I lived in the woods with Thunderbolt before you jined this fambly, Did. I know it's his nature to come to the sound of this horn after a chase. It's his nature to come home to his hot cornpone and his good bed."

"Maybe old Hot Foot went in a deserted coal mine," Did said, as Sparkie walked back and forth in front of Thunderbolt's empty kennel. "Maybe Thunderbolt went in after 'im and got hung up. Something could 've happened to keep him from comin' home."

"Not one chance out of a hundred that he's still alive." Sparkie paced up and down in front of the kennels. Fleet knew something was wrong with her master. She came from the kennel, jumped upon Sparkie and kissed his face with her thin red tongue. "Ye'd a-been gone too, Fleet," Sparkie spoke softly to her, "if ye hadn't come outten the chase when ye did. Lightnin' would have been gone too if I'd a-used him at two this mornin' instead of twelve midnight. Shootin' Star's lucky he's retired from runnin' the fox 'n days like these."

"Sparkie, come and eat some breakfast!" Arn stood on the porch smoking her pipe, watching. "It ain't no use to grieve, son," she said. "This has happened before. Come drink some hot coffee and ye'll feel better! Maybe Thunderbolt is still alive!"

"I don't want coffee, Arn," he said. "I got to find Thunderbolt. I got to find 'im, dead 'r alive. But I'm afraid," he wept, "I'm afraid I'll find him dead and bloated by a stream."

"Come on and eat some breakfast nohow," Arn pleaded.

"I don't feel like grub, Arn," he told her.

"Come to breakfast, Sparkie," Peg said as he came through the door and stood beside Arn. "Thunderbolt is dear to us too. He's one of the fambly."

"Think of the times I've fed him, Sparkie," Arn said. "Look at the hot cornpone I've fed him mornin', noon, and night, fer the last six years. Don't let yer heart be troubled. These things will come to ye. Heaps of troubled feelings and misery before ye die."

"But look at the empty kennels," Sparkie said. "Four empty kennels and Thunderbolt's makes five. Can't find young hound puppies sired of runnin' stock with good bottoms to fill my kennels. Too many good foxhounds have gone the way of Drive and Lead and Topper and Scout."

"It's this war among us, Sparkie," Peg said. "We are

a-fightin' one another and we are a-fightin' Greenwood. God only knows when it will ever end. Fox hunters are a-fightin' terbacker growers and all of us are a-fightin' Greenwood. And, maybe, who knows, we may have to fight two companies of the National Guard. That's the rumor. A terbacker barn is burned mighty nigh every night! The terbacker men are a-goin' to fight back. They think it's the fox hunters a-burnin' their barns. Maybe the only reason my barn has stood is because ye and Did are fox hunters and ye sleep in its hayloft."

"I'd better never know the terbacker grower that pizened my hounds," Sparkie threatened. "He'd never pizen another!"

"I've never seen the people a-livin' in these hills in so much misery," Arn said. "It's war, death, and ashes on every side. People are suspicy of one another. It's a lonesome time now even with the bright leaves frosted and blowed away from the trees in death-drops to the ground. It's war and misery, and tears and death and suspicy. Come and eat, son, and drink some hot black coffee to settle yer nerves. Ye will feel better. These are bad times among these hills. Maybe we'll git these men that's burnin' these barns and pizenin' these dogs. Spring will bring green back to kiver these dark lonesome mountains. Then life will be like it ust to be. Life will be good again."

"I can't eat," Sparkie said. "I got to find my dog. If I only knowed where he was. If I only knowed he was dead and I had his dead body. I'd fetch it back, Arn, and I'd lay it upon that hill yander," he pointed to the high hill with the path zig-zagging down to the barn, "with the others. Let's git the mules, Did, and go find 'im."

6

SPARKIE LIFTED HIS horn to his lips. He blew notes on his horn that Thunderbolt understood. He knew if Thunderbolt could hear, he would start running as fast as his legs could carry him. He knew that Thunderbolt would come barking every breath. The echoes of the horn came back to Sparkie. In the far distance, toward Possum Hollow, they heard another fox horn blowing mournful notes for a lost dog. They heard a horn sound faintly in the direction of Shackle Run Valley.

"I believe our hounds got pizened last night," Sparkie said. "I can tell by what the hunters are a-sayin' on their horns. They're a-callin' fer lost hounds."

"It's a sad sound, calling for lost dogs," Did said.

"Let's go down the path the way we followed the trap lines," Sparkie suggested. "That's where they were a-drivin' old Hot Foot when we last heard Thunderbolt at three this mornin'."

Did and Sparkie rode Dick and Dinah in a trot down the path that led to the polecat country. They rode across the old deserted fields, where brown broomsedge waved in the November wind. They rode, a hundred yards apart, across these old fields looking right and left for the blue-speckled body of Thunderbolt. They rode under the leafless persimmons, through the barren pawpaw thickets, on and over little hills and across ravines.

"A dead crow," Sparkie shouted, bringing Dinah to a stop.

Sparkie jumped down from his mule, picked up the crow, and ruffled its feathers.

"Not a mark on it," he said. "It's not been shot. 'Spect it's got pizen taters."

Then he threw the crow down on the broomsedge and leaped into his saddle again.

"Another crow," Did shouted. "Here's a dead snowbird too."

"The pizen must've been spread in this direction," Sparkie said. "Did, this was the way the man was a-runnin' the night Shootin' Star was shot. Remember," Sparkie pointed, "that's Eversole Ridge. That was the night Tid Barney's barn burned."

"I'm all turned around, Sparkie."

"Let's ride on to Possum Hollow," Sparkie said. "Maybe we'll find Thunderbolt there."

On their way to Possum Hollow, they found more dead crows. They found three dead snowbirds and a dead cardinal.

"If we find Thunderbolt," Sparkie spoke softly, "we'll find him dead."

As they rode toward Possum Hollow, they met Glenn Shelton. Glenn Shelton was a fox hunter and he hadn't come to the corn shucking.

"Have ye seen old Bomber?" Glenn asked.

"Nope, we ain't," Sparkie said. "Have ye seen my Thunderbolt?"

"Ain't seen 'im," Glenn said. "John Fultz found his old Monk. He was pizened. Guess thirty-seven hounds, maybe more, got pizened last night."

"We've just come from Buzzard Roost Ridge," Did said. "We've looked all along the fox path and we didn't see a dead hound."

"Then I'll ride across the ridge to Nellievale and go down Sleepy Hollow," Glenn said. "I'll follow the stream. If I see yer Thunderbolt, I'll fetch 'im home to ye. If ye find my Bomber, will ye bring 'im home to me?"

"Shore will," Sparkie said.

"I never set fire to a terbacker barn in my life," Glenn said as he rode away. "What terbacker man would be so low as to pizen a hound?"

"This might cause more barns to burn," Sparkie said to Did, as they rode over the low hill into the valley of Possum Hollow. "The hunters'll go to work after this."

"Come to think about it, the hunters have been riled for a long time," Did said. "You didn't see many of 'em at Peg's corn shucking. You didn't see Glenn Shelton, Jimmie Dennis, Ivan Nicholls, Brier-patch Tom and Cief Eversole, or Henry Keeney there."

"I didn't expect to see that crazy Brier-patch Tom and Cief there," Sparkie said. "It's jest as well they didn't come."

Sparkie rode up one side of Possum Creek and Did rode up the other. They looked to their right and left from the water's edge upon the hills that slanted down. They rode over big stones, through thickets of grapevines, black shoemakes, greenbriers, saw briers and locusts. The mules leaped over deep ravines with them and over big boulders that had rolled from the high cliffs above. They leaped over two fences. Not anything stopped them until they reached the head of the hollow. They found two more dead crows.

"We're a-goin' to find Thunderbolt," Sparkie said. "We can ride out this ridge to Little Tunnel. If we don't find Thunderbolt there, we can ride over to Nicholls Hollow and up Nicholls Branch. A pizened dog wants water. If we don't find Thunderbolt at any of these places, we can ride past the Reeves Pond, down Little Sandy, and up Shackle Run!"

Sparkie and Did rode on to Nicholls Branch. They followed this stream, riding on each side from its mouth to its source.

But they didn't find Thunderbolt. Then they dashed across the Sandy River bottoms to the Reeves Pond. They didn't find Thunderbolt.

They rode down the east bank of Little Sandy. They looked down to the water's edge. They looked high upon the rocky bluffs. Now that the leaves had fallen they could search the brown carpet of leaves for a blue-speckled hound. When they came to where Sleepy Hollow Creek emptied into Little Sandy, they found Glenn Shelton roping Bomber behind his saddle.

"I found 'im," Glenn said softly. "I rode over the Nellievale hills and down Sleepy Hollow. I found 'im right here where the fox crosses."

"Thunderbolt is somewhere on Shackle Run," Sparkie said, as he gave Dinah more rein. "He's a mile or more ahead."

Sparkie and Did rode in a full gallop until they came to the Shackle Run Ford.

"Did, ye ride up that side. I'll ride up this 'n," Sparkie directed.

Sparkie looked behind each rock and tree. He looked upon the rocky slope and down to the water's edge. Did forded Shackle Run and rode up the jolt-wagon road, looking to his left on the stubble fields where there had been corn and tobacco and on his right to the edge of the stream. They rode searching behind each fodder shock, roadside tree, and rock for more than a mile.

"I see my dog," Sparkie shouted. "I've found Thunderbolt. Jest as I'd expected to find 'im—dead."

Sparkie jumped down from his saddle and ran to Thunderbolt. Did forded Shackle Run and dismounted. Did and Sparkie stood beside the dog whom they had heard lead a pack of seventy hounds until three o'clock that morning. He had died on the fox path, pointing the way old Hot Foot ran. Thunderbolt's front paws were thrust ahead as if he were trying to take another step. He was lying there as silent as one of the gray stones that dotted the dark earth. His eyes were glassy in the sun. Sparkie's eyes filled up. Little streams ran down his autumn-colored face.

"I'll put him in the sack and strap him behind my saddle," Did said.

Sparkie couldn't speak. He stood silently for a minute looking on. Then he climbed into the saddle and rode away. Did put Thunderbolt in the big sack and strapped him to the saddle. He mounted Dick and followed the Shackle Run road. Did soon overtook Sparkie riding slowly, staring straight ahead. They rode along together through the slanting rays of a sinking sun, up the hollow, under the giant beeches by the spring, and up to the barn. Peg and Arn were standing there waiting for Thunderbolt.

"We'll put the mules in the barn," Sparkie said. "They're tired. They've not et anythin' since morning. Then we'll take Thunderbolt up on the mountain and let him rest."

7

THE SLOW PROCESSION of silent people walked in single file up the narrow winding path. Sparkie carried Thunderbolt and Did came next with a spade and mattock. Arn and Peg followed. Since the path was rocky and steep, Arn had to assist Peg. Once they had to stop to rest. Finally, the procession reached the mountaintop where the sun's faint rays lay softly on the land.

"Here's where we'll bury ye, Thunderbolt," Sparkie said. "Here beside Drive, Lead, Topper, and Scout."

There was a row of four graves with field stones at their heads and feet.

"It's a good place to bury 'em here, Sparkie," Peg spoke softly, "up here above the other hills where they can still hear the hounds a-runnin' the fox."

Sparkie dug into the hard mountain dirt and Did shoveled the dirt from the shallow grave. They made a neat grave in the hard crust of the mountaintop.

"I want to see Thunderbolt again," Arn said.

Did untied the sack and slipped it from over his body.

There lay the once powerful Thunderbolt. Arn, Peg, Did, and Sparkie gathered around and looked at him in silence.

"He was a stay-dog. He'd chase all night," Peg said.

"Think of the times I've fed you, Thunderbolt," Arn said.

"I never owned a dog like Thunderbolt," Did said. "Now I know I sure missed something."

Sparkie wiped tears from his eyes with a bandanna. They slipped the sack over Thunderbolt and laid him in his grave. They covered him with the dark mountain dirt and carried heavy rocks and put them on his grave. Then they set a big flat stone at his head and one at his feet. They left Thunderbolt up near the sky in the heart of the Plum Grove hills. They left him where he could hear other foxhounds chase the fox through the rugged hills.

8

EIGHT DAYS AFTER Sparkie and Did had made their selections from the *Wish Book*, they rode Dick and Dinah back from Nellievale with a large coffee sack in front and a large coffee sack behind each saddle. They balanced the big sacks across the mules' backs in front of their saddles and they roped the sacks behind to the rings in their saddles. These sacks were filled with light bundles and boxes. This time Dick and Dinah carried precious loads.

Since Did and Sparkie arrived after the sun had set, bringing the short November day into semidarkness, Arn was in the barnyard pouring buttermilk into the trough for the possums. Peg was filling his feed basket with big ears of yellow corn for the fattening hogs. When Did and Sparkie rode up the path by the spring from Shackle Run Valley, Arn finished pouring the buttermilk into the possum trough in a hurry and walked over where Sparkie and Did sat on Dick and Dinah. They had ridden at a fast pace to get home before dark. Little streams of white vapor were rising from the mules. The chilly evening wind was drying the sweat on their hot bodies. Peg left his basket of corn in the crib door and walked over.

"Ye'll haf to have some hep," Peg said. "Let me take the front sack down fer ye."

"All right, Peg," Sparkie said, as Peg braced his good foot

and placed the sharp end of his wooden leg on a little rock so it wouldn't sink in the ground and throw him off balance.

Sparkie bent over and lifted the corner of the sack up, and Peg shouldered it as he had done the heavy rye seed when Sparkie and Did brought them from Nellievale on muleback.

"W'y, it's almost light as a feather," Peg said.

Sparkie and Did laughed at the joke they had played on Peg. Arn's lips slowly curved in smile showing her long front teeth.

"Don't ye know what's in this sack?" Sparkie laughed. "Clothes!"

"I want to see yer clothes," Arn said. "Did, let me take the sack down fer ye."

Did handed the sack to Arn. Then Sparkie and Did jumped down from their mules and untied the ropes that held the sacks behind the saddles.

"Sparkie, ye take the sack," Peg said, "and I'll take keer of the mules. They're sweaty and need to be outten this November chill."

Sparkie carried one sack under each arm. Did carried one sack of his own and Arn carried the other. Peg limped toward the barn leading Dick and Dinah by a bridle rein in each hand. "Not so fast, Dinah," Peg complained. "Don't ye step on my good heel. I'll git ye to yer barn stall."

"Arn, ye won't know me in this suit," Sparkie said. "It don't fit me like the green bark fits a tree. That's the way my overalls have always fit me. This suit fits me like the loose dead bark fits a dead chestnut tree. Ye've seen dead chestnut bark loose and comfortable around a dead chestnut pole, ain't ye?"

"I've seen that, Sparkie."

"Did took my measurements this time. Did knows how to measure clothes."

"How do ye know yer suit fits like that?" Arn asked.

Peg hurried through the door with his wooden leg tapping

against the hard bare planks like a small sledge hammer. Peg was in a hurry to see Sparkie and Did's new clothes. Sparkie and Did had untied the strings and opened the sacks.

"We talked about our suits as we rode home," Sparkie said. "When we got to Whetstone Creek, we reined Dick and Dinah off the jolt-wagon road, up a little road. We rode on until there wasn't a path. Then we got behind a rock cliff where nobody would see us. We took off our clothes and tried on our new suits. Did bragged on me until I followed the Whetstone Creek to find a hole of water where the afternoon sun was still a-shinin'. There I sat and looked at myself. I couldn't believe I was the same Sparkie that I'd seen just a few days ago when I looked at myself in the spring at the lower side of the cornfield."

"Reckon Lucy will know ye now?" Peg laughed, his brown eyes laughing too as Sparkie took the long paper box from the sack.

"I doubt that she will," Did said. "Sparkie sure looks swell in his new clothes. Wait until you see him."

"I've got plenty of room to git my hand in my hip pocket," Sparkie said. "I always thought my hands were too big fer my body and that was the reason I ripped my pockets a-gittin' my hands into 'em. Did showed me how to git the right kind of clothes."

"Did, reckon Pollie 'll know ye in yer new suit?" Peg teased.

"I don't know," Did said. "Sparkie said it looked good on me. It's the first suit I ever ordered from the *Wish Book*," he said with a chuckle. "I never even got many suits from Father's store. Father has a tailor in Cincinnati, Ephraim Snyder, who has always made his clothes and my clothes. I didn't go to the hole of water with Sparkie to look at myself. I held the mules while Sparkie went."

"This is the first real suit of clothes ye've ever had in yer life, Sparkie," Arn said, as Sparkie opened the box.

"Oh, how purty," Arn bragged as she looked at the salt-

and-pepper-colored tweed. "Jest let me feel of that purty suit."

Arn put her hand on the suit. She rubbed her rough hand gently over the suit. Then she felt of the cloth between her thumb and index finger.

"It's so soft, Sparkie," she said. "I'm a-dyin' to see ye in it."

"That shore is purty, Sparkie," Peg said. "Dogged if I believe Lucy Howard will know ye in this suit."

Did had not opened his suitbox. He stood holding it in his hand while Peg and Arn looked in amazement at the beauty of Sparkie's suit. Did had never in his life seen parents more pleased with clothes for one of their children. He was happy that he had some part in helping Sparkie order this suit. Did had told Sparkie that he was tall and lanky and he thought a tweed suit would be the thing for him. Then Did had taken his measurements for the suit, since Sparkie had never worn a suit of clothes before.

"What kind of a suit did ye git, Did?" Peg asked.

"I got a teal-blue suit with a shadow-checked plaid," Did said. "Least that's what they told me it was."

Then Did took his suit from the box and showed it to Arn and Peg.

"Oh, ain't it purty," Arn soothed it with her rough hand. The calloused skin of her hand caught on the suit. Arn felt its thickness between her thumb and index finger. "Ye won't look the same, Did. I'd love to see ye and Sparkie in yer new suits."

"Then go into the kitchen," Sparkie said. "Wait till we tell ye to come in."

Arn walked out and Peg got up from his chair to follow her. "I'll go with ye," Peg said. "I want the surprise too. I jest want to see if I'd know old Sparkie all triggered-up in a new suit!"

Sparkie and Did dressed from the skin out in new clothes. They put on new suits of underwear, socks, shoes, shirts, and neckties. Then they dressed in their new suits. Did had to tie

Sparkie's necktie for him. They looked in the little mirror above the dresser at themselves.

In the kitchen Peg turned to Arn. "They didn't say anything about work clothes and brogan shoes. I wonder if they got themselves any?"

"What did they have in the big sacks?" Arn whispered. "Must've got a supply of everything."

Arn and Peg didn't have long to wait to see what Sparkie and Did had ordered from the *Wish Book*. When Sparkie came to the door and told her and Peg to come in, they saw something they had never seen before.

"Sparkie, ye're a better lookin' man than County Judge Burton," Peg said.

"Ye're better lookin' than the Governor of Kentucky," Arn said. "I ain't seen 'im, but ye're better lookin' than the picture I've seen of 'im."

Sparkie walked the floor in his new clothes while Did stood by and looked on. Did thought: He's a new Sparkie, all right. Wouldn't he be somebody in Greenwood City schools! Did had never seen Sparkie dressed in store clothes from head to foot before. Sparkie took long strides up and down the room in front of the fire in his new salt-and-pepper-colored tweeds, white shirt, red tie, and shoes that looked long as sled runners and squeaked when he walked.

"When new shoes squeak, they're a-tellin' the price, Sparkie," Arn said. "Yer shoes are a-sayin' 'Five dollars. Five dollars.' "

"My new shoes are wrong about the price," Sparkie laughed. "They ought to be a-sayin' 'Seven dollars. Seven dollars. Seven dollars.' Maybe they are a-sayin' 'A redfox hide.' I don't know exactly what they're a-sayin'."

"Gee, Did, that's a better lookin' suit than ye wore out here," Arn bragged on Did. "The color of yer face has changed since then. Yer face is brown as an autumn oak leaf."

Did had dressed in many new suits before. Getting a new suit wasn't a novelty. But his ordering a suit, one he hadn't seen before, was a novelty to him. Earning his own money to buy his suit was something new for him too.

"We won't know our boys now," Peg said with a wink.

"They shore look purty," Arn smiled, looking first at Sparkie, then at Did. "That suit is jest exactly what Sparkie needs. That suit Did's wearin' suits 'im same as the poplar leaf suits the poplar tree."

Arn happened to take her eyes off Sparkie and Did and look toward her bed. She saw there a pile of shoes and bundles of clothes.

"Look, Peg," Arn said, pointing to the bed.

"I'll be dogged," Peg said. "Look at that, won't ye."

"Did will be able to hide his nakedness now," Sparkie said.

"Wind felt awfully good on my legs when I was plowin' the big cornfield on the mountain," Did said. "I'll never forget how soothing and good your old work clothes felt to me, Sparkie."

Arn and Peg looked at the new work shirts, dress shirts, work pants, overalls, socks, shoes, handkerchiefs, underwear, gloves, scarves, and work shoes. There were three unopened boxes lying on the bed.

"I'll open those boxes now," Did said as he walked toward the bed in his new suit. Did's new shoes screaked too.

" 'Possum hides, possum hides, possum hides,' Did's shoes are a-sayin'," Sparkie laughed. Arn and Peg laughed too as Did opened the box.

"What's that, Did?" Sparkie asked. "Fishin' net? What kind of a big ball is that?"

"Basketball," Did said. "These are the baskets!"

"What's that?" Arn asked.

"It's just a game for Sparkie and me," Did said. "After I saw 'im throwing pumpkins with such deadly aim at the fodder shocks, I thought he would have a good eye for the basket. I played basketball at Greenwood High School. It's a wonderful game."

Then Did opened another box.

"Oh, that's a football," Sparkie said.

"We're going to do some passing, Sparkie," Did said as Arn and Peg looked on. "I want to see how far you can throw this ball."

Sparkie took the ball from Did and gripped it in his big hand. "Not as far as a pumpkin. It's too light."

Did laughed and opened the third box.

"A little book," Arn said.

"Who's it fer, Did?" Sparkie asked.

"It is for you, Sparkie," Did said. *Learn to Read in Ten Easy Lessons.*

Sparkie laughed. "Ye a-goin' to larn me to read?"

"Git all the book eddication ye can, Sparkie," Peg said. "Don't go through life a-missin' it like I have. Wouldn't know my name if I's to meet it in the Shackle Run jolt-wagon road."

"If ye get an eddication, ye may be county sheriff or county jedge some day, Sparkie," Arn said. "Look what a proper young man Did is. He's different to us. It's because he's got book larnin'. Fixed the tags in fancy writin' when you sent the hides to the Good Fur Company."

"Book larnin' comes in right handy," Peg added.

"I never took to books," Sparkie said. "I had my chance at Plum Grove."

"Ye were young and foolish then, Sparkie," Peg told him. "Now ye're older and ye've changed a lot. Ye've changed fer the better too. Ye may take to book larnin' like a duck takes to water."

"We'd better get our clothes and take to the hayloft, Sparkie. It's past Peg and Arn's bedtime."

" 'Spect we had," Sparkie agreed, as he started putting his clothes into the sacks. "We'd better sack up."

"It's a shame to sleep in them purty suits in the hay," Arn said.

"Don't worry about that, Arn," Sparkie said, as Peg opened the door for them, "we'll change our clothes again before we bed in the hay fer the night."

PART EIGHT

I

PEG WAS NOT the same when Sparkie and Did sat down to breakfast next morning. He did not laugh and joke with Sparkie and Did as he had always done when they came from the barn loft for their breakfast. There was a serious expression on Peg's beardy face.

"What's the matter, Peg?" Sparkie asked after he had comfortably seated himself at the table. "Is somethin' ailin' ye?"

Arn looked over at Peg while she poured a glass of sweet milk for Did. Then she poured steaming hot black coffee in the cups for Sparkie, Peg, and herself.

"Peg, ye don't seem to be at yerself," Arn said. "Ye were all right when ye got outten bed and dressed. Ye laughed and talked like ye've always done. But after ye fed the livestock and come back to the shack, ye've not been the same."

"When ye all sit down at the table, I'll tell ye what's wrong," Peg said. "It's enough to make a man have sad feelings."

Arn carried the coffee pot back to the stove to keep the coffee hot. Then she walked over to the table and sat down.

"Last night after ye showed us yer nice clothes, I did a lot of thinkin' before I could go to sleep," Peg said. "Arn was a-sawin' soft poplar timber while I lay there a-tossin' on that bed like a dry oak leaf on troubled water. I thought about all the nice things ye boys were a-totin' to that barn loft. How ye'd ridden the mules to the trap lines, skinned wild varmints, boarded the hides, and watched the seasonin' of 'em. I thought about the way ye had worked to buy yer clothes. Then I thought about how thirty-seven hound-dogs were pizened a few nights ago. I thought about a lot of things I shouldn't a-been thinkin' about, but I couldn't keep the thoughts from comin' to my mind. I couldn't keep from a-thinkin' about all the barns that have been burned and the great lights up against the sky at night from every holler and mountain side in the Plum Grove hills. Then I thought about my barn out there and ye boys in it. I thought: What if a barn burner climbs that log wall and sticks a torch to the hay when my boys are asleep! I had these thoughts until about midnight. Then I must 've started sawin' oak logs. I don't remember anything more."

"Ye didn't sleep well last night," Arn said, pouring her coffee from the cup into the saucer. "But ye seemed in a rightly speret when ye got outten bed this mornin'!"

"I've not finished tellin' ye what happened, Arn!"

"I didn't mean to backsass, Peg," Arn apologized, as she saucered her coffee.

"I left this shack," Peg continued his story, "to feed the livestock. I went through that door right there," he pointed with his knife, "and I saw my terbacker barn go up in a puff of flame. I saw that flame jest as plain as I can see yer faces around this table," he said, staring at Sparkie, then at Arn and Did. "And when the flame shot up toward the stars and God blew it out with a great puff of His breath, I looked down where the barn had once stood and there was a heap of embers that brightened to livin'-ember-red when the wind blowed. In the wink of God's eye it was a pile of cold ashes. Among the ashes were yer ashes, Sparkie," Peg said, staring wildly at Sparkie, "and yer ashes too," he said, turning to Did and staring at him. "The ashes of Dick and Dinah, our good mules, Boss and Daisy, our cows, all our livestock and my terbacker were in that cold heap that looked so dark and dreary there beneath the stars."

"Ye didn't tell me about it, Peg, when ye come back to the house."

"I waited to tell Sparkie and Did. I didn't want to tell it to ye and then haf to tell it to them. At the breakfast table is the place to tell all of ye."

"Then, ye had a token, Peg."

"I'm not through yit, Arn," Peg told her while the coffee got cold and Did's glass of milk sat before him untouched.

"Jest as I opened that gate and the hinges creaked and the plowpints jingled," Peg said, "a voice on the wind as plain as one of yer voices around this table said to me: 'That barn will be set on fire. Take heed.' I was so nervous that I stood there tremblin' like a tough-butted white-oak leaf in the November wind. I was stunned fer a minute as much as any Greenwood man hit over the head with a cornstubble. Finally I got my leg to move from the track where I was standin' and I walked on toward the place where I had seen the flame shoot to the stars and the heap of cold ashes a-layin' there beneath the stars."

"Oh, a real token, Peg," Arn spoke with a trembling voice.

"What is a token?" Did said. "I've never heard of one before."

"Jest what I've been a-tellin' ye, Did," Peg said. "It's a warnin' of something to come. When a body gits a token, he'd better take heed."

"Ain't ye never been warned by a token or a dream?" Arn asked Did.

"Not that I know of," he said. "Have you ever been warned, Sparkie?"

"Warned in a dream in the hayloft about old Thunderbolt. I didn't tell ye about it, Did. I thought ye'd laugh. But I dreamt of carryin' Thunderbolt in my arms over the fox-huntin' woods. Dreamt a big fire had burned down every livin' tree, every dead leaf and log from the ground. Dreamt I waded through cold ashes to my knees over a dark land where there wasn't any life, not a crow, bird, owl, or fox. When I waked, I was mistaken. Thunderbolt was not in my arms. But it's a bad sign to dream of cold ashes beneath the stars. This was the reason I was so shore Thunderbolt was dead when he didn't git home from the chase."

"There's somethin' to dreams and tokens," Peg said. "I believe everybody gits the warnin' before the real thing comes along."

"If ye had only heeded the warnin' ye got about Thunderbolt," Arn said. "He might 've been alive out there in his kennel now."

Did didn't say anything. He let Peg, Arn, and Sparkie talk. He had never been warned by dreams and tokens in his life, he thought, as he sat looking at Peg's serious face. Arn's face was serious too as she looked at Peg and listened to the words of warning he had received.

"I tell ye boys, ye'd better git down from that hayloft," Peg said. "If ye don't, I'm afraid we'll be a-tryin' to untangle yer ashes with the long-handled shovel from the rest of the fambly's ashes."

"But where would we go, Peg?" Sparkie asked.

"Ye can sleep in this room with us," Peg said. "This shack is plenty big fer two more. It would hold a dozen if need be."

"We can't do that," Sparkie said. "Haf to undress and dress under the kiver."

"I've been a-thinkin' that we could move the corn from the crib to the hayloft and ye could live in the corncrib!"

Arn nodded her head in approval.

"No hay to sleep in?" Sparkie said. "We'd freeze to death in that corncrib!"

"If we can find a stove someplace, we could put it in there

215

and run a stovepipe up through the roof and fasten it with hay wire like we got on this kitchen."

Sparkie didn't say anything. Everybody sat silently while the food and coffee got cold.

"Thirty-seven hound-dogs pizened," Peg said. "Everything so quiet now. It's like a summer lull before the storm."

"I wouldn't like to live in the corncrib, would ye?" Sparkie said, turning to Did.

"It wouldn't be like the barn loft," Did said.

"That barn loft is home to me, Peg," Sparkie said. "Token or no token, I'm a-goin' right on sleepin' there. Even if Did leaves me, I'll still sleep there. I'm not afraid and I can tell ye why!"

"Don't ye believe in tokens, Sparkie?" Arn asked, turning to Sparkie.

"I believe in tokens and warnings," Sparkie said. "I'm not disputin' these things I've seen come to pass. But I do believe," Sparkie reasoned, "if anybody tries to tiptoe to that barn on a night when the ground is froze, one of my hounds will hear 'im. If the hounds are fast asleep, one of the fattening hogs will hear him and start gruntin'. If the hogs and hounds are both hard to wake from sleep, Dick or Dinah will hear 'im and bray. Even the roosters will make quirkin' noises in the trees. The hens will cackle or the cattle will low. Too many livin' things around that barn to warn us. They will warn us too. It will be hard fer anybody to git to the barn to set it on fire on a night when the ground is froze."

"But what if the ground is thawed?" Peg asked.

"The barn burner will rustle the leaves," Sparkie said. "He'll wake someone in the barnyard fambly. The tough-butted white oaks around that barn keep on a-droppin' their leaves until they bud in the spring. There'll always be the leaves around the barn. And never one time did I go into the barn loft on any night—spring, summer, fall, or winter—that I didn't wake somebody up. Most of the time everybody is awake and talks to us in his own words. Ain't that right, Did?"

"That's right, Sparkie."

"Did ye ever go out there in the mornin', Peg, when ye didn't rouse every livin' thing?"

"Come to think about it, I don't believe I have," Peg said. "Everybody is soon wide awake a-astin' fer his breakfast. But remember, Sparkie, a token as plain as I heard on the wind at the gate this mornin' is a warnin'. Something is bound to happen after I saw the flame shoot to the sky. Something is bound to happen after I saw the wind-fanned embers and the cold ashes beneath the stars."

"The coffee is cold," Arn said. "It ain't been teched. I'll pour the cups of cold coffee back in the biler."

"Why hasn't somebody set fire to that barn before now?" Sparkie asked.

"That's something I've thought about," Peg answered. "I'm a terbacker grower by choice. I love the foxhounds and I love to hunt. Ye and Did are fox hunters by choice. Ye sleep in that barn. That's the only reason I believe it's not already a heap of cold ashes."

"I feel safe in that barn, Peg. Maybe I feel safe there because it's home to me. Do ye feel safe in the barn, Did?"

"Yes, fairly safe," Did admitted shyly, trying not to get into the argument. He didn't want to be forced to say how he felt about tokens and warnings. He just couldn't believe in them.

"Did and me have got plans fer our home. When we work the barn loft over, we'll pull the hay back from the cracks between the logs so if a barn burner does get past the animals, he can't climb up the log wall and set fire to the hay."

"I'll be uneasy about yer sleepin' in that barn after Peg has had this token," Arn said, as she brought the pot of hot coffee back to refill the cups. "It will be hard fer me to sleep a-knowin' ye are up there when so many hound-dogs have been pizened, the hills and hollows so winter-dark and with all the people riled and so full of misery."

2

"I CAN'T KEEP from thinkin' about the token Peg heard on the wind this mornin'." Did held his pitchfork in his hand as he watched Sparkie's pitchfork bite deep into the hay. "I don't believe Peg was tryin' to scare us. I wonder if we are safe out here!"

"Peg wasn't tryin' to skeer us. Peg heard the words on the wind. Peg saw the flame, the wind-fanned embers and the cold ashes. It was a warnin' all right. Peg's been warned by too many tokens in his lifetime. He's seen a lot of ghosts too."

Did watched Sparkie's pitchfork handle bend as he came up with a forkload of hay. Did thought he would break the pitchfork handle. Sparkie tossed the hay against the north side of the barn loft. Did had never seen any youth as powerful as Sparkie. He had thought, and this thought came back to him now, when he plowed the big cornfield in eleven days, beating Sparkie's record by one day, that someday he would be as big and powerful as Sparkie. He had dreamed as he plowed behind the big mules, crumbling the dark cornfield dirt over the moldboard, that he too would have shoulders wide as an ax handle is long. Now he wondered why he had had such thoughts as he watched Sparkie lift the forks of hay, bending his pitchfork handle to the breaking point, while he worked to clear one side of the barn.

"What kind of a ghost did Peg see?" Did would always be dubious about such things as ghosts.

"A woman ghost ust to worry Peg. Remember where the old well is kivered over with logs at the oxbow-turn in the Shackle Run jolt-wagon road? Right there is where he saw her three or four times before he married Arn. One mornin' Peg was a-goin' to dig coal and he was a-walkin' down that road before daylight. This woman ghost swooped through the air in a long white robe and lifted the coal-bank cap from Peg's head. She blew out Peg's carbide lamp. Then she gave Peg's cap back to 'im. At another time Peg met her in the road face to face. Peg said she was as purty as a chinee-eyed doll. Twice more she come from nowhere and walked beside Peg a hundred yards or so and then she jest disappeared into nowhere. After Peg married Arn, he never saw 'er again.

"Funny about that woman ghost," Sparkie continued, as they forked the hay back from the south side of the barn loft, "every person that saw 'er was an unmarried man. Peg was the unmarried man that saw her the most. See, Peg and Arn didn't marry until they's almost forty. Lacie Howard saw this woman last year. She lifted his hat from his head when he passed that old well. It's become the token around here when a man sees this woman in white at the old well that he ought to git married. Lacie is nigh onto thirty years old. Sam Eubanks saw her twice. He'd been a-sparkin' Dollie Young about seven years and he up and married Dollie in a hurry. Eurea Smith saw 'er the third time after he'd wronged Bee Burton, and he went back and married Bee and took his own flesh and blood young'un to honor and to father.

"Peg is the seventh child of the third generation," Sparkie continued. "He can blow three times in a baby's mouth and cure the thrash. He can raise knockin' sperets. Peg has heard the rattlin' of chains in dark places and he's seen lights come on and go off all over these hills. It ain't that Peg wants to raise knockin' sperets and cure baby thrash and see lights and ghosts; it's because he's born that way."

"I never heard of that," Did said. He had a creepy feeling.

"Glad I'm not the seventh child of the third generation," Sparkie said.

"Hope I never see that woman at the old well," Did said.

"I've heard the people say that she lived in the old shack that stood near that well. Ye can see the old foundations rocks there yet. Said she was supposed to marry a man that lived in Lonesome Cove over where Greene Howard lives now. Said the man jilted 'er and she jumped into the well and ended 'er own life. Now she spends all her eternity a-skeerin' the life outten the Plum Grove men that are slow to git married, that go with girls too long or that wrong the girls they go with. I'm skeered of 'er. I never want 'er to appear to me. That's one place I never passed after night until ye come here to live with me, Did."

"You do believe in all these things?" Did said.

"Shore I believe," Sparkie answered.

"Then you believe somebody will come to set this barn on fire?" Did said. "You believe Peg got a warnin' and this barn will burn?"

"I don't know whether it will burn or not," Sparkie said. "I won't be surprised if somebody *tries* to set it on fire. That's what we're workin' against now. If we throw all the hay on the north side of this barn loft, it will be hard fer anybody to git to the hay. It's the south side of this barn loft I've always worried about. Big cracks between the logs and the hay a-stickin' through the cracks like long brown rabbit ears. Barn burners are as sly as foxes. One could run up the log wall on that side and fire the hay with a torch. We've just got two chicken roosts on that side of the barn. On the east side we got the cattle stalls. On the north side we got chicken roosts and we got the fattenin' hogpen. On the west side we got the hound-dog kennels. It'll be hard fer anybody to git past the hounds. When we git the hay moved from this south side, there won't be any hay a-stickin' through the cracks. If he tries to git through on the north side, the east or west end of the barn, he'll run into trouble, Did. Ye can put yer faith in animals that love ye. They won't let ye down when they know something strange is a-goin' on that shouldn't be."

"Maybe you're right, Sparkie," Did said. "I don't know whether the dead return to warn the living or not. I don't believe they do. I can't make myself believe all of that. I'm not afraid of those passed on, but judging from what has happened since I've been here and what happened before I came, there is danger in our sleeping in this barn loft. But you're a light sleeper, Sparkie, and the way we are arranging the hay in this barn loft makes sense. Besides, it will be hard for anybody to get past the animals."

Sparkie gripped the ball in his big hand. His long fingers were like the brace roots of a poplar tree. They held the football as securely as the brace roots held the poplar. Sparkie drew back his arm and let go. The spiraling football rose like a pheasant in sudden flight, arced across the clear November sky, and came to rest against the barnyard fence nearly fifty yards away.

Did gasped. "That's the longest pass I ever saw!"

"It's jest like a pumpkin, only lighter. Too light to throw a far piece."

"Just wait'll I take you back to school. What a team we'll have!"

"School," Sparkie muttered, kicking at the turf. He spat. "Tried it once; didn't take to it. If a body could jest have the football without the booklarnin'. I like to play this game—an' fox huntin' ain't the same anymore without old Thunderbolt. It ain't any fun to have a burnout dog like old Lightnin' and a cheater like old Fleet without havin' Thunderbolt. I love a hound-dog with a good bottom like old Thunderbolt."

Did was still thinking of Sparkie performing glorious deeds for Greenwood High. "You'll hit the ends with the football just like you hit the fodder shocks with the pumpkins." He watched Sparkie stuff a golden leaf of light burley into his sun-tanned jaw. It puffed out his cheek as big as a turkey egg. "Of course you'll have to stop chawing. There's no place to spit in the classroom. Maybe the inkwell." He stopped and scratched his head. "No, it wouldn't do to spit in the inkwell." He laughed.

Sparkie went loping down to the fence after the ball. He picked it up with one hand. Did thought: It looks like a marble; his hand is so big the ball looks like a marble.

Later they sat in the hay under a hunting lantern. The hunting lantern hung from a piece of baling wire which was fastened to a rafter under the barn roof.

"Now ye take this little book, Did," Sparkie said holding *Learn How to Read in Ten Easy Lessons* in his hand. "I can hold it like this and ye can't see any part of it. I can measure its thickness with my thumbnail. I could bite through it with my teeth. I could almost eat it. This book that is so little—" he held it up to the lantern—"and yet we sit here and go over it night after night after night. Ye take to it, Did, like a quail takes to the rye field when the grain is ripe. Like a possum takes to the pawpaw after the frost has ripened the fruit. But me? I'm a-sittin' here with this little book in my hand jest a-listenin' to the wind in the bare treetops an' a-wishin' I heard the hounds barkin' on Buzzard Roost Ridge."

"But it's easy, Sparkie. Letters are little things, and easy to learn. Anyway, you already know your letters. You put letters together to make words. You speak words. You put words together into sentences."

Sparkie brushed Did's words aside with a sweep of his big hand. "It's yer nature to larn and say them things. Every livin' thing has a nature—a lizard, a mule, a hound-dog, a possum. Even me, I have a nature. And mine and your'n ain't the same."

There was silence in the barn loft. The hounds were asleep in the kennels. The hogs were full of swill and slept on their bed of dry oak leaves. The November wind spilled over the dark breadloaf hills of Plum Grove and sang a language in the pine needles that Sparkie understood. He stretched back into the hay and crammed another tobacco leaf into his jaw. *Learn How to Read in Ten Easy Lessons* dropped from his hands.

PART NINE

I

WHEN SPARKIE HEARD Shooting Star send up a lonely howl, he moved restlessly in the hay. Since this was a warm night and he and Did were not sleeping with their hounds, Sparkie wondered if Shooting Star wanted to sleep with Did in the hayloft. When Shooting Star sent up his second howl, Sparkie got up from his warm bed of hay. He slept in his shirt, long underwear, and socks. He put on his pants. He laced his shoes hurriedly in the starlight that filtered through the cracks at this early morning hour.

When Shooting Star let out one howl after another, Sparkie instinctively reached up in the crack between the logs, grabbed a leaf of burley he had laid away after Did had persuaded him to stop chewing, crammed it into his mouth, and held it behind his jaw.

I wish he'd stop that howling, Sparkie thought, as he walked softly over the hay to where Did was fast asleep and snoring.

"Did, wake up!" Sparkie whispered, reaching down in the hay and shaking Did's shoulder. "I believe Shootin' Star's a-warnin' us."

Did rose from the hay, rubbed his eyes with the backs of his hands, and yawned.

"All right, Sparkie," Did whispered.

Sparkie tiptoed over the hay to the wall beneath the gable door. He crouched beside the widest crack. He cupped his hand behind his ear to catch more sound.

He could hear the sound between Shooting Star's howls. But he wondered if it were the sound of a mule's hoof stirring the stall bedding below. He wondered if a cow had got up to stretch in her stall or if one steer was butting at another sleeping too close. Unconsciously he manufactured a supply of tobacco juice for ammunition. Sparkie drew a long breath and waited to catch the direction of the sound.

It's not from the barn, he thought, as he picked up the sound again between Shooting Star's howls. It's in the direction of the beech grove.

"Hurry, Did," Sparkie whispered. "Git into yer pants and shoes!"

"I'm hunting one of my shoes."

Sparkie put his eyes to the crack and looked in the direction Shooting Star was barking. He could no longer hear any sound since Shooting Star was making so much racket, charging against his chain, barking, growling, and kicking the dirt up with his hind feet.

"Did, I see 'im," Sparkie whispered excitedly. "I see a man. He's a-comin' this way."

"Hope it's not Father," Did answered softly. "Hope he's not after me again."

Sparkie's eyes followed a tall man as he stepped cautiously on the frosted leaves. It's not Mr. Hargis, Sparkie thought, as he watched the man dodge around the hogpen, then go quietly like a cat from chicken roost to chicken roost. He's too tall fer Mr. Hargis. Besides, Mr. Hargis would have Sheriff Watkins with 'im.

"It's not yer pappy, Did," Sparkie whispered. "This man's a-comin' to the barn."

Sparkie squared himself so he could watch both the scuttle-hole and the gable door. Then he heard the man's footsteps on

225

the logs. He could hear his hands taking hold of the barn logs as he climbed the wall. Sparkie's heart beat faster, and he motioned with his hand for Did to stop digging in the hay for his shoe.

"Sparkie, shouldn't we yell for help?" Did hissed.

"Wait'll he gits closer," Sparkie's jaws worked hard on his tobacco, "close enough to ketch."

The man climbed to the gable door. He was familiar with the barn, for he knew where this door was. He tried to open it but couldn't, for the hasp was fastened on the inside. He knew the hay was piled on the north side too. With one hand he held to a barn log, while with the other hand he pulled a pine torch from his pocket and stuck one end of it in his mouth. He got a match from his pocket, raked it gently across the gable door, and lit the torch. Sparkie watched the light from the torch through the tiny cracks between the gable-end planks. When the man bent down to put the flame through the hay, Sparkie saw a masked face and eyeholes in the mask.

Squirt.

The ambeer spittle came from nowhere, for the man couldn't see Sparkie in the darkness. It filled the eyehole of his mask, like a warm soft bullet. Before Sparkie could squirt into the other eye, the man had ducked his head beneath the crack.

"Come on, Did," Sparkie yelled as the barn burner dropped his pine torch and scrambled down the log wall.

"Found my shoe," Did shouted. "Be right with you."

Sparkie jumped down the scuttle-hole, ran across Dick's stall, and out the barn door. Did followed him. When Sparkie ran around the barn, the barn burner was running toward the beech grove.

The mules jumped up from their soft-bedded stalls and brayed. The cattle lowed in their stalls. Lightning and Fleet came from their kennels and charged against their chains, barking and growling.

"Yander he goes!" Sparkie shouted. "Come on, Did!"

226

"What's the matter out there?" Peg yelled from the window.

"It's the barn burner," Did screamed, loud enough for Peg to hear as he streaked across the barn lot in the direction Sparkie had gone.

2

"THE BARN BURNER, Arn!"

"The barn burner," Arn repeated, jumping out of bed, dragging the quilts with her.

"Light the lamp, Arn!"

By the time Arn had lighted the lamp, Peg had found his horn he kept hanging to a nail on the wall.

"Hep me to the door, Arn!"

Peg supported himself with one hand on Arn's shoulder. With the other hand he lifted the horn to his lips. He blew a quick mournful long and two shorts. The weird sounds penetrated the barnyard noises far beyond into the stilly steel-blue night.

"Hope the folks git that message," Peg said excitedly.

"Send the warnin' again, Peg! He didn't fire our barn but if he gits away he'll fire others."

Peg sent the message again.

On the high hill above the barn where Sparkie had buried his foxhounds came four long mournful notes. Peg and Arn stared at each other. Everything was happening tonight. The grapevine said the enemy was coming.

"I'll bet that's Bill Hargis a-bringin' Sheriff Willie Watkins and a posse to git Did," Peg said.

In the direction of Buzzard Roost Ridge another horn blew four long mournful notes. South of the barn another horn sent the same message. North of the beech grove a horn sent the message that the enemy was coming.

"Speak to me, Peg," Arn cried. "Air we a-dreamin'?"

Then the horns started blowing in all directions while Peg and Arn hurried to get dressed.

"Our enemies have us surrounded," Peg said as he pulled the big leather strap around his waist and buckled it to hold his leg and pants in place. "Bill Hargis ain't a-goin' to let Did git away this time. Men are a-comin' toward this shack from all directions!"

"Misery, trouble, and death," Arn said. "I see 'em every mornin' in my coffee grounds."

Peg ran to the door.

"There's fire in the barn," he shouted.

Peg ran from the shack toward the barn.

"The livestock," Arn screamed as she followed Peg.

"Save us, Lord," Arn prayed as she stumbled over Peg, whose leg sank deep in the soft ground and he sprawled forward on his face.

3

"DIDWAY! DIDWAY," CALLED the familiar voice of Bill Hargis. "Are you in that barn?"

All over the Plum Grove hills, to the mountaintops and down in the deep valleys, horns were sounding four long mournful notes. The grapevine was saying that the enemy was everyplace.

"To the fire, men," shouted another familiar voice above the distant echoes of the mournful horns.

"Save the barn, Sheriff Watkins," Arn pleaded, as she rose to her feet to help Peg up. She knew Sheriff Watkins's voice.

Armed men came running toward the barn from all directions.

"Every time we come to take Didway Hargis home, somethin' happens," said a man, as he ran past Arn and Peg. "This time it's a fire."

"Stack your guns in a hurry, back from the fire," Sheriff Watkins ordered above the roar of men's voices. "Let's save this barn!"

"Where's my boy?" Bill Hargis shouted above the wild confusion.

"The boys are not in the hayloft," Peg answered. "They're after the barn burner."

"I wouldn't be afraid to bet that outlaw Sparkie set this barn on fire and took off when that first horn started blowin'," shouted a Greenwood man. "Who knows? He might be the real barn burner."

"Come on, men," Sheriff Watkins commanded. "We'll find out later who set the fire! Let's get it out!"

"Let it burn," someone shouted.

"I deputize you in the name of the Law to fight this fire."

The chickens flew from their roosts around the barn. They sailed in every direction. Many hit the branches of trees and fluttered through space to the ground. Many flew a safe distance away and when they alighted on the ground, they were running.

"My cows," Arn wept as she reached the barn door that opened to their stalls.

The cattle lowed pitifully when they smelled the smoke and heard the wild confusion around the barn.

"My mules!" Peg shouted. They were braying and kicking the barn walls.

Two Greenwood men opened the barn door and rushed ahead of Peg to get the mules out.

Bill Hargis shot by the men and mules like a bullet. He made a wild leap for the manger and climbed up through the scuttle-hole like a cat.

"Come down from there, Mr. Hargis," screamed a Greenwood man. "Peg told you Didway wasn't up there!"

"He's told me lies before!" Bill Hargis retorted.

The fire had started in the cornstalks, scattered hay, and oak-leaf bedding in the mules' stalls directly beneath the gable door. It was burning knee high and spreading toward the log walls where there was loose dry bark. A few flames were leaping high as a man's head.

"Come down out of that hayloft, Mr. Hargis!"

"Didway's not up here," Bill Hargis shouted.

"Are you crazy, Mr. Hargis?"

"The fire is spreading, Mr. Hargis! The flames are climbin' up!"

The barn was filled with smoke. The mules brayed excitedly. When a Greenwood man tried to drive Dinah from her stall, she charged at him with her forefeet. Old Dick bit at the ear of the Greenwood man that tried to drive him from his stall. Then Peg went into Dinah's stall. He laid his hand gently on her neck.

"Come, Dinah," he said softly.

Dinah followed Peg from the burning barn. When Dinah went out with Peg, old Dick followed. Then Peg rushed toward his hogpen.

"Is my boy hiding in one of these stalls?" Bill Hargis asked Arn, as he rushed inside the shed where she kept her cows.

"I told ye where he was," Arn snapped. "He's after the barn burner."

Bill Hargis looked in every stall. Then he ran out at the door.

Arn took her cows out all right. With the help of two Greenwood men she got all the cattle from the barn. They took off lowing, butting, and snorting into the darkness.

"Any buckets around this place?" asked a man with a black mustache.

"On the porch ye'll find four buckets of water," Arn answered.

Then two men, with beads of sweat standing all over their fire-reddened faces, took off running toward the shack. Since the mules were out of the stalls, a dozen men rushed in their stalls to fight the fire. They tried to stomp the flames out with their feet. They tried to beat them down with boards, clubs, anything they could get their hands on. One man rushed in with a pine bough he'd broken from a tree and started swarping the flames.

"Come on, men," Sheriff Watkins screamed, as he beat the flame with a club.

"There's a empty barrel under the raindrip," Arn shouted as she fought flames with a pitchfork. "Will some of ye fetch a barrel of water from the spring? The spring is down under the bank," she said, pointing in that direction.

Four men with sweat running down their faces took off into the cool night air to bring a barrel of water.

"Watch these hogs, men, they don't run into ye," Peg shouted when he opened the hogpen door.

The fat hogs with little tails curled up over their fat rumps ran helter-skelter, squealing as they ran. They ran beyond the reflection of firelight and heat. There they started rooting contentedly among the oak leaves for acorns. Then Peg ran toward the possum pen.

"I fergot the boys' new clothes are up in that hayloft," Arn screamed.

"Can't get 'em now," Sheriff Watkins shouted. "This fire's gettin' out of control."

"Fire! fire! Help over this way!"

"Don't let it get to the hay!"

"Beat the flames down!"

"Help! help!"

"Help!"

Men moved in all directions. Approximately fifty Greenwood men were fighting this fire. When one shift of men rushed in, stomped the fire, beat it with sticks, clubs, and pine boughs until they could no longer stand the heat, they stepped back and another group of men rushed in to take their places.

Two men rushed by with a bucket of water in each hand. They dashed the water on two barn logs that had caught fire. Then they ran toward the spring to refill their buckets. Four men rushed in with a barrel of water. They poured the water on the bedding in the mules' stalls. It seeped through the dry bedding and quenched a portion of the fire that was threatening the hay on the north side of the barn loft.

"Where are you goin', Bill Hargis?" Sheriff Watkins asked.

"To the shack to see if Didway's hidin' there."

"Think he'd be a-hidin' there and this barn on fire?" Arn

shouted as she continued to beat the flames with her pitchfork. "He'd be here a-fightin' this fire."

"Let this barn burn," Bill Hargis shouted. "It'll be one good riddance!"

"Bill, I deputize you in the name of the Law to help fight this fire!"

"Bill Hargis, we've tried to help you."

"Mr. Hargis, we're ashamed of you!"

"Don't step on a possum, men," Peg shouted as possums ran in all directions, seeking again the freedom of the wild land they had once known and loved. "All livin' things have been freed, praise the Lord."

Bill Hargis stood a minute watching his friends fight to save a barn that belonged to a mortal enemy. He watched the sweat run from Arn's face in little streams while she continued to fight the fire without a rest from the heat. A little midnight possum ran past Bill Hargis, fleeing for its life. He watched it run away to the darkness. The words a friend had said to him flashed through his mind: *Bill, we've tried to help you.* Bill Hargis reluctantly joined the fire fighters.

"That's more like it, Hargis!"

"That's right, Bill!"

"Let's save this barn," Greene Howard shouted, leaping from the saddle. Lacie jumped down from behind the saddle. "We've almost run old Toller till he's got the thumps since we got yer message that the enemy was a-comin'. We didn't know the barn was on fire."

Greene turned Toller loose and he and Lacie threw their guns on the ground when they saw Bill Hargis with his sleeves rolled up fighting fire with as much determination as Arn.

Tid Barney rode up on a mule that was getting his breath as if it had the heaves.

"Thought it was the enemy. Didn't know the barn was on fire," Tid shouted as he went into action. "Any old quilts, blankets, coffee sacks we could get to smother the fire?"

"I'll go fetch all I've got!"

Arn dropped her pitchfork and ran toward the shack.

Tim Gilbert jumped down from his saddle and let his mule go free. He carried a pistol in a holster on each hip.

"Let's fight to save this barn," Tim shouted, unbuckling his holster and throwing his pistols on the ground when he saw Bill Hargis and the Greenwood men fighting the fire to save Peg's barn.

Tim went to work beside the Greenwood men he had up-ended with his fist and had been upended by them seven weeks before at a corn shucking. Tim took an order from Bill Hargis, who was giving more orders to the men now than Sheriff Willie Watkins.

Glenn Shelton, Jimmie Dennis, and Ivan Nicholls rode in from Eversole Hollow.

Just then Greene and Lacie Howard and two Greenwood men passed with a barrel of water. Arn came running from the shack with an armload of quilts.

"Here's the quilts," she said, giving them to Ivan Nicholls.

Ivan ran through the barn door. He spread the quilts over the flames to smother the fire. Glenn Shelton used Arn's pitch-fork to throw stall bedding that hadn't caught fire from the barn. Lacie and Greene Howard and two Greenwood men dashed water from the barrel to quench the flames.

A dozen more of Peg and Arn's neighbors rushed up to the barn. Without question, they joined the Greenwood men fighting the fire.

4

"THEY'VE GOT 'IM," Peg shouted. "They've got a masked man!"

Peg was the first to see Sparkie and Did walk slowly up the little path from the spring. Sparkie and Did's clothes were covered with mud. Their mouths were open and they were breathing hard. Did's tongue was over his lower lip. They were so tired they could hardly walk. They had the barn burner's hands tied behind him with Sparkie's red bandanna. The masked man walked between them with Did holding one arm and Sparkie the other.

"They've got the barn burner!"

"Where is he?"

"Did and Sparkie 've ketched the barn burner!"

These words went from mouth to ear of the sweaty red-faced fire fighters who had battled the fire down to charred embers and smoke. These words leaped from person to person like ripples spread when a rock is thrown into a mountain pool. Only these ripples of words spread faster than ripples on a pool.

"How'd they ketch 'im?"

"My son Didway helped catch the barn burner!"

"He's wearin' a mask!"

"Shoot 'im betwixt the eyes."

"Stomp 'im in the ground. My barn in ashes!"

"Let 'im die the way my livestock died."

"Order in the name of the Law," Sheriff Watkins shouted above the angry shouts of the Plum Grove tobacco growers. "Men, pick up your guns. Preserve Law and Order. Let's see there's no bodily harm done this man!"

Sheriff Watkins and his men moved swiftly to take up their arms. The tobacco growers were closing in around the two tired boys and their prisoner.

"We'll see who he is," Tid Barney shouted. "Here goes his damned mask."

Tid Barney ran in and jerked his mask off while Sparkie tussled with Tid.

"Brier-patch Tom Eversole!"

"Can ye believe it!"

"Old Brier-patch Tom!"

Men and women ran in with clubs and pitchforks, others with guns. The Greenwood men, greater in number, rushed in, pushing back the angry tobacco growers. When they formed a circle around Tom Eversole, he laughed as they had never heard a man laugh before. The threats of the Plum Grove men, whose barns, livestock, and tobacco had been destroyed by fire, made him laugh hysterically. Although his hands were tied behind him, in one hand he held a little dirty rag that he fondled nervously between his index finger and his thumb.

"Stand back, men," Sheriff Watkins pleaded.

"What do ye think of yer friend now, Mr. Hargis?"

"It's a good thing, Mr. Hargis, ye showed a willingness to help fight the fire."

"I never approved of a barn burning in my life, I'll have you know," Bill Hargis interrupted in self-defense. "I didn't know this man would do that. I never dreamed that he was a scoundrel and an arsonist. I didn't know that he is a potential murderer trying to burn my son up in the hayloft! Do you think that I would knowingly aid such a vicious character?"

236

"Stand back there!"

"Don't come any closer!"

"We don't know yet that this man has burned a barn," Sheriff Watkins said.

"I know he set this one on fire," Did spoke wearily from the center of the circle of armed men. "We followed this man straight down the hollow. We caught him just below the Plum Grove church in the middle of Shackle Run Creek."

"He emptied his pistol at me," Sparkie said. "He might've shot me if he'd a-had two good eyes. The bullets stung the trees a-near me and singed off into space! He didn't have time to reload the pistol when we reached the open road. I was too close to his heels!"

"He was a hard man to take," Did said. "Sparkie had to goose 'im all the way here."

"Speak fer yerself, Brier-patch Tom."

"Did ye try to burn this barn?"

"I ain't a-sayin'," Tom chuckled to a circle of mad people wanting to get to him.

"Just a minute, we'll see if my evidence hasn't burned," Sparkie said, as he pushed his way through the crowd and walked wearily toward the barn.

"Eversole, I'm surprised at you," Bill Hargis said. "I didn't know you were this kind of a man."

"I told ye what he was, Bill Hargis," Arn said.

Then Brier-patch Tom laughed hysterically and fondled the rag in his hand, as everybody looked on and listened.

"Hold up yer right foot, Brier-patch Tom!" Sparkie had returned with a stick in his hand. "Let's see if it's got a patch on it!"

He wouldn't raise his foot. When Sparkie started to lift it, he kicked like a horse. Then he laughed like a braying mule. Two of Sheriff Willie Watkins's deputies helped Sparkie lift his foot.

"Look, Did," Sparkie said as he measured the patch by the

notches on his stick. "The patch is wore thin but it's still there."

Then Sparkie measured Tom's shoes.

"The night Tid Barney's barn burned we were possum hunting on the hill above," Sparkie said. "We saw the fire. We heard somebody shoot three times. My Shootin' Star was shot that night with a soft-nose .38 bullet. That's the kind of bullet that tears a hole. Tonight I got Brier-patch Tom's pistol when we captured him." Sparkie showed the pistol to the people who were now listening to his story. "He also fired soft bullets tonight! I've got 'em here to show ye."

"One of 'em would have ruint ye, Sparkie," Arn interrupted, now that she had lighted her pipe and was smoking contentedly.

"We heard a man runnin' from the fire across the ridge ahead of us the night Tid Barney's barn burned," Sparkie said. "I was suspicy he was the barn burner. I found his tracks and I measured 'em. They are Brier-patch Tom Eversole's tracks!"

"Why were ye a-runnin', Brier-patch Tom?" Peg asked.

"We're not havin' his trial here," Sheriff Watkins said. "He's under arrest. We'll take 'im to Greenwood."

"Ye'd as well confess, Brier-patch Tom."

"Tell the truth. Ye were a-tryin' to burn Did and Sparkie up, weren't ye?"

"What about his son Cief?" Arn asked. "I'd as liefer think he's mixed up in this too!"

"My Cief never even set a brush pile on fire," he said. "I've always handled the fire. I like fire. It's powerful stuff."

"What about Tid Barney's barn?"

"I burned it," he laughed. "Who'd ye think burned it?"

"Let me to 'im," Tid screamed. "He'll never burn another barn."

The Greenwood men, armed with Winchesters and pistols, held Tid back.

"What about my Shootin' Star?" Sparkie asked. "Did ye shoot him that night?"

"I shot some old stray dog that night," he said.

"What about my Thunderbolt?" Sparkie asked.

"What about my Bomber?"

"What about my Rifle Bullet and Lady?"

"I pizened yer dogs too," he confessed casually. Then he gave a little wild laugh.

"Now stand back, men," Sheriff Watkins said. "A jury will decide fer this man!"

There was a great ripple of words that spread among the people gathered around Tom Eversole and those that remained to watch the smoldering embers of the barn fire.

"What, Brier-patch Tom pizened the dogs too?"

"Stand back, Glenn Shelton!"

"Stand back, Jimmie Dennis!"

"Let the Law handle this man, Ivan!"

"We're the Law!"

"Leave 'im to us."

"Ye hunters thought one of us kilt yer hounds," Tid Barney said.

"Now we see," Greene Howard said.

"We've been fooled," Peg admitted.

"A terbacker grower and a fox hunter a-burnin' barns and pizenin' hounds," Tim Gilbert said. "Did ye ever hear of sich before?"

"Now, my boy Cief never done a thing." Brier-patch Tom spoke as if not much of anything had happened. "My boy Cief is lily-white and pure. I burned the barns and pizened the hounds."

The Plum Grove people were stunned. They stood looking at Brier-patch Tom, who seemed proud to be the center of attraction.

"Now if ye ever want to do anything to me fer pizenin' yer hounds and burnin' yer barns," he continued in a soft voice,

239

"don't hang me up with a rope. I wouldn't like that. I'm afraid of a tree. Jest put old Brier-patch Tom over a powerful fire until his blood biles and his flesh sizzles. Ye ain't got the nerve but I have. Fire is powerful stuff. I love it."

"That man's crazy," Glenn Shelton said.

"I'll admit he's just a little bit left of center," Tid Barney, a hill Republican, admitted.

"Let's go with the prisoner," Sheriff Watkins said. "Let's get 'im to jail."

"Stand back, men! You're not goin' to do anything."

"Nothin' will happen here."

"Let 'im tell it to the jury."

"Sparkie and Did will git a thousand dollars."

"They deserve it."

"They've captured the biggest arsonist, thief, and cutthroat of all time," Bill Hargis said. "It makes my blood boil to hear him talk. If I had known his true character, I wouldn't have got closer than a mile to that man!"

"Come to take Did back to Greenwood and look who they've got."

More Greenwood men picked up their guns and joined the men who were protecting Tom Eversole.

The procession of men started moving up the long mountain path in the twilight hours of morning, while the stars set and light streaks came in great shafts from the east, silhouetting the barren oaks against a soft blue sky. Bill Hargis did not follow the procession as it moved slowly up the steep mountain. Did stood beside Sparkie and they watched the procession move away, while Plum Grove men, who had respected Bill Hargis on this night, looked on with eyes that stared from solemn serious faces.

"I'd like to speak to you, Didway, before I go," Bill Hargis said. "I'd like to have a talk with you."

"All right, Father," Did said. "I'll be glad to talk with you."

Did and his father walked down the path, out of sight,

where what they said could not be heard. They talked while the Plum Grove people watched the procession until it reached the mountaintop. They watched the men walk along the ridge path, silhouetted against the soft blue morning sky until they were out of sight. The Plum Grove people whispered to each other about what Did was going to do. Many said he would go home with his father, others guessed he would stay. Did and his father walked back to the barn and shook hands. Bill Hargis said good-by to Did and to the Plum Grove people and hurried up the path the way the great procession of Greenwood deputies and Sheriff Willie Watkins had gone with their valuable prisoner.

PART TEN

I

"NO, DID, I'M not a-goin' to tell ye what to do," Peg said, as he pushed his chair back from the breakfast table. Peg pulled a long cigar from the pocket inside his coat. "I'm a-goin' to tell now what I've told ye many times before. Ye can stay here with us as long as ye like. People'll always treat ye right out here. They like ye." Peg wet his long cigar with his tongue and stuck it between his beardy lips. "I feel toward ye as I do Sparkie. This shack is yer home. Ye're one of us."

Arn got up from her chair, walked to the woodbox, and picked up a stick of kindling. She lifted a cap from the stove with the caplifter, held the stick of kindling in the firebox until the end was flaming. She put the cap back on the stove, walked over to the table, and held the fire to the end of Peg's cigar. After Peg puffed a cloud of smoke, Arn lighted her own pipe.

"One thing we're a-goin' to git at this place soon as we sell the terbacker," she said, "we're a-goin' to lay in a supply of matches."

Arn sat down in her chair. She puffed clouds of smoke from her pipe while she looked at the coffee grounds in her saucer.

"I don't know what yer pappy said to ye the other night, Did," Peg continued. "I think he was awfully plagued when ye and Sparkie ketched old Brier-patch Tom and he confessed before everybody to his crimes. I'd as liefer think yer pappy didn't know old Brier-patch Tom was that kind of man. But when yer pappy come to his right senses and called ye away from everybody and talked to ye like a man, then I thought he acted like he was good enough to be yer pappy. I made up my mind then to put a good message over the grapevine telephone fer 'im after the Plum Grove people have time to cool off. It will take time, Did, after all this fight with Greenwood to git the people friendly with one another like they ust to be. We don't want to keep on a-goin' to Nellievale," Peg added, blowing a cloud of smoke up toward the ceiling; "we want to go back to the county seat town of Greenwood. Some of us will want to whittle on the telephone post while we talk to a neighbor like we've always done. But I'm not a-tellin' ye to go back to Greenwood or to stay here. I've always let Sparkie do a little thinkin' fer himself. Accordin' to the laws of nature and the *Good Book*, old Sparkie will be here when I'm gone. I think he'd as well be a-thinkin' fer himself now. And this is the way I feel about ye."

"Ye've asked me many times what to do, Did," Arn said, as she puffed clouds of smoke from her long pipestem and looked at the coffee grounds. "I feel the way Peg does about it. I'm a-goin' to leave that up to ye. But I can tell ye what I think ye're goin' to do," she said, looking closely at the coffee grounds. "I can see in this saucer a big house and a little shack. I can see at the big house three well-dressed people. I can see at the little shack three people."

"Are ye shore it's that way, Arn?"

"That's the way it's here, Sparkie!"

"I've not said I'm going back to Greenwood High School," Did said. "But if I do go back, would you care if Sparkie went with me?"

"Just as I told ye awhile ago, I'd leave that up to old Sparkie," Peg said. "Something has to be within Sparkie that makes him speak fer hisself."

"If Sparkie wants booklarnin' so he can write fancy and speak proper like ye do yer ownself, Did," Arn said, "I want him to have 'em!"

"Gosh-old-hemlock, what would ye do without me, Arn?"

"If ye want the eddication, we can do without ye, is what I'm a-sayin', Sparkie."

"We will do without ye," Peg added. "Ye must make up yer own mind, Sparkie."

"But if there are three people at the big house and three people at the shack, what is the use to ast me what I am a-goin' to do," Sparkie asked. "What's the use to ast Did? What's the use to ast when something has already come to pass? Didn't the barn burner set fire to the barn after Peg heard the warnin' in words spoken on the wind at the gate? Peg saw with his own eyes flames shoot toward God's stars. Peg saw God's breath quench the flame in front of his own eyes. Peg saw the heap of wind-fanned embers and the pile of cold gray ashes."

"If it hadn't a-been so ordered, there would have been a heap of cold ashes," Arn said. "Ye've ketched old Brier-patch Tom and there is peace. What I worry about now," Arn continued, "is all that reward money ye have fer ketchin' Brier-patch Tom Eversole. The money here and I can't go to sleep fer a-thinkin' about the danger in it. Ye're still a-sleepin' in the barn and the people a-knowin'!"

"It's time the mornin' light is in the terbacker shed," Peg said. "While the terbacker is in season, we must work to finish it ready fer market. We must be up and a-goin'."

2

PATCHES OF SNOW lay on the Plum Grove hills. This rugged land looked like a great white-and-black patchwork quilt Nature had quilted carelessly. There were great white patches on the north mountain slopes and in the valleys and patches of dark earth on the south mountain slopes and on the teacup peaks where the wind had swept over. There were large and small dark and white patches spread over the Plum Grove world where the monster mountains and their baby hills slept peacefully through the short December days and the long December nights. A wind, warm for this time of year, swept up from the south. White patches on this great quilt that covered the sleeping monster mountain and their baby hills were gradually being erased, leaving the mountains grotesque, dark, and winter-barren. White clouds of mists were riding on the soft warm wind, over the mountains, to the unknown world beyond.

"It's a real terbacker season," Peg said as he followed Did and Sparkie into the tobacco shed. "The soft warm mists go between the log cracks in this barn. The mists seep between the planks and between the terbacker plants on the sticks. They make the terbacker leaves as soft as wet oak leaves beneath the snow. Now's the time to finish stripping this terbacker. Now's the time to grade, tie in hands and have it ready for the next snow. Then we can put it on a sled, take it with the mules to Nellievale, and ship it on the Old Line Special to Maysville."

"It's a-gettin' about time fer old Santa Claus," Arn said, as she followed Peg into the shed. "It will soon be time to pay the debts we've made this year. Last month was the time to pay our taxes."

Sparkie and Did knew what they were to do. When they entered the tobacco shed, Sparkie reached overhead and caught hold of a tierpole with his big hands. He muscled himself up on the pole. He stood upright on this tierpole and reached to the next one and muscled himself up. Did was not tall enough to reach the tierpoles. He had to climb the barn post. Did climbed the post like a cat. He followed Sparkie up in the barn where half of the tobacco was still hanging. In the first and only season, they had not been able to strip, grade, and hand all of their tobacco.

Down on the ground floor Peg was lifting sticks of firewood from the high stack of long buff-colored fodder. The wood had been used for weights to keep the wind from blowing the fodder away from the tobacco. Peg stacked the sticks of wood in the corner of the barn while Arn moved the fodder over to one side. They worked together until they had uncovered the long heap of light burley tobacco that had long been ready for market.

Did lifted a stick of tobacco from the top tier down to Sparkie. Sparkie smelled of each tobacco plant along the stick. Then he took several whiffs from one bright burley plant. He lifted this one from the stick, stripped its bright leaves, and crammed them into the big loose hip pocket of his new work pants. Then he passed the stick down to Peg, who was waiting on Sparkie.

"Does that terbacker smell good, Sparkie?"

"Never smelt better, Peg."

"It's because ye've been without yer chewin' so long, Sparkie," Arn said, looking up. "Once you git the taste of the fragrant light burley, ye'll always have the taste, so they say. It's the same as drinkin' lonesome water! I know," she added, "when you once git the smoke from light burley, it's too pleasant ever to fergit."

Sparkie will never quit chewing tobacco, Did thought, as he handed another stick down from the topmost tierpoles. Sparkie smelled over it and didn't find a suitable stalk of tobacco. He passed the stick of bright tobacco down to Peg. Peg passed it on to Arn. Arn smelled of the bright plants and selected a plant for her own use.

"Ye missed on that one, Sparkie," she said, smiling up at him.

Sparkie is laying him in a supply of tobacco to chew, Did thought. He can't chew tobacco in the schoolroom. Where could Sparkie squirt the juice?

Arn's rough calloused hands pulled the bright leaves from the stalks. She laid the leaves in separate little piles. When she found a leaf that suited her, after she smelled of it, she laid it to one side for her own use.

"I tried to quit the weed," Sparkie said. "I know ye can't chew in school, Did. Honest, I broke down every sassafras on this mountain and stripped the bark from the wood. I chawed the tender sassafras twigs, bark, and bud. But I didn't git the satisfaction outten it I got from a good chaw of burley. I plucked the mountain tea leaves from all the stems that growed on Buzzard Roost mountain. I et the red mountain tea berries. And the juice was green like that of the sassafras bark, twig, and bud. I couldn't hit the knot on a tree ten feet away with it."

"Then choose the best bright leaves before we go to market, Sparkie," Arn told him. "Lay in yer supply to last until another season. That's what I'm a-doin'."

"I'm a-selectin' the best fer my cigars too," Peg said. "We'd better make our selections now."

"That's what I'm a-doin', Arn," Sparkie said as he smelled

the plants on another tobacco stick. "When I took that chaw the other night to use on Brier-patch Tom Eversole's eye, it tasted good as honey. I'd been so long away from the taste I thought I'd lost it. But I hadn't. After I took that chaw, I decided I wouldn't deny myself no longer of the fragrant weed."

Wonder if Sparkie could spit in an inkwell? Did thought as he watched Sparkie select more bright burley leaves.

Did watched Arn take her time and select the best burley leaves for her pipe. He stood upon the tierpole and looked down at the high pile of bright leaves she had selected from the good burley that she was preparing for market. He watched Peg select the darker burley leaves to make cigars for himself to last until his tobacco ripened in another season. While the short day wore on and they worked in unison to prepare the tobacco for market, Sparkie climbed down many times from the tierpoles and carried the bright leaves he had selected for himself to the barn loft to lay in the broad cracks between the logs.

3

"GOD IS GOOD to give us seasons," Peg said as he stood beside the sled. "He give us a season to put the terbacker in case so we could finish a-gittin' it ready fer market. God gives us a blanket of snow over the long road to Nellievale. Dick and Dinah will have an easy time of it this mornin'. Do be keerful to rough-lock down hills so the sled won't hit Dinah's heels."

"I've got the rough-lock chain in the sled," Sparkie said. "I've got the ax, to cut a dogwood, brace and bit to bore the holes, and a knife to whittle the pegs, so if we lose a half sole, Did and I can put another one on. We'll deliver the terbacker for shipment on the Old Line Special. It should be in Maysville tomorrow."

"Honey, we'll git our terbacker check in time fer Christmas," Peg said, turning to Arn. "Santa Claus will be a-seein' us, ye know, purty soon. Got to have a little money before old Santa Claus comes! Ye boys be keerful and don't have a runaway with that load of terbacker. That's all our money crop fer the season."

"I'm not a-worryin' as much about the mules a-runnin' away as I am about the money Did and Sparkie have on 'em," Arn said. "I'm afraid somebody might git his hand down in Sparkie's pocket and rob 'im. The hip pocket in his new suit is big. Sparkie couldn't feel a hand a-slippin' down in that big pocket to git his money!"

Sparkie and Did were dressed in their new suits. They were wearing gloves on their hands and bright scarves around their necks. Their hair was combed back over their heads and the winter wind had whipped color into their faces.

"Don't have fears about somebody a-robbin' me, Arn!" Sparkie spat a bright sluice of ambeer on the snow.

"I worry about you and Did with all that money," Arn said. "I don't see why you haf to go plum to Huntington to buy Christmas presents for Pollie and Lucy. Can't ye git something nice enough at Tom Flannigan's store?"

"We shore can't," Sparkie told Arn. "We've looked over everything Tom's got. We don't want to go to Greenwood. Not yet."

"Ye're not a-goin' to git married, are ye?" Peg teased.

"Oh, no! I mean—no." Did colored like a small boy.

249

"I will sleep better now since all that money is away from here," Arn said. "A lot of money is a worrisome thing that kills a body's pleasures."

"Ye have three terbacker crops in yer pockets," Peg told them. "Do be keerful about a-takin' up with strangers. Be keerful with the mules too. I'll worry until ye git back."

"We'll leave the mules in Tom Flannigan's new livery stable," Sparkie told Peg. "I'll see they're put in good stalls where they can't kick the planks down and come home. I know it's their first night away from home! It will be my first night away from home too!"

"We'll be back on the Old Line Special at two o'clock tomorrow afternoon," Did said. "We'll hitch the mules to the sled and drive straight home. We'll be here by six or seven unless we have more snow!"

"We'd better be on our way," Sparkie said, as he lifted the leather check lines in his gloved hands. "All right, Dinah, let's go, gal!"

"Be shore to buy yer gals purty presents," Peg teased, then he roared with laughter at his own words.

When Dinah moved, rattling the harness, Dick moved also. Snow flew up from their hoofs toward Sparkie and Did's faces as they moved away with the precious sledload of bright burley tobacco leaves that was covered with Arn's best quilts.

"Do be keerful," were Arn's last words as she waved to them.

"Don't have a runaway," Peg shouted.

Peg and Arn watched the mules trot down the gentle slope under the interwoven beech tree branches that were white arms of snow against a low gray winter sky. They watched them around the bend and out of sight.

4

"PEG NEEDN'T WORRY about these mules a-gittin' away from me," Sparkie said, as he reined Dick and Dinah down the narrow snow-filled unbroken road. "I can take this team any place a mule team can go. I can handle any kind of a mule team. But if they'd start to run and the check lines would snap, I'd stay on this sled and let 'em run. I'd let 'em run until they give out, then I'd run 'em some more."

Squirt!

"Did I hit that rabbit, Did?" Sparkie asked, never taking his eyes off the trotting team.

"What rabbit?" Did asked.

"It was a-settin' by that stump back there!"

"Oh, I see it now," Did said. "You hit 'im. He's running wild circles in the snow!"

"Terbacker is a powerful weed," Sparkie chuckled as he drove on.

Tobacco is all right for Sparkie, Did thought. He'll never quit it. If he's to play on a football line, he'd be squirting juice into his opponents' eyes!

When they reached the Shackle Run Road, just below the Plum Grove church, the knee-deep snow was packed by tracks of mules, sleds, and people.

"This road 'll be better," Sparkie said, as he gave Dick and Dinah more rein; "we can make better time here."

The ends of their bright scarves floated on the December wind as the mules galloped down the snow-packed Shackle Run Road. The raw wind whipped more color into their faces. The duck-egg-sized knot where Sparkie held his quid of burley looked like a ripe red peach in July.

"It's easy this year to take the terbacker to the market," Sparkie said, as a rain of little hard pieces of packed snow flew up from their hoofs. "Last year I had to take it over the mountain on Dick and Dinah's backs to the Plum Grove turnpike. Peg borrowed a wagon from Greene Howard, and I hauled it on to Greenwood. Dick and Dinah skeered at everything in Greenwood. Stood on their hind feet and pranced, but I held 'em. This year we can take it all the way to Nellievale in a sled and ride all the way ourselves. But last year," Sparkie added with a smile, "all eight of my hounds were alive and a-followin' my mules and the wagon. It was a purty sight, Did, to have eight hounds a-followin' the wagon."

Sparkie held the reins and slowed down for the oxbow turn in the Shackle Run Road.

"Here's that place I never want to pass alone at night. Here's where Peg saw that woman ghost. I'm not afraid of anybody or anything, Did," Sparkie said thoughtfully as he reined the mules around the oxbow turn and the slickworn sled runners skidded on the packed snow, "but I never want to see ghosts at night!"

"Don't wait too long to get married, Sparkie." Did chuckled.

"I've thought a lot about that too, Did. But something happens to a man after he gets married. After he's married he starts a-ridin' in the saddle. He lets his wife ride behind on the mule's bare back. I never want to do Lucy that way. I will always want her to ride in the saddle. I'll always want to ride behind with my arms around 'er. If marriage keeps me from a-doin' that, then I don't want to marry her."

"What if you don't marry Lucy?" Did asked.

"I 'spect somebody else will," Sparkie answered quickly. "That's why I say it's a problem. She's too purty fer me to go away and leave. Cief Eversole has always been crazy about 'er. That's why he doesn't like me. That's why he kicked Thunderbolt that night on Buzzard Roost Ridge and I tied into 'im!"

"Then you've been going with Lucy a long time?"

"Five or six years, I 'spect. She's the right kind of a girl, Did. She likes hound-dogs and mules, and the sound of the fiddle makes her feet move."

Did didn't answer Sparkie. He never had much to say about love and marriage and girls.

"Thank the Lord it's froze over," Sparkie said. "I was afraid if we had to ford Shackle Run we'd get the terbacker wet! The Lord is with us. Giddup there, Dinah. Ye ain't a-goin' to fall. Just a little ice! Come along, gal!"

While Sparkie and Did rode up the east bank of Little Sandy toward Putt Off Ford, there was silence between them. Sparkie slowed Dick and Dinah, for the little white cloud of breath they had exhaled through each nostril at the beginning of their journey had expanded into big clouds. Did sat comfortably, his mind in a deep study as he looked at the rock cliffs, Little Sandy River, the deep ravines and little streams he knew so well. He had ridden this way many times in the bright days of autumn when the leaves were multicolored; he had ridden over this land, walked and hunted over it after the frosts had ripened the leaves and the raw winds had swept them from the treetops to the ground. Did had watched these big leaf drops of yellow, light-yellow, red, and brown zigzagging slowly to the ground. Now he was riding over this land that was blanketed in snow, where he heard the December wind sing mournfully in the barren branches of the bankside sycamores along the Little Sandy River.

This is Sparkie's land, Did thought, as Sparkie let the mules walk up the narrow winding road. This land is part of his heart. It's his flesh and his blood. This is my land too. I've learned to love this land. His thoughts flashed to the corn shucking, the square dances, fox hunting on the mountains, and the music of the hounds. Then he remembered how he and Pollie had ridden old Dick together, the mule that was there in front of him, helping his mate, old Dinah, to take Peg and Arn's money crop to Nellievale. Old Dick is my mule, he thought. He's my sure-footed mule.

"I've been a-thinkin' about what ye said about us a-goin' someplace to school together," Sparkie said to break the silence. "I know I'd like football and basketball even if I didn't like booklarnin'. But I've been a-thinkin' about what my hound-dogs would do without me. What would Dick and Dinah do without me? What would Peg and Arn do without me? Lucy too," he added. "Where would we go, Did? Could we fox hunt on the ridges under the stars and listen to the music of seventy hounds? Could we square dance? Could we roast sweet taters in the ashes? Where could we find sweet tater patches in the city, Did?" Sparkie chuckled. "Where could we empty our revolvers at old Eversole in the moon or at a low floatin' cloud of white mist over the valley? Where could I spit my terbacker, Did?"

They laughed together. "I've thought of that," Did said, "and here's the only place I know where you can do these things."

Sparkie reined the mules around the bend at Putt Off Ford. He was now driving up the Sleepy Hollow road.

This is Sparkie's world, Did thought. It's a good little world too. I love it. Then his mind went back to his home in Greenwood, the Greenwood High School, his mother and his father. His mind went back to the talk that he had had with his father.

"No, Did, I can never leave here," Sparkie said. "Ye know how hard it is to grub a yaller locust from the ground. It's hard to pull up all its roots. They go deep into the ground.

There are many of 'em and they are hard to git up. I'm like a yaller locust tree a-growin' in the dead-leaf loam."

"I agree with you, Sparkie," Did said. "This is your land. This is your world."

"What are ye a-goin' to do, Did?" Sparkie asked.

"I'm going back to Greenwood High School the second semester," Did said. "I'm staying with you until after Christmas! Then, I've made up my mind to go back and finish school."

"Booklarnin' is in yer nature, Did. I've always knowed that. Then Arn was right. She did see three at the big house and three at the shack."

"But when school is over, I'm coming back to be with you, Arn, and Peg," Did told him. "This is my land too. I love it. I love the people that live on these rugged slopes and in the deep valleys."

Sparkie took the quid of burley, reduced in size and juiceless, from behind his jaw. He threw it onto the snow.

"Then ye'll not be a-leavin' Pollie?"

"I'll not be leaving any of you."

"Gosh-old-hemlock," Sparkie said with a smile, "I've often thought it would be wonderful, Did, if you came back here to settle down. We could have hound-dogs, mules and we could hunt, plow, dance together until our legs got too stiff to do more of it! Ye're like a brother, Did. But that booklarnin' is part of yer nature, Did. It's like lonesome water to ye. Ye've got the taste. Ye'll never leave it."

Sparkie pulled a long dry leaf of burley from his coat pocket and crammed it into his mouth. Sparkie and Did were now driving past the big honey-locust tree on the left of the road. The long red honey-locust beans no longer swished in the wind. The barren interwoven honey-locust branches were white tracery against the fodder-blade-gray sky.

"Have ye told Peg and Arn ye're a-goin' back to school in January?" Sparkie said.

"Not yet," Did said. "I'll tell 'em after Christmas. I've not even told Father yet. He left it up to me to decide. I'm going to surprise him. I'll surprise Dee and Dennis Delmore too," Did added with a chuckle, "if they jump on me again. I can take care of myself now."

They drove around the bend onto the Plum Grove turn-pike. They could see Nellievale where a half-dozen men were unloading tobacco from sleds.

PART ELEVEN

I

"YE'D BETTER HANG yer socks up tonight, Peg," Sparkie said, as he raked among the wood ashes with the long poker for sweet potatoes. "Old Saint Nick may be here to see ye!"

"Think he will?" Peg said, laughing as he had never laughed before. "Why do ye think he'll come?"

"Ye've been a good boy, Peg," Sparkie said, as he raked the roasted sweet potatoes out on the rough-stone hearth to cool. "Ye've worked hard and ye've been good to Arn, Did, and me! Ye've been a good boy, Peg." Sparkie picked up a hot potato from the hearth and juggled it to keep it from burning his hands.

Peg laughed some more and patted his brogan shoe on the hearth.

"You'd better hang up your stockings, too, Arn," Did reminded her, as he picked up a potato from the hearth.

"My stockin's are too full of holes to hold what Santa might fetch me," she laughed.

Arn knocked the ashes from her pipe. She broke the skin on a roasted potato.

"Gosh-old-hemlock, that smells good," Sparkie said. "Here, Peg, ye take this one and I'll git one from the hearth!"

Peg threw the short butt of his cigar into the fire. Then he began breaking the skin on his potato. The four of them sat before the big wood fire and ate roasted sweet potatoes.

"Ye ever spend a Christmas away from home before, Did?" Sparkie asked.

"No," he answered.

"Ye never slept on the hay in a barn loft when there was fourteen inches of snow on the ground either, did you?" Sparkie asked.

"Never slept on the hay in my life until I came here," Did said.

"Will ye need a quilt in the barn loft tonight?" Arn asked.

"No, the hounds will keep 'em warm," Peg answered.

"Honest, with hay over me and under me and old Shootin' Star beside me, I nearly burn up," Did laughed. "I don't want a quilt. What about you, Sparkie?"

"It's warmer in the hayloft with the hounds than it is in here," Sparkie said.

"This is the life," Did said as he threw sweet potato peelings into the bright blaze that shot from the forestick to the throat of the chimney. "I never tasted anything better than Sparkie's roasted sweet potatoes!"

"Glad ye like 'em," Sparkie said.

"Now fer another cigar." Peg had finished his last potato. "Then I'll hang up my sock and git in bed! Santa's a-comin' to an old man like me because I've worked hard and been good to Arn, Sparkie, and Did." Peg laughed and slapped his wooden leg.

"Another pipe of terbacker and I'll hang up my stockin'," Arn said.

"We'd better get to the barn loft, Sparkie." Did got up and stretched his arms high over his head. Watching him, Arn thought, Somehow he don't look like the white-faced little city feller anymore.

The December winds sang lonesome songs through the leafless branches of the chicken roosts around the barn. The wind

258

was cold and good to breathe. They could feel it go into their lungs. The deep blue sky was filled with bright stars. A sickle moon was just above the grove of pines whose green arms were laden with snow. Did had never seen a prettier picture on a Christmas card than was this night. As for Sparkie and Arn and Peg, they had never received a Christmas card. They didn't know about Christmas card scenes. But Did had seen hundreds his parents had received over the years. He knew as he stood beside Sparkie outside the shack and breathed the cold December air deep into his lungs that he had never seen a Christmas card as beautiful as this winter night in the Plum Grove hills.

"We've stood here long enough and looked at the night," Sparkie said. "Come on, Did, let's git our hounds and git to the hayloft."

2

EARLY CHRISTMAS MORNING Sparkie and Did were the first to rise. They dressed and hurried to the shack. Sparkie built a fire in the big fireplace and the bright flames leaped from the dry wood and warmed the room.

"Merry Christmas," Peg said, rising up in bed.

"Merry Christmas, Peg," Did said.

"Merry Christmas to ye and Arn," Sparkie said. "We'll go outside while ye git up and dress. Ye ought to see what Santa Claus's fetched ye."

Did and Sparkie went outside while Arn and Peg got up to dress. They walked over the frozen snow to keep themselves warm.

While Sparkie and Did walked around the barn in the light of the morning stars with the frozen snow crunching beneath their feet, the roosters began crowing, the cattle lowing, the mules braying, and the hounds barking. Did listened to these early morning sounds. It was the first time in his life that he had lived close to animals. At first he had only been curious about them. It was interesting to watch Dick and Dinah pull the plow. It was fun to stand near the hogs as they stuck their long noses into the trough of swill. Now he had more than just curiosity for the animals. He felt a kinship for them. They were part of Peg's "fambly."

"Sparkie! Did! Come 'ere!" Peg shouted wildly from the shack. "Come and see what Santa Claus has brought me."

When Did and Sparkie went inside the house, Peg stood before them in a new suit of clothes. He was wearing two shoes instead of one. His eyes were filled with tears.

"First time since I was seventeen years old," he said, weeping with joy, "I'm a-wearin' two shoes."

"You look wonderful, Peg," Did said.

"None of yer friends will know ye now, Peg." Sparkie stared at Peg's new foot.

"It didn't take me long to larn how to put it on," Peg said. "It's jest a fit. It feels wonderful! I'm a new man! How did Santa Claus manage to git such perfect fit?"

Arn looked at Peg as she stood there holding her dress and coat and new pair of shoes. She looked admiringly at Peg while tears streamed down her wrinkled cheeks.

"Don't fergit, Peg, that Sparkie is very good at measuring tracks," Did smiled.

"Did can talk to Santa Claus too," Sparkie explained. "He can tell Santa Claus exactly what a man needs. He told him what a fine man ye were and how long ye'd been on one good leg and what a time ye'd had with yer wooden one. Did even explained how ye once nailed a block on the sharp end of yer wooden leg to keep from sinking in the soft ground. He told how he'd seen you fall on yer face many a time. Santa Claus ast Did a lot of questions. He ast me a lot of questions too since I had the measurements. After we talked to 'im and told 'im we wanted the best fer ye, he went out of his way to git what ye needed!"

"I'm a new man," Peg said. His brown eyes were as bright as wind-fanned embers in the dark. "I can walk without Arn's heppin' me! I can bear my own weight on my own two feet! I'm a new man!"

Peg strode back and forth across the room in wild excitement. Then he walked to the mirror to look at himself. Arn showed Sparkie and Did the beautiful dress and coat she held across her arm.

"I never had clothes as purty as these in my life," she said. "I've never had shoes on my feet that felt better. I tried 'em on. I took 'em off. I want to save 'em to wear when I go places. They feel so soft and good to my feet it's like leavin' a rocky path when a body's a-walkin' barefooted and a-steppin' on the tender green April grass."

"The shoes that I thought good enough Did wouldn't have," Sparkie said, watching Peg stride first to one side of the room and then the other, in wild excitement. "Did would say to the clerk: 'No, we don't want them. Let us see something better.' And it went on like that until I saw so many shoes I got to thinkin' ye was a thousand-legger."

Peg and Arn gave Did and Sparkie what had been their customary Christmas treat ever since Sparkie could remember. They gave each a coconut, an orange, two bananas, and peppermint stick candy. These were delicacies at the Sparks' shack. Peg gave each of the boys a pair of work gloves. He had bought Arn a ready-made gingham dress. He had bought himself a box of inexpensive factory-rolled cigars. This was a big Christmas for Peg. This was more Christmas than the Sparks' had ever had before. When Peg sold his tobacco, he didn't have much left after he paid his taxes and his store bills. He just had enough to tide him over from one tobacco season to the next. He couldn't spend much for Christmas. Arn and Peg had forgotten all about cooking breakfast, feeding the livestock, and milking the cows. Tears were streaming down Arn's wrinkled face. Tear drops hung to the beard on Peg's face. They shone as brightly in the lamp light as dew drops hanging to grass in the early morning sun.

"Santa Claus has got something for you in the hayloft," Did said to Sparkie. "You didn't know that, did you?"

"Santa Claus has left something fer ye in a hollow log," Sparkie said to Did. "I'll bet ye didn't know that either!"

Together they ran out of the shack and raced toward the barn. Did went inside the barn and up through the scuttle-hole while the cattle lowed and the mules brayed below. Sparkie ran to the hollow log where he kept his firearms, knives, shells, money, and the stick he had used to measure Brier-patch Tom Eversole's tracks.

When Did came around the side of the barn, he was carrying a box under each arm.

"Let me carry one," Sparkie said, taking the larger box from under Did's arm. They carried the boxes into the shack and put them on the floor. Peg was still walking back and forth across the room. Arn still gazed at her new dress, coat and shoes.

"Open 'em up, Sparkie," Did said. "See what you got!"

Sparkie tore open the box he had carried inside.

"What is it?" he asked, lifting a smaller box from inside the big box. There were shavings packed between the two boxes.

Sparkie opened the second box and Peg and Arn stopped admiring their own presents long enough to look on.

"It's a music box," Peg said.

Sparkie lifted the portable up and held it in his hands.

"It—it plays?" Sparkie looked confused.

Sparkie set the victrola down on the dresser. Then he opened the second box.

"You'll like those records," Did said. "Wait until you hear some of this fiddle music!"

Did selected a record and put it on the portable. There had never been anything like this in the shack. Sparkie patted his feet to the music.

Peg stared. "Why, it'll be jest like a-hearin' Lacie Howard and his bull fiddle here all the time!"

"You've got plenty of music now," Did said.

"Ye couldn't have got me anything I'd take to more, Did," Sparkie said. "Listen to that fiddle lead! Listen to the guitars and that's a five-string banjer too!"

Peg said, "I'm the happiest man in the world! I've got what I always wanted but never expected to git in my lifetime."

"It's so good to tech," Arn smiled as she went back to rubbing the soft coat with her calloused hand.

"Did, here's what ye got," Sparkie said, unbuttoning his coat. Did, Arn, and Peg stared at a brand-new holster and the bright handle of a .38 Special sticking out of it.

"Wait till ye git the feel of it," Sparkie said. "The right feel of it is when ye know exactly how much it weighs and just the right way to hold it when ye shoot. You'll love to carry it on lonesome dark nights. Ye'll git to the place, Did," Sparkie told him, "that ye can't do without it. That pistol will feel like it's a part of yer body. That's the way I feel about one of mine. Jest love the feel of it. Ye'll feel that way too, Did!"

Did stood before the fire fondling the shiny pistol, hypnotized.

"I've seen ye at the square dance not properly dressed," Sparkie said. "All the boys had their pistols, but ye didn't have one, Did. Ye'll look good on the dance floor now when

263

your coat flies up and the girls and boys can see the bright handle a-showin' from a leather holster. If ye ever go to another dance, ye won't haf to go half dressed."

"Pistols are purty things," Peg said. "No harm in one till ye make the harm yerself!"

"We ain't et," Arn said suddenly. "I'll git breakfast." She walked toward the kitchen.

"Just a minute, Arn," Peg said, "I forgot to put a fire in the kitchen stove."

"I'll build the fire, Peg," Did said. "You'll mess up your new clothes."

"That's thoughtful of ye, Did," Peg laughed.

Did went into the kitchen with Arn. Sparkie put another record on his portable.

Before the record had finished playing, Arn came to the door with a plate of cold cornpone in her hand.

"Sparkie, yer hounds are hungry, so give 'em this cold cornbread," Arn said. "It'll stave off their hunger until I can bake 'em some hot."

Sparkie took the plate of cornbread and dashed across the snow toward the kennels. Arn and Did stood by the window watching him. When he reached the kennels, Shooting Star and Lightning and Fleet charged against their chains to greet him. Then while Sparkie was dividing the cold corn pone among them, a blue-speckled hound pup came out from Thunderbolt's kennel. It struggled weakly against the chain and barked a high puppy-bark. Sparkie stood speechless staring at the pup at first. Then he threw the rest of the corn pone to the hounds, sat down in the snow, and wrapped his long arms around the little dog.

Peg and Arn and Did stood on the porch watching the boy and his new dog. Even from the shack they could see tears glistening on his brown cheeks. To hide his embarrassment, Sparkie reached for a leaf of tobacco and crammed it into his mouth. The hound pup made playful leaps at his face.

264

"That boy couldn't be sech a bad boy," Peg said. "Shucks, bad boys can't cry."

Did felt something like a twinge of regret as the last bit of tobacco leaf disappeared in Sparkie's big jaw. He thought: There sits Greenwood High's greatest football player—but he'll never play because it's not his nature.